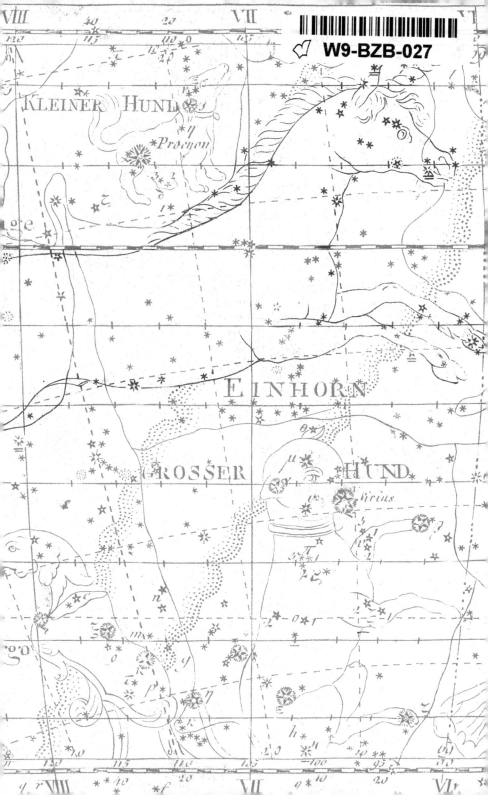

Monoceros

a novel by Suzette Mayr

Coach House Books
Toronto

first edition

 Canada Council Conseil des Arts   ONTARIO ARTS COUNCIL
for the Arts   du Canada   CONSEIL DES ARTS DE L'ONTARIO   Canadä

Published with the generous assistance of the Canada Council for the Arts and the Ontario Arts Council. Coach House Books also acknowledges the support of the Government of Canada through the Canada Book Fund and the Government of Ontario through the Ontario Book Publishing Tax Credit.

LIBRARY AND ARCHIVES CANADA CATALOGUING IN PUBLICATION

Mayr, Suzette
    Monoceros / Suzette Mayr.

ISBN 978-1-55245-241-7

    I. Title.

PS8576.A9M64 2011   C813'.54   C2011-901015-1

For Tonya Callaghan,
and in memory of D. S. and others like him

My skin presses your old outline.
It is hot and dry inside.

— Maxine Kumin, 'How It Is'

Make a hawk a dove,
Stop a war with love,
Make a liar tell the truth.

— Theme from *Wonder Woman*

DE MONOCEROTE.
Figura hæc talis est, qualis à pictore illius feré hodie pingitur, de qua certi nihil habeo.

A.

Monday

The End

Because *u r a fag* is scrawled in black Jiffy marker across his locker. Because after school last Thursday, the girlfriend of the guy he loves hurled frozen dog shit at him, and her friends frisbeed his skateboard into the river. Even though he stomped and cracked through the ice shelving the banks, waded in to rescue it — after the shouting and shoving, they're stronger than they look, all those girls with their cello- and violin-playing fingers, yanking him back by handfuls of coat, handfuls of hair, hooking with their elbows and digging with their fingernails as he scrambled after his skateboard — the banks too slippery and shattered with ice, the current too swift, the water too cold and deep and brown. Freezing river water up to his chest, the water and ice shards wicking into his armpits, scratching his heart. His black coat wet and sucking him down into the current. His skateboard buried in the river.

Because the Tuesday before that horrible Thursday, the guy he loves gave him a kiss so electric electrons shot into his penis, his toes, it was like he discovered Planet X, and he ejaculated into his pants, luckily they were black, luckily it was dark outside, luckily when he got home his mother was squealing into the phone about how she wanted to replace the new stone kitchen counter with a newer, stonier kitchen counter, and his father's face flickered blue before the TV, mouth open and tongue like a leftover slice of roast beef drying out with snoring, his arm triangled behind his head.

Because in a text the girlfriend of the guy he loves said, *we're going 2 kill you.* Because she knew he lived at 2279 Moth Hill Crescent sw; knew that when he wasn't in school he was playing *World of Warcraft* or the faggy JRPG *Divinity XII* with his imaginary, online, why-not-just-buy-a-blow-up-doll loser friends; knew Monday nights he watched his favourite TV show, *Sector Six*; knew that every Tuesday, Thursday and Saturday, like a wobbly-assed soccer mom trapped in a dead marriage, he ordered a large iced cappuccino from the drive-thru at the Tim Hortons on

12th Avenue; knew that anytime he could, weekends and week-days, nighttime, daytime, he'd yank it in his cubby-hole bedroom, splattering himself like the *devient* he was because he was a loser with no friends *n thats Υ u deserve 2 di u Fkng fag cocksucka fuckface royal sht eater.* In the text, she has almost all of his days right, except for two things she'll never know: 1. he's not watching *Sector Six* — they're all reruns in February, and 2. one or two pockets of time he's on secret dates hooking up with her boyfriend when she and her foot soldiers have their junior serial-killer cadet training classes. Lucky him. And the spelling is *deviAnt*, not *deviEnt.* Though it still means he's a dead boy.

Because that last glorious Tuesday, Ginger, the guy he loves, met him at their special place in the cemetery, halfway between their houses. Their breaths misted in the cold air, little white ghosts dissipating in the light of the tall lamps that lined the graveyard, the ache evaporating when they finally touched, their lips colliding, eating, so much time had drained away since they last met. The dead boy pulled away, burrowed into the front of his shirt and brought out a heart-shaped locket in a pool of gold chain, the dead boy smiling so hard his face nearly cracked heart-like in two, the metal heart a hot star in his icy hand.

— I'm wearing it this time, said the dead boy. — See? I haven't lost it.

— You lose it and my granny's ghost will haunt you forever, said Ginger, and he laid a hand overtop the locket, over the dead boy's hand, pushing against the dead boy's chest. Kissed him again, bit the dead boy's bottom lip. Ginger wearing layers, a blue sweater on top of a striped T-shirt on top of a long-sleeved white shirt; all the layers still showing off his flat, gorgeous abs, the smooth mounds of his pecs. The soon-to-be-dead boy, smiling, clicked open the heart, snap.

— When will you give me your picture for it? asked the dead boy.

— You crazy? asked Ginger, his eyes darting over the graves, his mouth blowing on his cold hands, on the dead boy's. — What if you lose it? Anyways, you don't need a picture, we see each other in the halls. But see the rose engraved on the front? It's red. Red means love.

— No it's not, said the dead boy. — The heart's the same gold metal as the chain. It's red because you say it's red? Are you on crack? The dead boy laughed, his voice erupting in the marble and granite forest.

— Yeah, it's red. I am telling you it's red.

— So love is red, said the dead boy. — Then why can't you red me at school?

— That's stupid, said Ginger.

Layers peeled and discarded, Ginger's and the dead boy's lips and tongues and bodies fitting puzzle piece into puzzle piece, skins moulted in the dead grass, the gold locket pressing skin into skin.

The dead boy and Ginger fumbled their clothes back on in the dark, chilled their bodies dizzy as newborn kittens, Ginger hurrying into his jacket, the dead boy pulling on Ginger's sweater, then his own long coat, the smell of Ginger knitted to his skin.

Now Monday. Because today, nearly a week since that starlit Tuesday, the dead boy doesn't want to leave his house because Ginger will still be cold to him like he always is in the days right after hooking up in the cemetery, because he doesn't want to leave his house in case today is the day the girlfriend and her hive finally kill him. His mother gnaws at him with her mandibles to hurry up, — The sun doesn't beam out of your bum even though *you* seem to think so, she says, and she gulps a spoonful of bran flakes.

He hates the way his mother says *bum* like he's a kid, like he doesn't know what you can use it for. He crunches his cereal, one sugary shamrock, one star, one diamond, one Lucky Charm at a time, and listens to his parents drink their orange juice, their swallows loud and revolting, watches his mother x-ray the Monday morning paper, sometimes her lips moving, the heart-shaped locket swinging on the outside of his three T-shirts and a blue argyle sweater, where she can see it, where his father sloshing his coffee into a travel mug can see it. He watches his parents not watch him, drive away in their separate, oversize pollution machines. His father slinging a briefcase stitched together from an endangered species, his mother meandering out to buy hunks of dead animal for supper before barricading herself with paint, paintbrushes and canvasses big as sails, small as stamps, in her studio in her fashionable yoga pants, made by tiny brown children for less than a nickel a day.

Because the Friday right after the horrific Thursday, he fought to see the principal to tell him about his skateboard thrown in the river. The dead boy had to scramble up the fortress wall of secretaries and vice-principals. The principal straightened his tie, rolled forward his chair, jingled the keys in his pocket, said, — If they purloined your skateboard when you were all off school property, there's nothing I can do. That would be more of a matter for the police. The principal clearing his throat emphatically to indicate the matter was Closed.

Because the dead boy ran into his English teacher at the Pita Pit after talking to the principal, in her black clothes punctuated with her own white, chalky handprints, her face splotchy white and pink. The only teacher who ever says anything like, — That attitude smells worse than poo, when someone says *The Glass Menagerie*'s a gay play. He told her about the principal, and she said, — He really said that to you? You've got to get out of this deadbeat school.

Her eyelids and pinked lips twitched.

Because the dead boy and Ginger wrestled into scorching sex in the dead grass, hot enough to start a grass fire, their bodies flaring in the dark, in the middle of a February chinook, the smell of chinook wind and Ginger in his nose, Bed Head shampoo, blue wool sweater the dead boy pulled up over Ginger's head, Ginger's sweaty silky ribcage, flowery fabric softener from all six of their shirts, Ginger's tongue pushing bright as a meteor into the dead boy's, Ginger's nipples, the warm salt of him, behind a tombstone that said, *Lél Somogyi Gone But Never Forgotten 1987–2004.* Ginger's torso naked and slick, dead grass and twigs sticking to his skin. Afterward, the dead boy accidentally on purpose pulling over his head Ginger's blue sweater in the dark, and Ginger was so sweaty and hot he forgot the sweater, tugging on his other shirts and his jacket in a rush because he was late for home. The next morning in the hallway, Ginger's fingers sticking in his girlfriend's tangled hair, stroking, while they prodded their way through the waves of students pushing, bumping and clanging lockers around them, the dead boy wading toward them as though by pure cosmic coincidence, Ginger hovering over a tangle in his girlfriend's hair, and not catching the dead boy's eye, not for a second even though they had agreed last week that occasional eye contact was not completely verboten, they could kiss and fuck with their eyes, no one could tell if they just fucked with their eyes. Ginger's irises radiating aurora borealis from Hershey Kiss brown into caterpillar green, a hazel colour meant for kissing. Their bodies' protons and electrons zinging across the shortening space between them; Ginger staring at the top of his girlfriend's head. The dead boy and Ginger, each of them a sun, each of them a planet in orbital thrall to a sun, the dead boy hugging himself, suddenly cold, in Ginger's blue knit sweater. The body slam of Ginger twisting away from the dead boy, not a single eyekiss, like the dead boy was already dead. Though not a surprise: Ginger frozen sub-zero like he always was in the days following a cemetery date.

Because on Friday, Valentine's Day, an envelope with the dead boy's name on it was slipped into his locker, just a corner of it peeping out from the metal crack between the locker's metal frame and the locker door, and when he pulled it out and ripped it open starting at the crumpled corner, he found a card — a painting of a bowl of fruit, circled by a ballpoint-pen heart. Inside, scrawled in more ballpoint, *Happy Valentine's Day Faggot. Love, G.* Calling him *faggot* was Ginger's idea of a joke. An exhausted, pathetic joke.

Because Ginger's girlfriend hissed at him, she is such a dyke-in-training and she doesn't even know it, so he hissed back and he was doomed. Once, a long time ago, he overheard her playing a waltz on the piano in the band room. He had to fight not to cry, the song tugged at him so.

Because he scraped himself down the crowded walls of the cafeteria, past a jughead accompanied by a jughead parasite who said, — Out of my way, homo, as they chewed their way into the middle of the cafetcria lineup.

Because on his walk to school this morning — he's a dead man — a cat pads across the dead boy's path with a grey and yellow bird in its mouth, stepping into human boot steps pressed into the ice and snow, neat, like a dog carrying a newspaper.

Because today, tromping his way to school through mushy cigarette butts, a lost comb in the muck, waiting at this intersection as the cars slop by exhaling exhaust that burns his eyes, his phone chirps, Ginger: *i cant hang out wit u any more this time its 4 real ... I want my locket back*

Ginger will never change.

Because the crosswalk light shines its red eye, refuses to blink into green, cars spitting gravelly snow, one slap to his face after another on this Monday that refuses to start and refuses to end, he has to stand and stand, waiting for the light beside the brick wall spray-painted *Ava is a muff muncher*. Ginger wants the locket back, the only thing Ginger's ever given him, the only thing that keeps the dead boy going through all the days of Ginger pretending he doesn't exist. Monday. He can't bear it. He turns and tromps back home, ignoring cars, his frozen rubber soles scuffing iced concrete. The wind slathering cold, his exposed throat, the locket a hunk of metal pounding against his sternum, the chain winding winding round his neck.

Because he can't bear it.

He can't bear any of it. It will never get better.

Because he wants to be in charge of his own ending.

Tuesday

Faraday

Until Faraday settles into her desk and the news about Patrick Furey whacks her between the eyes, all she can think about is the tuft of evil frizz above her ear that day, what a toolshed her brother George M. is, hiding her straightening iron and not giving it back no matter how much she shrieks, and how she's finally going to buy that brocade bag with the medieval unicorn tapestried on the side and the humongous silver clasp (also unicorn-shaped) after school, and if someone else has already bought that perfect bag, and the metal shelf where it normally sits is empty dust in the shape of the bag instead of crammed with the delicious bulk of the bag itself, she will kill herself. She will.

She swings through the school bathroom door into the swirl of flushing toilets, gushing faucets and girls tit to shoulder at the mirrors lacquering on mascara and lip gloss, the smells of perfume and deodorant and freshly washed hair poofing into the air, and she tries to clamp down that frizz with another barrette, brushes on another lick or two of mascara. She tries to prepare for this day: how to not spill on herself, or have a menstrual calamity, or call her *Teacher Advisor* her *homeroom teacher* like she did last week like some junior high school loser. When she drops into her desk, the barrette clipped crooked and poking at her scalp so hard she's seeing a galaxy of stars, a boy at the back of the class neighs at her and his posse all laugh. She hooks her unicorn pen out of her unicorn pencil case and clicks it once just as her *Teacher Advisor* Mrs. Mochinski rattles out the announcements in her tin-can voice, — Yearbook club meeting in roooooom 210, graduation committee meeting at 3:15 in the band rooooooom, math club meeting tomorrow at lunch in compuuuuuuter lab 14, and Madison, the girl who sits behind Faraday, not a friend of Faraday and her unicorns, taps Faraday on the shoulder and whispers, — Patrick Furey's dead. That's why he's not here for a second day in a row. Look!

Faraday whips around in the direction of Patrick Furey's desk, her hair fanning out in the sudden wind, Patrick Furey's desk empty, Madison sucking on the corner of her cellphone, already murmuring to Jennifer next to her. Madison tucking the cellphone into the dark valley of her cleavage. Faraday clutches both hands around her pen. Jennifer's leaned over to Juana, who leans over to Maurizio, who leans over to that boy Ginger who sits at the front and who's juggling erasers and grapes from hand to hand as though they are stars and planets. His erasers and grapes abruptly bounce and zing to the floor.

Faraday raises her hand neatly, her elbow tucked in, spine straight.

— Mrs. Mochinski? she asks. — Where's Patrick today?

— Patrick? answers Mrs. Mochinski, busily fitting a new stick of chalk into its metal holder. — I don't know. He's away obviously.

Mrs. Mochinski's chalk snaps, so she fishes another one out of the box. — Okay, time to call attendance, people, so listen up! she says.

Ginger raises his hand to ask to go to the bathroom and bolts out the door, his backpack hooked over his shoulder.

Then Mrs. Mochinski calls attendance and the bell drones, and Faraday and all these alive people get up and traipse to their different classes, crowding and bottlenecking each other out into the aisles between the desks, out the classroom door as if Patrick Furey isn't dead. Faraday neatly prints the biology teacher's chalkboard notes about human kidneys on a sheet in her binder, her letters round as cherry pies, the vertical and horizontal lines straight and strong, her diagrams of Bowman's capsule and the loop of Henle each the exact width of a quarter, her fingers touching her barrette, the lined paper, the bag, a bisected kidney including cortex, medulla and nephron the width of a quarter, her hair, the boy, click the pen, her hair, that boy, her barrette, her bag, unclick the pen, her bag, her hair, the loop of Henle, click, a boy, the boy, that boy, unclick, oh boy, why that boy, the jarring rumour drilling her between the eyes, suddenly that boy, her hands crashing down from the barrette and her hair, the pen unclicked, an illustration of a kidney belonging to a dead boy, the size of a silver quarter.

The buzzer sounds, a thumb jabbed into the back of her skull, and knapsacks sprouting from backs, book bags like blood-engorged ticks swinging from armpits, the occasional jutting wheelchair handle in the hallway groping her, oomphing her in the ribs, jabbing her in the loop of Henle; she weaves toward social studies class and she cannot believe she now personally knows a person who is dead. Except: no minute of silence. No silent prayer. No special assembly. Rumours fluttering and roosting in the hallways. The walls of the school echoing and hammering with unicorn hooves only Faraday can hear.

— I heard he fell off the balcony in his building.

— Garrett said he was hit by a car.

— Accidentally poisoned when he bit into a poinsettia plant left over from Christmas.

— Crushed in a trash compactor!

Faraday blows her cheeks out into balloons of frustration.

— Maybe he's on a train to Antigua! she explodes to Madison right after lunch in the bustling lineup outside their classroom. — Maybe he's not dead at all!

Madison, chewing on the corner of her phone, shrugs her shoulders.

Mrs. Mochinski, in her chalk-splotched black pants and lady's feathery moustache, rattles out after them in the hallway to keep the noise down please, while fiddling with her brooch. But throughout the day — as they scarf down their lunch, after biology, social studies, math and religion, when Faraday has to bound from one end of the school to the other across the cracking tiles, the fresh gobs of chewing gum, around a janitor's yellow mop bucket — she doesn't see Patrick Furey anywhere. After lunch, in chemistry, French, then English. In English, again with Mrs. Mochinski, the chair where Patrick Furey normally sits, angled away slightly from its small table so it looks like he's just stood up to go to the bathroom and will be right back.

And, except for Madison's tiny gigantic rumour, Tuesday is as predictable and unkempt as any other. Almost. She learns that the ancient Greeks placed coins under the tongues of their dead loved ones, about afferent and efferent arterioles, though she knows she will forget the difference before the next test. What should be remarkable is that, for the first time ever, Madison is talking to her, a lot of people are talking to her, and she actually has a conversation with the goth girl who sits across from her. But instead, what's remarkable is that goth girl whispers that she's sure as fuck the boy killed himself because why aren't any of the teachers announcing that he's died?

— Like, if he'd been in a truck accident they would have said, says goth girl. — If he'd been randomly shot on his way to the snowboard shop, fuck, man, they'd be like, *he's been in a drive-by shooting*, but they're not. No one's saying a fucking *thing*. As if him not coming to school because he killed himself is something *ordinary*.

Goth girl drums her nails on her desk as she whispers, each of her fingers drumming on the fake wood surface, her fingertips galloping across neurotic fields. And goth girl's parents switched her to this school, a fucking Catholic school, on purpose because Catholics are supposed to be more disciplined, right? They aren't allowed to commit suicide. Right?

Tap tap tap tap tip tap, goth girl's fingers say.

— Right? Goth girl's eyes wide in the rings of charcoal eyeliner. — Right? Fuck! Right? She reaches over and grasps Faraday's arm.

— Yes, exhales Faraday, her eyes prickling at the clammy touch.

— Suicides go to hell. It's a sin for Catholics. It's a technicality with no loophole, says goth girl, her fingers drumming a hole in the cover of her paperback copy of *Romeo and Juliet.* — Well, a girl drank something in the bathroom of my last fucking school and a janitor found her still fucking *twitching* on the floor, a fucking non-Catholic school this was, and maybe I'm cursed, fuck, I'm hoisting this curse with me everywhere I go, like I thought hiding among Catholics and their fucking crucifixes would protect me, how wrong was I? I blame society! You can't run away from society, no matter how fucking hard you try.

Tiny spit bubbles fleck goth girl's lips, Faraday stares at the goth's black, chipped fingernails, the flecks of dry skin in her moonless black hair.

The goth's eyes, globby with eyeliner, abruptly turn shiny, her tapping fingers trembling and uncertain, so Faraday turns away, scribbles the first words of the notes on the board with her unicorn pen on an empty lined page near the middle of her notebook.

Goth girl's fingers resuming their synchronized, millipede-foot tapping.

Faraday would like to go to the funeral, but will the dead boy's family be upset if a stranger crashes in and plunks herself down in one of the grieving pews? She wishes goth girl's fingers would stop running, that goth girl would stop trembling and streaking her makeup and saying the f word. Mrs. Mochinski should have announced the date and time of the funeral in the daily announce-ments, should have announced the dead boy. Maybe Faraday will light a candle for the dead boy next time her parents make her go to Mass.

— Fucking Petra Mai and her skanked friends told him they were going to kill him, goth girl whispers, her black lips turning pinker as she chews off her black lipstick, voice so low Faraday can hardly tell it from the whistling in the heating vents. Petra.

Ginger's girlfriend, Petra, copying notes about Mercutio and Tybalt also like it's all ordinary, her long dusty hair a shaggy cur-tain spilling over her anorexic shoulders, snapping her gum. Ginger's chair empty too. Goth girl draws a pentacle in the margin of her coiled notebook. — That's why he hung or poisoned or shot himself, goth girl says.

— Or maybe she managed to kill him, says Faraday. — She got to him.

— Oh, fuck! exclaims the goth, her hand flinging to her raw mouth.

— *Hanged himself* is the correct grammar, the dead boy's English teacher says. — This will be on the next quiz. Fumiko, quit swearing! ... This will be on the next quiz!

The class bursts into whispers. Petra flicks her hair over one shoulder and scans the class. Jésus at the back of the class stands up and whinnies into his hand.

— You at the back of the class, you can raise your hand like everyone else, bellows the dead boy's teacher, and then she coughs, croaks.

Jésus raises his hand.

— Yes? asks Mrs. Mochinski.

— Because he was a homo-sek-shhhhyoo-al, says Jésus.

Jésus's posse howls.

Faraday looks at Jésus.

— What's *your* problem, Unicorn Girl? Jésus smirks.

— Jésus .. That attitude smells like poo, says Mrs. Mochinski. — Where have all the manners gone? ... Romeo was a homosexual? ... Please.

She holds her hand up in the air as though to say *Stop*. Coughs again.

— What's wrong with the word *unicorn*? asks Jésus. — Is it pronounced *unicorn-ee*? Shit!

The teacher flings her arms around her copy of *Romeo and Juliet*, around her drooped monobreast.

— Homosexual? says Jésus. — What's wrong with the word *homo-sek-shhhhyoo-al*? Well, he was.

— You can talk about that with the veep if you keep pushing it, Jésus.

— All right! I'm *sorry*.

— Now, says Mrs. Mochinski, — Can someone please ...

— So what if he was gay? Faraday says. Her paper one giant mess of unicorn ink.

— It's a sin, says Madison.

— Where on *earth* does it say in this play that Romeo was gay? splutters Mrs. Mochinski.

The class sizzles with whispers, a popping of *sssss* and *sssssh* as students lean forward to speak, lean backward to hear, hunch forward to click text keys to buzz to each other about the dead and dying Romeo who up until today went to their school.

— Listen, hisses goth girl, leaning across the aisle, — This is what happened: those girls from the chamber ensemble murdered him. Fuck. The ones who hang out with Ginger's girlfriend when she's not fucking sitting on Ginger's face, they're the ones. I think I've accidentally warped into the wrong Catholic dimension. I am torrentially fucked. This is so torrentially sad.

She lays her cheek down on the top of her desk. Closes her eyes. Her eyelids scarab-wing blue. Murmuring all around them.

The teacher swivels back from the board and coughs at her buzzing, whispering, humming class. She slams her copy of *Romeo and Juliet* down on the desk, another chalk breaks as it hits the floor, and she jams her hands on her hips.

— That's it! I have *had* it. You people! Stand for prayer please, staaaand for praaaayer.

The students scrape, shuffle and skulk themselves to standing.

— InthenameoftheFathertheSonandtheHolySpiritAmen, she says, crossing herself. — Our Father who art in Heaven ...

— Our Father who art in Heaven, the students say with her.

After the prayer she enforces Silent Reading until the bell.

— And by Silent Reading, says Mrs. Mochinski, — I mean Silent and Reading. Stop doodling, Faraday. Now that's a nice waste of paper and ink. Fumiko, she says to goth girl, — *Try* to stay awake for longer than a minute!

Faraday would like to hold Fumiko's hand.

Jésus jumps onto his desk and gives a loud, juicy belch.

The time is 3:19, and then that droning, time-for-home-and-dysfunctional-family bell. Faraday and her asymmetrically frizzy hair dawdle on the front steps of the school, other students in puffy coats and parkas shoving her into the sandstone door frame in a continuous herd as they crash through the doors, cascading, coursing, dribbling down to two students at a time, the occasional one cantering down the snowy carved stone steps and leaping to the bottom. Faraday leaning into the stone, scarf drawn up over her nose, not because she's cold, but because she is afraid to breathe. Clicking and unclicking a unicorn pen — the cold starting to pluck at the fingers on her clicking hand — she is afraid to walk, worried how to place her toes on each step so she won't fall and crack her head open like a snow globe on the school steps. Madison sucking her phone and telling her that rotten, indisputable thing that Patrick Furey is not in school and probably dead.

The Canadian flag whips against the grey winter sky; her head is bubble-clear on her neck. The flag isn't at half-mast like it was at her brother's school last year when that Grade 7 kid died on a downhill skiing field trip.

She breaks the spring in her pen because she has overclicked it, and nearly tumbles down the school's front steps.

She takes the bus to Bettie's Bag Boutique, the bus windows foggy with condensation. Faraday listening to staticky piano music as she stands in line at customer service with her brand-new unicorn bag. Paying for the bag, jamming her papers, books, emergency menstrual equipment — and her old bag — into the new bag, clicking closed the silver clasp in the shape of an anatomically correct unicorn — billy-goat beard, lion's tail, cloven hooves, the shadowy angle of a penis, not the kiddy, neutered, Disney horse-with-a-horn version. Leaning into and through the front door of the boutique to stand on the sidewalk and wait for her bus. The people around her walking, blabbering, spitting, begging, complaining, farting, buying, selling, and a boy from her English class. Most probably dead. Did she serve him his last large iced cappuccino? Did he die Monday morning or Monday night? Or Sunday night? Maybe she was the last person to see him alive. Should she go to the police?

She wants to plop down on the gritty, icy concrete and cry.

She remembers how he had not a single zit on his entire face. Once she knocked her eraser off her desk and it bounced across the floor. He had to reach from an awkward angle to pick it up, his face reddening as he hung upside down. Did he know he only had a month and three days to live? He exhaled a breath when he tossed the eraser to her, his face scarlet — a crack in the veneer of him.

She never was his friend. She said *Thanks* when he threw her the eraser but that was all, she was so afraid she would miss catching it. If she'd known he was going to die she would have said something or written him a note saying *Hi*. She would have donated her virginity to him even though it would have meant giving up her chance at having a unicorn lay its head in her lap as her life companion, its pearled alicorn spiralling smooth and nourishing in her hand, its shaggy lips nuzzling her other palm. Even though he would never have slept with her because he was gay, but whatever, she would have liked to give. Let him know that soon a blessing of unicorns would be here to save them all.

She wonders how many days she has left to live. If sitting on this revolting sidewalk is one of her final acts. Formaldehyde stews behind her eyes. She clasps her bag in her arms, its stiff new-car smell.

Walter

Way back on Monday, 4:17 a.m., Walter, the guidance counsellor — stone-cold irritated at his boyfriend Max because of their fight the night before, stone-cold awake hours before the alarm clock is set to shriek them awake — hauls himself out of bed and shakes open the newspaper in the dark of the kitchen. His boyfriend Max now awake too, bumps into the wall on his way to the bathroom. Walter hears the toilet flush, so he flicks on the coffee machine. The coffee almost done gurgling as Walter cranks open a can of cat food while their cat, Lieutenant Fong, twines her tail around his shins, and Max sucks in his morning smoke on the back porch, wrapped in his parka, his boots trailing their laces. They spoon low-cal cereal and skim milk from their bowls, drink the coffee, bite into toast with peanut butter, Max still oppressively silent like a great big pouting man-baby, his silent fury left over from last night because Walter accidentally marked the coffee table with a ring from his glass of orange juice. The Cold War all over again because of a bit of marked varnish on the *coffee table*. It's 5:32 a.m. as they knot their scarves and pull on their toques and boots. Walter stuffs the book he finished this weekend into the papers spilling from his satchel: Max's secretary, Joy, recommended it, *The Pride and the Joy* it's called, and he loved it. *Loved* it. He hasn't cried so much since he read *Sounder* when he was eleven.

Max about to yank open the front door.

— Wait, says Walter. — Where's my goodbye kiss?

Max purses his lips, his arms crossed. Leans forward and pecks Walter on the mouth.

— That's right, says Walter.

— Doesn't fix the goddamn table, spits Max, furiously shooting back the lock on the door.

— Oh bugger off, says Walter. Max pounds his feet into the snow.

— *You* bugger off.

Max violently brushes snow off the car windshield, the hood.

— No, *you* bugger off, whispers Walter, stepping through the front gate and out onto the slushy sidewalk.

That Monday morning before all the bad things happened. A normal Monday. Monday. Monday. Monday.

Monday, Walter decides to walk to work instead of taking the bus while the diapered and swaddled giant squalling baby Sir Max, His Royal Highness, the Sulking King of Coffee Tables, who as principal of the school and so technically Walter's boss, drives away and onward to his special, reserved parking space at the school. Excruciatingly early for work. Walter estimates it will take him an hour and forty minutes to walk to school. Two hours maximum.

Walter forced to run the last fifteen minutes to work, he broke down and jumped on the bus part of the way there, his clunky boots nearly kicking off his feet as he lumbers through snow-banks, leaps icy gutters, his coat flapping wide open, his armpits soggy, his knees creaking, his lungs raw and heaving, socks sliding down inside his boots, his heels naked and rubbing against the felt lining. Bursting through the doors only one minute before the first bell which means he's twenty-nine minutes late.

Walter mops and blots himself down in the bathroom with paper towels as best he can, his shirt drenched with sweat; ten minutes later, sauntering casually, his lungs still smouldering, to the main office to refill his coffee cup, *The Pride and the Joy* under his arm, when Joy the secretary says, — *The Pride and the Joy?* No no, I said *The Pride of Provence!* It's a book about a man from Ontario who decides to renovate his country house in Provence. Look at this picture I took of my husband and son when we did a bus tour of Provence. More like an eating tour!

Walter crinkles his lips, — That's awesome! he says, tucking *The Pride and the Joy* behind his back. His chest pings. His book a different book entirely.

She flips through her little plastic book of pictures twice, so he won't miss the white canvas cap her husband is wearing, how tanned she is in her striped tube top, camera case slung over her shoulder, an irritating Frenchman who pops his head into the picture at the last second. Her son's round face and barbed wire teeth blocking the view of a stone church, the outline of a quaint bakery window neatly arranged with iced pastries and loaves of bread. Walter gazes at the pictures, gazes at the bobby pins criss-crossed on the back of Joy's head from where he is hunched over her shoulder for her exciting pictures.

— How wonderful! he says. — Awesome!

He grins when she swivels in her chair to watch the delight on his face. He's read the completely wrong book — a dreadfully wrong book, a sentimental, gloopy, ridiculously happy-ending gay love story that he read for twelve hours straight on the weekend while Max was out, and which made him bawl.

— You should go to France! exclaims Joy. — You can borrow our Michelin guide. And the French women are beautiful. Beautiful! Very stylish. Find yourself a girlfriend in no time. In fact, I have a girlfriend in my book club, Yolanda, recently divorced ...

— Getting too old for that kind of nonsense, Walter grins. He grips the wrong book, tucked even more firmly, behind his back. She's new, been working here for less than a year. He's a fat black man in his fifties, an old bachelor, who eats alone in his guidance counsellor office every lunch hour. Doesn't she know to leave him alone?

He points at a picture of her son doing a grinning handstand in a fountain to distract her from Yolanda, from the book burning his hand. His spilling desire, his longing to talk about *The Pride and the Joy* with someone, anyone, in this relentless place, who might understand just one word. Max so absorbed in the damn coffee table, he refused to listen when Walter tried to tell him about the book this weekend. On the way back to his office,

Walter grasps the book, title in, against his chest, its pages slippery with inadvertent radioactivity.

Walter puffs into his office, then realizes he forgot his coffee cup in the main office. He opens the Tupperware container on his desk, a jumble of carrots, celery pieces and cherry tomatoes. He pops a tomato into his mouth and bites on it while he scrolls his emails, flips through his appointment book, scratches his beard hard all over, beard dandruff flakes fluttering, then remembers with a start that graduation is in less than four months. He fritters the morning away printing up Grade 12 transcripts and trying to come up with a more time-efficient plan for the graduation ceremony.

After a lunch spent eating an egg salad sandwich from the machine in the cafeteria and looking out his office window at a snowy honeysuckle hedge, he meets with two students, Laura Giardini at 2:30 p.m. who wants to argue about her aptitude test, — I don't want to be a hairdresser, I want to be a lawyer, why doesn't the test show that I should be a lawyer? Can I take it again? How many times?

Josh Gatchalian at 3:00 p.m. who doesn't want to talk about anything, — My mom told me to come, he says. — Nope, don't know why I'm here. So what if I'm failing band, I never wanted to play the trombone anyway, only fags get good grades in band, Mr. Boyle.

Only a half an hour left in this Monday. Walter opens files on both Laura Giardini and Josh Gatchalian, adds their file icon selves to his list, types in Laura's history from her pink Grade 10 sheet, figures out Josh's aptitude test results say he's suitable for the police or law enforcement or party planning. Walter leaves a voice mail on Josh's parents' phones, — I think it would help Josh if we all had a meeting to talk about why playing the trombone is vital. Okay. Awesome. Hope you have a great evening!

Sequestered in his office, he opens his Tupperware again, a piece of carrot crunched in half when he picks up the ringing phone and Max is calling him from down the hall, — Mr. Boyle. Walter, I need to speak with you immediately. I need you.

A piece of carrot half-bitten, half-chewed, the secret thrill he gets when he has to interact with his boyfriend at work. Their dangerous, exciting secret.

Thirty seconds later, his hand on the principal's doorknob.

The door opening, the vice-principals Morty and Gladys standing at attention on either side of the principal, a carved wooden crucifix hanging on the wall behind his head. Their silence cool metal. Walter's heart falters.

Walter's Monday should have been the tedious photocopy of every other Monday, but Max the principal tents his pale fingers and breaks open the rotting egg of Patrick Furey's suicide to him and the two vice-principals, turning this Monday into a Monday of unique suffering.

— A student in our school has made the disastrous decision to end his life, Max says, his voice quavering. — I have already begun taking the appropriate measures.

It's okay to cry, Maxie, Walter wants to say. *You blubber away.*
— I'll draft a memo for the teachers and staff, Walter says instead.

— And put in your memo, says Max, — that staff and teachers are forbidden to discuss the death with the students until I have all the facts. We'll let the students know on Wednesday.

— In my position as head guidance counsellor I have to ask if you really think that's a good idea, Max, says Walter. — Better to give them the facts as we know them as soon as possible because the students will figure it out themselves but they'll figure it out all wrong. We know enough already about how he died, don't we? Today's Monday. By tomorrow afternoon the rumours will be out of control. Better to get the grief counsellors in first thing Tuesday morning.

— Get that memo written up, says Max, turning to his desk and picking up a stack of paper. — You may go now, Walter.

Walter exits the office like a butler instructed to go scrub the chamber pots, his face and feelings sutured tight as he trudges back down the hallway, slams through the drawers on his office desk, prepares to write his memo, Monday fucking afternoon.

He tries not to dissolve into the 98 percent water he is made of when Joy rushes into his office and grips him in a bosomy hug.

— Oh Walter, she says, as she grips his upper arm, his overflowing waist, — You looked so sad. Like you needed a hug.

— Sometimes it is hard to understand God's plan, gasps Walter, trying to pull himself away. — We just have to trust He knows what He is doing. The boy's in a better place now.

He accidentally touches her bra strap through her blouse, yanks his hand back, pulls himself away from Joy. Clumsily pats her on the shoulder. Joy's crinkled eyes squish out tears.

— I never understand how that's supposed to make someone feel better, she says in a flannelly voice, her nose bright red.

Walter starts to draft the memo that Joy will slip into all the teachers' mail slots Tuesday morning. He tries to hunt down the right words for the memo, thumbing through his thesaurus, settling for appropriately vague, consoling words: *unfortunately* rather than *tragically*, *passed away* rather than *died*, *please refrain* rather than *forbidden*. His face to the computer screen in his office, he swallows, his Adam's apple sliding up his throat, tipping further up into his sinus cavity, cutting off his breath.

They meet Monday night in the front foyer of their house, Walter and Max, when Max finally swings closed and bolts the door behind him. He kicks off his winter boots, the air heavy. Walter puts a hand on each of Max's shoulders.

— This day, exhales Max.

— I'll crack you open a beer, Maxie, says Walter. He kisses Max's temple. The skin sticky.

They eat from the bowls of stew in front of them, Lieutenant Fong perched neatly in Walter's lap, studying every movement of his spoon from the bowl to the mouth to the bowl. Max inserting spoonfuls of stew into his own mouth as though administering to an assembly line: deposit, chew, swallow, deposit, chew, deposit, swallow.

Walter's lips slack, Max's lips tight.

— At least it didn't happen on school property, says Max, his words clipped and cauterized. — That's one good thing.

Walter's ears pop. — *What* did you just say? Walter's spoon clattering into his bowl. Lieutenant Fong skitters to the floor from Walter's lap.

The growing puddle of stew in Walter's belly sour, coagulated.

— It didn't happen on school property. It's technically not a school issue.

— You know what? says Walter, — This stew tastes like diarrhea. It looks like diarrhea too.

— My mother made this stew, snaps Max.

— Lucky she didn't make it on school property.

Max's jaw clicking rhythmically, the scrape of his metal spoon on the bottom of the ceramic bowl. Walter tosses his bowl in the sink, grabs the pot from the stove.

— Oh, and by the way, I don't appreciate the way you talked to me today, says Walter as he scrubs the glutinous remains of the stew from the pot with steel wool, his man-boobs bobbing under his T-shirt. — We have enough facts about how the boy died. What other details do you need?

Max stands up from the table, rattles cups and plates in the dishwasher as he inserts and reinserts them, his elbows jabbing, stabbing the air.

— Do I need to remind you of suicide contagion? says Max, his face swivelling from the dishwasher to Walter, pencil-dot eyes. — Or are you having some kind of neuron seizure? You cannot even *begin* to conceive of the damage this will do to the school's reputation, can you?

Walter harrumphs as he slops the dishrag back and forth across the counter, knots up the plastic bag of garbage, the bag sloppy and heavy as he trudges it out the back door. He swings the green garbage bag in an arc into the trashcan, the metal clanging, the bag landing with a tinny squelch. He clumps back into the house, snow squeaking under his feet.

— The students will not find out ahead of Wednesday that there was a death, says Max. — Or any erroneous details about the death, if news management is done correctly. News management is your job. He slams the dishwasher door closed, his elbows folding back to his sides.

Walter sloshes water into the kettle for a cup of instant decaf.

Walter regards Max in his old sweatpants, his oversize T-shirt proclaiming *Don't Mess with Sulu* drooping over his ass, Max locking the dishwasher door, stabbing the On button.

— Tell me, says Walter. — What are you feeling? It's okay to cry.

— One moment please. I can't hear a word you're saying with the water on, Max says in that strident principal's voice that makes Walter want to set his own hair on fire as he double-checks, triple-checks the lights on the dishwasher. — What did you say? asks Max.

— Oh forget it, says Walter, turning to the cupboard for a coffee cup. He stops. His hand rests on the cupboard door.

Something suspended inside him has just dropped. Lieutenant Fong meows.

Max adjusts the single magnet on the fridge, a mini replica of the Starship Monoceros from his favourite television show, *Sector Six*. He brushes past Walter on his way out of the kitchen and into the TV room because tonight is Monday night and Monday night is *Sector Six* night even if it's just mid-season reruns and a boy died today. Max dusty, mouldy, plumped on the couch.

Sunday, Saturday, Thursday, Friday. Last Friday.

Walter should have noticed, should have hooked the dead boy Patrick Furey back from the edge of that cliff. He should have stood at the bottom and let the boy bounce off his belly. Walter never met the parents, he never met the dead boy really except to squirm across the desk from him last Friday as the boy insisted on opening his mouth and confessing his obsessions into Walter's ears. Patrick Furey was addicted to another boy. I'm in love, he told Walter. Patrick's voice jumping and squeaking as he creaked forward on the chair opposite Walter, Walter nervously spooning out globs of canned therapy-speak as fast as he could in the direction of the boy, — Is that so? How do you feel about that? Really? Mm-hmm.

Walter noting every papery curl, every ragged edge of the posters pinned to the wall behind the boy's head: the poster of the *Hang In There* ginger kitten clinging to a fence, the Black History Month poster trumpeting *Inspiration* in rainbow colours. Walter still managing to blob out platitudes, a horse shitting in a geometrically perfect line in a parade.

But as the dead boy talked, his problem mushroomed between them, the boy blowing his problem into a giant word balloon that squished them into opposing corners, — He's in my English class, said the soon-to-be-dead boy. — I really love him. He gave me his grandmother's necklace. I can't sleep anymore, Mr. Boyle. This school is an insane asylum. They stole my skateboard. Mr. Applegate says that because it was off school property the school isn't responsible.

— *Insane asylum* is a bit harsh, don't you think? said Walter.

The chair's hiss as the boy leaned forward, fingers at his chest, fiddling with the heart pendant on the long chain around his neck, his sweater on inside out, his eyes wet and wide. He said, — *You* know what I mean, right?

The dead boy wearing a girl's heart-shaped locket around his neck. His fingers tangling in the delicate chain. His heart exposed outside his clothes.

— I don't know what you mean, said Walter.

— Well you're — you're —

— No, Walter said. Because he would not lose his job for this kid. — Let's focus, he said. — This isn't about me. Sounds like your problem is a lack of focus. You don't know what your feelings are. You're distracted from your schoolwork. Keep focused on the important things.

Walter caught up a pencil from his desk, started tapping his front teeth with the eraser end. He dropped the pencil, slid open his desk's top drawer and crinkled open a package of Sezme Sesame Snaps. Crunched a Sezme wafer loudly.

The boy leaned back in his chair. His mouth a straight line.

Walter finished chewing his Sezme. Swallowed. Picked sesame seeds from his teeth with tongue, then cleared his throat. He picked up his pencil. — Life is all about focus, Walter said, resuming tapping the pencil against his teeth.

— Mmm, said the boy.

— Awesome, said Walter. — Thanks for the talk. Good luck!

And the boy slipped from the office. Walter too sweaty to call out a goodbye, his hands clasped in his lap to clamp down on the shaking.

The boy left the door ajar so Walter wheeled over in his desk chair and pushed it closed himself. He turned to his computer and clicked open a new file. The boy's name, *Furey, Patrick* under the file icon. Under category *Hobbies*, Walter typed, *Likes skateboarding*, into the electronic file. He clicked the file closed, then turned to his lunch bag for another package of Sezme Snaps. He jammed all the Snaps in at once, the sharp corners piercing his gums.

Saturday, Sunday, Monday, Tuesday, Friday, Monday. Monday. Monday. Monday.

The boy having solved his problem then.

Mrs. Mochinski

As Mrs. Mochinski pulls open the door to the school Tuesday morning, she smells that familiar smell of floor cleaner, basketball rubber, gym socks and chalk, the smell that tricks her into believing every time she walks into the school that she hasn't yet received her Grade 12 diploma, that she hasn't yet gotten past high school or scored a high-paying corporate job like the ones they always give advice about in the newspaper's career section. She grabs her mail from her pigeonhole, scuttles through the hallways, traversing the long, wrong, subterranean way to her classroom because she doesn't want to talk to anyone. Anyone. She unlocks the door of her classroom, inadvertently slams it behind her. She found the divorce papers in her mailbox this morning. Her husband's inky signature scrubbed into the papers. He dropped them off last night, in the dark, like a coward. When she signs the papers she will be a single woman, and her life will be over.

Then she reads the memo, the paper limp in her hand. Reads that she and all the other teachers are to 'Please refrain from discussing the tragedy with students until Principal Applegate has gathered all the facts.' For a moment, she can't even remember who Patrick Furey is, is sure she's never taught him, and then her head threatens to cave in.

In her ten-minute Teacher Advisor group first thing this morning, the unicorn girl who always sits in the front shoots her hand into the air.

— Mrs. Mochinski? she asks, and Mrs. Mochinski dreads the question she knows will come, she just knows it. — Where's Patrick today?

— Patrick? answers Mrs. Mochinski, scrambling with her chalk, her chalk holder, trying to stop her hands from trembling. — I don't know. *He's away obviously.*

He's away obviously. What is she? An android with a microchip instead of a heart? The stick of chalk in her hand snaps

in half. She shakily fishes another one out of the box. Coughs.
— Okay, time to call attendance, people, so listen up! she says.
And, accordingly, the rest of the day spirals down the shithole.
— *Hanged himself* is the correct grammar, Mrs. Mochinski corrects the goth girl in the afternoon English class, and immediately she wants to kick herself, correcting grammar about hanging on this day of all days, the dead boy's desk a gaping hole in the middle of the classroom. The goth girl swearing like a trucker.

— This will be on the next quiz, she continues, trying to recuperate some kind of control. — Fumiko, quit swearing! And by the way, you people, Romeo killed himself with a vial of poison, not through hanging. Pay attention. This will be on the next quiz!

The students' antennae spring up and they all write down *Quiz* on shreds and sheets of paper, backs of books, backs of hands. Then the class bursts into whispers. The worst little fucker of them all at the back of the class stands on top of his desk and whinnies into his hand.

— You at the back of the class, says Mrs. Mochinski. — You can raise your hand like everyone else, she says, and then her vocal cords kick back so she coughs. — Let's have some respect around here, she croaks. Her voice dying early today. She tries to inhale a deep yoga breath, yoga breaths are supposed to keep the anger away.

Jésus raises his hand.

— Yes? she asks.

— Because he was a homo-sek-shhhhyoo-al, says Jésus.

The baseball caps at the back of the room howl with laughter, and she wants to shove a bar of Irish Spring soap in his mouth and scrub until it foams. She chokes on her yoga breath.

— What's *your* problem, Unicorn Girl? he smirks to the unicorn girl.

— We don't talk that way in class, Jésus. You know I think that attitude smells like poo, says Mrs. Mochinski. She grabs up her copy of *Romeo and Juliet* from the desk. — Where have all the manners gone? And there is no obvious indication in the play that Romeo was a homosexual, but if you have proof to support your statement, by all means educate us — using respectful and appropriate language. Please —

Her voice too shrill, the control seeping away, she coughs again, these students make her sick!

— What's wrong with the word *unicorn?* asks Jésus. — Is it pronounced *unicorn-ee?* Shit!

Mrs. Mochinski crosses her arms over her copy of *Romeo and Juliet.* She wants to boil Jésus's guts in a pot. She wants to go home and pour herself a salad-bowl-sized glass of wine.

— Homosexual? says Jésus. — What's wrong with the word *homo-sek-shhhhyoo-al?* Well, he was.

— You can talk about that with the veep if you keep pushing it, Jésus.

— All right! I'm *sorry.*

Jésus and his little crew giggling and poking. She will get through this day. She will live to the end.

— Now, asks the dead boy's teacher, pretending her students are nothing but the hum of the furnace, the buzz of the fluorescent lights, — Now, she repeats. — Can someone please tell me how we know Romeo's love for Juliet is the *real* thing?

Mrs. Mochinski does not want to die on this Jésus hill, her hands full of paper and chalk dust. God, her underwire bra is stabbing a major artery and she may be dead before the last bell, the thousands of students trampling her body as they buffalo-jump out the door. The dead boy's desk sits in the middle of the room and she isn't allowed to say anything to the students because the principal doesn't have all the facts. Why would having the facts matter?

She turns her back to the class, her copy of *Romeo and Juliet* clutched in her hand. She rolls a piece of chalk between the fingers of her other hand, the many eruptions in the classroom only a background hum. Her face to the board, her fingers picking up then clinking down roll after roll of chalk. Her nose moist, just on the verge of running, her wedding ring dull under the dust. The dead boy a homosexual.

Romeo and Juliet. Two dead teenagers. This is what she needs to concentrate on. Even though who besides their parents cares? Even these kids in her class care only about the sex.

— So what if he was gay? says the unicorn girl.

Good for you, Mrs. Mochinski wants to say. *A++*.

— It's a sin, chirps the chinless one behind her.

That's an F for you, Chinless, thinks Mrs. Mochinski. *F*–!

— Where on *earth* does it say in this play that Romeo was gay? splutters Mrs. Mochinski.

The class dissolves into a buzzing like she has stumbled into a flight of mosquitoes, an infuriating whine needling every nerve in her body.

Mrs. Mochinski whirls from the board and wheezes out another cough. She slams the play down on her desk, the chalk in her other hand jumps, shatters on the floor. Hands on her hips. — That's it! I have *had* it. You people! Stand for prayer please, stand for prayer.

The students rumble and screech their chairs to standing.

— In the Name of the Father, the Son and the Holy Spirit, Amen, she says, making the sign of the cross, accidentally chalking her left boob. Then she leads them in the Lord's Prayer, squinting through her partly closed eyes at them, ready to quash any hijinks.

— So sit down and do your Silent Reading. And by Silent Reading, says Mrs. Mochinski, — I mean Silent and Reading. Stop doodling, Faraday, she says, suddenly remembering her name. — Now that's a nice waste of paper and ink. Fumiko, she says to goth girl, — Try to stay awake for longer than a minute.

Little Jésus fuckface jumps onto his desk and belches.

At 3:45 p.m., Mrs. Mochinski beetles through the icy school parking lot to her car, yanks open the door and dives into the driver's seat. Back to her own life. The divorce papers in their neat manila envelope lie on the passenger seat. She left the car unlocked this morning on purpose, hoping someone might steal them. The only thing she cared about this morning. Patrick Furey gone for good, then. A boy she hardly knew in her third-period English class. Grade 12, then. Nearly at the end. Gripping the cold steering wheel, she coughs and coughs, lets the coughs erupt unimpeded, the tears gushing and streaming from her eyes.

Walter

Tuesday morning, with the memo with its bullshit instructions sent out to every teacher, the news of Patrick Furey's suicide flinging itself against the bars of its cage, Walter strides busily through the school hallways, checking the bulletin boards for inappropriate material as a way to avoid his own office.

Finally in his office, he snacks on a power bar and sips tomato juice. He sucks up the juice too fast and droplets splash out his nose onto the keyboard. He stares at the bloody drops, breathes the stale air in his little pod of an office. Walter's back crawling because that dead boy is sitting in that chair, still and silent, sweater resolutely inside out. Walter keeps his back to the dead boy, slides the binders back into their correct places above his desk, but it makes no difference: the surface of his desk, the computer screen with its hundreds of rows of tiny folder icons, are a multiplying landfill. Patrick Furey's tiny folder icon smoulders on the screen, a disorderly tic, a rogue wave, a cigarette butt screwed into the middle of a strawberry-rhubarb pie. Walter clicks the dead boy's folder icon open. *Hobbies: Likes skateboarding.* Walter prints a copy for the parents.

This Tuesday. This Monday that refuses to end. Every day a stretch of endless Mondays.

— Have you solved your problem then, Walter whispers to the dead boy. — Awesome.

He leans his chin on his fist.

The radiator ticks.

He stuffs *The Pride and the Joy* deep into the outside pocket of his briefcase. He will abandon the book at a bus stop on the way home. Maybe someone will read it and it will change his life. Or drive him further to the brink. It will end up in a landfill. As a hunk of trash in the sea. A skateboard in a river.

When Walter finally unlocks the front door of their house Tuesday evening — Max still muscling around at work making phone calls, writing agendas for Wednesday morning — the first thing Walter does is gobble down one of the two foil-wrapped Grandpa burgers with added bacon and cheese he bought on the way home, the warm meaty treasures at the bottom of the paper A&W bag, one for him and one for Max. He unpacks the burger, unhinges his jaws and bites into it, one bite so big the burger he draws away from his face is only a quarter its original size, a chubby crescent moon. He chews through the juicy meat patties, wipes ketchup, meat-juice drips, bacon fat from his beard with a paper napkin, slurps the stringy, wet lettuce splattered on his cheek. Lieutenant Fong leaps onto the table and perches next to his plate, her tail whisking, head cocking side-to-side as she assesses the waning burger, the cardboard container of disappearing french fries percolating with grease. Walter takes a long, freezing slurp of his chocolate shake, the ice cream chilling his tongue, the roof of his mouth, his throat; he waits for the fat from the burger to give him a great big hug from the inside, but today the hug doesn't come.

The cat yawns, her mouth bristling with fangs. He tries to pet her, hopes she might curl into his lap, but she squirts away from his outstretched hand.

When he's crammed the last of the burger into his mouth, landslid the rest of the french fries down his throat, he scoops up the chocolate shake and screeches his chair away from the table.

He unfolds himself onto the carpet in the basement den; his upper half releases so quickly he falls straight backward and his head bounces. He lies on the carpet, his head bloated, his joints hardening, tears streaming from his eyes, pooling in his ears. A very nice pose for a man of fifty-two, only three years away from retirement. How terrific for a man whose job it is to advise young people about career choices, course schedule timetabling, how to participate in the world as upstanding citizens, and how not to kill themselves. The cat licking her anus right next to his face, her leg sticking into the air like she's offering it for supper.

His heels grilling on the heat register, he can smell sweaty stink billowing out the collar of his shirt. He reaches for

Lieutenant Fong's left paw. She lets him take it in his hand, she spills onto the floor next to his face, her body hot and solid. He strokes the pads' cool, soft leather, the furry knuckles. She pretends to sleep, her eyelids slightly parted. She presses her other leathery palm against his chin. Listening to the furnace sighing, belching through the vent at his feet, smelling his own shame, eyes sticky with tears, resting his hand on Lieutenant Fong's back as she clambers up onto his stomach and curls herself into a warm turd.

His stomach flip-flops. He has to tug open his eyes, gummed together as they are.

He lurches to standing, Lieutenant Fong swinging to the carpet, a claw hooked into his sleeve, and he lumbers to the kitchen to eat the second Grandpa burger, the second set of french fries he's stowed in the warm oven. Max won't be home for ages. And burgers don't taste good cold.

Walter is not the dead boy's mother. He is not the dead boy's father. He was just his guidance counsellor. What was the last thing he said to the dead boy? *Good luck.* Or *Perk up.*

Max

Today is Tuesday. The day is one elongated blob. A temporal Möbius loop that makes him so dizzy he might vomit.

Saturday night Max the school principal drives his parents to a female impersonator show. He inhales his cigarette to the glorious, bitter end, grinds it into the ashtray on their porch, then ushers them into his car.

— Mother, you've slammed the seatbelt in the door. Mother, the door, Mother, no, the door, your seatbelt. Right. Good.

And his car spins off into the snow.

Before he leaves home to pick them up, he pecks Walter goodbye on the top of his thinning curly black hair, Walter haloed by the lamp next to the couch.

— Mmm hmm, says Walter. Walter wearing his bifocals and thumbing pages in his novel, chewing his moustache. Not until Max's key is turning in the lock does he hear Walter yell, — Bye, Maxie!

Max would rather be sitting beside Walter, his bony toes tucked under Walter's warm buttocks, watching old DVD reruns of *Sector Six* or *Star Trek* or *Battlestar Galactica* with a Guinness at his elbow, but it is his parents' fiftieth wedding anniversary and his father specifically requested that Max come along, said, — Your mother and I won't have anything to talk about, you're a terrific buffer, sonny.

So even though he would rather be stuck on the wrong end of Satan's pitchfork than watch men mincing around in miniskirts for two hours, he drives his parents on the bitterest night in February, the windshield brittle and bumpy with ice from falling wet snow. The star female impersonator is named Crêpe Suzette — *how original.* Obviously Max has accidentally stumbled into 1977. The waitress deposits their drinks, a giant strawberry daiquiri in front of his mother, a White Russian for his father, a club soda for him — no, he doesn't care if it's a lemon or a lime slice,

— Surprise me, he says to the waitress. He jingles the keys in his pocket while his parents order their food, quesadillas for his mother and spaghetti and meatballs for his father, then he stands up and straightens the crease in his pants. Sits down again. He could roar for a cigarette. — I'll have the salmon steak, he says, then he puts his head in his hands.

He lifts his head from his hands and nearly faints when a brown female impersonator in a Wonder Woman costume checks him out first thing, before the show has even started. She glides into the room on her red stilettos, jerks to a stop, her shoulders and long black hair flinging back, and violates him with her neon-blue contact lenses from under her impossibly long, curling eyelashes. Does she recognize him, he doesn't recognize her, he hasn't been to a bar in decades, *oh God please make it go away*, and his father's face is chubby and wide with smiling when Crêpe Suzette kicks her back heel and sashays a perfect forty-five-degree angle toward their table. Jazz-stepping toward Max, she glides right past Max so she can stroke Max's father's bald head with one long, golden brown finger. She cradles his father's face right next to her gold bald-eagle breasts. His father almost exploding right there, his mother smiling wildly into her strawberry daiquiri. Walter would laugh hysterically if he were here. He thinks Max's parents are secretly swingers.

During the show, Crêpe Suzette and the other men in dresses swan around a giant leopard-print high heel set right in the middle of the stage. They single out men in the audience — the ugliest, dweebiest, oldest men who are sitting next to delighted, laughing wives. The drag queens crack jokes about Prince Charles, balls, princesses, balls, tiaras, balls, balls, balls. Max, the soon-to-be-dead boy's principal, drinks his club soda. He could be smoking on his back porch right now, or at his desk, his fingers ragged with typing. Among the important items:

• Choose a guest speaker for this year's graduation ceremony. It isn't too late to get that female newscaster. The
one who reported on the big fire last year.

• Phone the bishop and run interference between him and the mother who complained that her son said his teacher was forcing them to read pornography in English class: *The Wars* by Timothy Findley.

• Have that carpet in the basement bedroom removed and figure out what type of flooring he and Walter want down there.

• Manipulate the budget data so that he can find the money to deal with the graffiti in the north stairwell.

• Purchase a carton of cigarettes. He is down to three packs and only if he rations will they last the week.

He tries not to pull back his sleeve to look at the glowing hands on his watch because his mother will ask him if he isn't enjoying himself and he'll have to stammer out, *Of course, of course, I adore the dance routines!* but the soon-to-be-dead boy's principal can't help nudging up his sleeve just once: 10:36 and 17 seconds. The soggy slice of lemon disintegrating in the bottom of his glass.

— Aren't you having a good time? asks his mother, her icy hand clutching his.

He has to void his bladder, but he doesn't want any of those lousy transvestites to direct their heat-seeking-missile, faux mammary glands in his direction. His bladder is about to pop when Crêpe Suzette starts a routine about how he can tell the straight men from the gays in the room by what kind of socks they're wearing; Max feels the blood drop from his head to the soles of his feet, feels the urine suck right up out of his bladder and flood his already toxic system. Suzette moves from foot to foot to foot and calls out — Straight! Gay! (the audience laughs) Straight! Straight! Oh honey, you're *so* straight! (the audience laughs again) Straight! Straight! Max's ankle grasped in Crêpe Suzette's hand, Suzette yanks up his trouser leg and evaluates his sock. Even though every strand of hair on his head is already white, Max can still feel his hair bleach, has a desperate child's wish that he could just teleport out of here. Suzette shouts out, — White tube sock!

Straight! and Max wants to weep. He blinks quickly to barricade the tears, he is straight, thank God he is straight, he would lose his job if anyone found out the truth, the snow razoring outside the lounge windows, and his father claps Max on the shoulder, his mother waves for another daiquiri, the dead boy's principal sizzles in the liquid gleam of his almost-horror.

He sees the dull, damp ring corroded into the surface of the coffee table top before he even makes it completely in the front door of his house, the table his grandfather made with his bare hands from a fallen maple tree, and the surface gleaming except for the now-permanent ring just off to the left, where Walter must have set down a wet glass or a hot mug, and he wants to clutch his bare hands around Walter's neck and squeeze, then kick him in the stomach, kick the entrails right out of him. Watch Walter sob and expire because he ruined the only beautiful family heirloom Max owns.

Max pulls off his argyle socks, brushes his teeth, pokes his scruffy toothbrush around in his mouth. He's so angry his mouth almost locks shut while he bawls Walter out after Mass on Sunday for ruining the varnish on the coffee table, his back to Walter in the bed for the entire Sunday night, his head brimming with vermin, fucking Crêpe Suzette and his father, his father's face practically buried between some tweaked-out faggot's tits, his mother chewing on the umbrella from her strawberry daiquiri. And now the coffee table. Wrecked and destroyed. Just like everything else.

Monday afternoon, so abruptly it pains his teeth, so loudly he doesn't even have the chance to take his keys out of his pocket, take off his coat, not even his scarf, he has one glove off, only one, he got to the school at 6:19 a.m., he's been downtown at meetings all day, biting down his lunch during a bathroom break, and he just wants to decompress in the imaginary holodeck in his office, but his secretary, Joy, rushes to him, sails into his office on a punch of perfume and says, — Patrick Furey's father called in that Patrick won't be coming to school tomorrow, then said he killed himself this morning.

Max stops pulling off his second glove, his hand still hot from the first glove, a boy in Grade 12 killed himself, Max feels strung up by the neck. He gasps.

— How did he kill himself? he asks Joy. — Do they know where?

— Oh, she says, a box of paper clips showering silver from her hands. — Oh. His father didn't go into details. And she shakes her head. — Now why would that boy want to go and do that?

— Mr. Boyle, he says into the phone. — Walter.

The school week is only five hours old but already assassinated. Max *hates* Mondays.

Notify the crisis team immediately, then phone the parents, pass on his condolences and delicately get the facts around the death. Both vice-principals shuffle into his office. He will need the details, every one, because soon the phone calls will start jangling in, and he will have to know what the suicide has to do with his school, his staff, his student body, did it happen on school property, he has to know because he will be running the front line, dodging, catching, lobbing reporters, parents, teachers, the superintendent. He will need to know the circumstances of the death better than he knows the hairs and wrinkles on the backs of his hands. The school's inhabitants a simmering mob. He will need to clamp the lid down on this boiling pot. He will need to burn this witch until not even ash remains. He snaps his fingers at Joy for the crisis team phone number, then immediately apologizes; she is new and doesn't know when he is being efficient rather than rude.

— I had a restless sleep last night. Do accept my apologies, Joy.

Joy's comma of a mouth sagging open in distress, her eyes limp. He could kill this kid. What was his name? Furey. Max's family heirloom absolutely decimated.

He will have to buy Joy chrysanthemums or a box of chocolate truffles. She sits at her desk, poking pens into a jar, her mouth melting into an upside-down U.

The smooth running of his high school disrupted, ruined — a hole punched in the walls he practically put up with his own hands.

He pulls out his chair and holds the phone number between his fingers. Fumbles his bifocals out of his pocket.

Because it might sound odd and he would never tell anyone else this — well, Walter perhaps — but a school *is* like a spaceship, just like on *Sector Six*, the best fictional example he knows of a well-run organization with a leader who is firm but personable, effective. And all the smaller parts have to work together to make the greater machine function. He is the captain of this ship, the crank in charge of the wheels and cogs. Colonel Shakira from *Sector Six* never has to buy Lieutenant Fong a box of chocolates to apologize for speaking too gruffly when she issues orders, but there you go.

Time for red alert.

The ringing of the crisis team's phone burrs in his ear. He props the phone between his head and his shoulder, smooths and straightens his tie with both hands, jingles the keys in his pocket.

Tuesday he is still on the phone. He swears he never went home.

Ginger

Because people in school were spreading an inconceivable rumour.

Ginger bangs out the front doors of the school — he doesn't care who sees him — and he slides over ice and hurdles over snowbanks all the way home. Just in case it's true. Is it true?

— Home already? asks his grandfather, reading a Czech newspaper on the computer. His trifocals sliding off his nose. — Interesting, he says.

Ginger texts Furey. Then after five minutes he thumbs in the phone number. Language leaks from the phone and burns in his ear, not Furey's moonlit voice but a man's voice with too much breath between the letters in the words. — Yessss? Whooo? Were you a friend of his? asks the plastic chunk, the sun, the past tense, exploding in Ginger's ear.

His grandfather clicks off the computer and tells Ginger that if he's decided he's home for the day, he can shovel the sidewalk. Snowed almost as deep as his knees last night, the mail deliverer will refuse to make it past the gate. Grampa might throw his back out again if he tries to shovel it himself so be a good boy and clear the walk, yes?

Because Furey told Ginger he loved him while they were doing it the last time, and what could Ginger do with that information? He had no idea what container to put those words in, how to hold them without them depositing their ooze all over. He just wanted to get away, he needed him and Furey to be done. He wishes he could push the words, all in a clump, back into Patrick's mouth, that he could clump them into an icy snowball and whing them back.

Because his girlfriend Petra guessed the truth. And Ginger didn't deny that he wasn't sure he wasn't sort of maybe in love with Furey, even though for sure he was still in love with *her*. But he had to tell Furey it was over anyway.

Petra is the gentlest soul on the planet — too gentle, he sometimes thinks as he listens to another song she's written for him, this one about the first time she touched his penis, and plays for him on the cello or piano, and sometimes she sings too, she sang for him in front of his friends and he nearly folded from embarrassment. The kind of girl who whines *ewwwww* and points her toes around earthworms and spiders and slasher movies and sucks him off in her parents' bedroom even when she knows her parents will be home any minute. But she has no gentle feelings around the dead boy.

Sleep no longer visits Ginger after his girlfriend scribbles *u r a fag* on the soon-to-be-dead boy's locker, and then announces the graffiti to Ginger like it's something to be proud of, the discovery of a wormhole, smiling so hard it looks like the dimples in her cheeks are touching in her mouth.

Because Monday morning, he texted Furey, asking for his grandmother's locket back. It seemed the right thing to do. He would give the locket to Petra. The normal thing to do.

Ginger wonders, if he'd just let Furey keep the locket, sucked up the fact that he'd been weak and given Furey a present like Furey and he were a real-live couple, would Furey still be alive? Ginger wouldn't have to see or feel that dead desk in the middle of his English class, know the absence of that subtle, muscled odour winding toward him from the other side of the classroom. The missing Furey like the missing tooth in his grandfather's mouth. An empty hole, no smooth pink gum to grow over, what can grow over such space? He pictures Furey not slinking around, not sneezing, not cramming for departmental exams. (Not kissing him, fingers not undulating over every bump of Ginger's spine.) Wonder blisters the roof of his mouth, what does Furey look like right now? This very instant? Would Furey still have lips and what do the lips feel like? Is there a suicide note? Is Ginger in it? He cups his nose with his hand. Smells the damp wrinkles in his palm.

His nose is running.

He wrestles the shovel out from the basement, knocks over a rake, the push-mower handle bangs against the wall. His teeth bang together.

— Aren't you going to put on proper pants, Tomáš? his grandfather calls, wedging himself between the screen door and the door frame, his hands twisting the architecture of the newspaper. His grandfather yells something else, the sound ricocheting off the streetlight pole, but Ginger is already scraping the shovel hard against the concrete, clanging it against car tires submerged in snow, pinging it against chain-link fences, the shovel's metal bowl clanking the sides of the steps, Zamboni-ing down the driveway, scooping, punishing the sidewalk. He heaves new snow, heaves grey honeycombed snow beneath a layer of dirt and gravel. His breath hurtles out. The slap of the cold clashes with his heat, his blood cells speeding past valves and sphincters. He whams and scrapes the shovel down the neighbours' sidewalk: the woman with the refrigerator-white skin and red hair who growls at him in unison with her three pug-nosed dogs, the bus driver at the end of the block whose car got set on fire. The couple with the Trans Am and the dead Chevy sedan parked on their lawn. The two tiny kids cocooned in snowsuits who roll out of the house each morning shouting insults in Burmese. He bulldozes piles from the gutter and hurls the snow and dirt into the middle of the street, onto people's lawns, over the fence into their backyards.

— Greetings, snow angel! shouts a woman with skin brown like an old-fashioned kitchen table, a woman he's never seen before, his shovel having led him blocks past his house; he squints against the fluffy snow-white of her hat, scarf and mittens, the gleam of her teeth. She waves one of her mittens at him, her mouth shining with her smile; he scrapes and scoops so he won't have to look at such awful happiness.

He pushes the shovel past raging Rottweilers, whining German shepherds. Pit bulls, Labradors and Heinz 57s; supercilious cats supervising from their windows, their tails snapped around their feet; an iguana on a windowsill lolling under a heat lamp. The more packed the snow the better, because he can hit at it with the shovel's sharp edge and stab at the broken sheets of snow, peel it like scabs off the concrete, bash its edges, slice into its core.

— Don't gouge my grass! barks a mottled pink-skinned man in a hat high as a bread loaf. — You're digging up my grass.

— Cheers, mate! Ginger sobs as he shovels, his mouth stretched and gaping, his throat leaking the words.

The clouds burn and smoke in the setting sun. How many houses, businesses, city blocks? He shovels on, his shoulders and arms bursting off his torso, his back one long band of pumping blood. But better this, better splinters and calluses, liquefying shoulders and frozen cheeks, than sitting wedged into a desk, buzzing at a hole in the middle of the classroom floor, bonking his forehead against the windowpanes like a fly, not breaking anything at all.

He stumbles through the front door and kicks off his boots to find his grandfather peering into a giant bubbling pot, stirring with a long metal spoon. Swing music belching from the radio.

Where r u? beeps his phone. A text from Petra. He turns his phone off.

The phone in the kitchen rings.

— Your girlfriend's on the phone, says Grampa.

Ginger holds the telephone receiver up to his frozen face and he says to Petra, — I feel like a jar of Cheez Whiz. Way past the due date. What does that mean, Petra? Exactly what it sounds like.

No, he's not falling out of love with her, of course he loves her, will always love her. He needs to get off the goddamn phone.

Grampa boiling up a giant pot of goulash, Grampa stomping around the kitchen with his favourite T-shirt stretched over his potbelly, sweat stains blossoming, browning in his armpits. Ordering Ginger to sit.

Ginger contemplates the steaming meat and gravy puddle on his plate. Pokes it with his fork, then sets the fork back down.

Later, Ginger falls backwards onto his bed, each one of his eye-lashes sticking up like spikes on a dog collar, he is freezing but sweating so hard he can feel his skin frying, sweat punching out every pore.

He noses his fingers for just one ghost of Furey's perfume.

Wednesday

Walter

These crisis team professionals — more credentialized than Walter — long, slow flaps of their borrowed angels' wings as they descend on the school, drop their bags, hang their coats in the Guidance office. They perch, freshly showered and combed, in his office, then they perch in a placid row in this room.

They all sit — students, crisis team, counsellors, the drama teacher — in their plastic chairs in the debriefing circle, barnacled to the floor. Chewing on cookies and celery sticks, quaffing orange and green unnameable-fruit drinks, in this choreographed circle of grief. The three members of the crisis management team are assembled in their chairs with their dour, stone faces, and Pam, the other guidance counsellor at Walter's school who elected to be on the crisis team this year, polishing all the moist, pink students' faces with her whispery voice as she explains the facts of the death: — His mother found him in his bedroom. He hanged himself. He left no note.

Pam's voice stinging as she goes about cleaning and sterilizing, embalming and stitching up the violence. — Not a single person in this room should feel any guilt. No one is to blame, she says. Pam folds her hands in front of her chest, her eyes blinking quickly. — Not his friends. Not his family. She closes her eyes for a moment. What she doesn't say: *Not even the dead boy.* Her words hang chest-level from her praying fingers.

Walter sits upright in the hard plastic chair, made for a person much narrower than him, hands resting on his thighs. His body arranged like a test-drive dummy's hurtling at a concrete barrier, his body swaddled and trussed in layers of spiderweb, his inside scraped clean as a corpse's on an undertaker's table.

All the crisis team members except for Pam wear neatly ironed ties and foreheads, their slacks creased, the lap of the one woman's dress shiny, her pregnant belly bulging and smooth as a beetle's back, like these people never sweat or sit down, never spill ham sandwich crumbs or mango juice on themselves like Walter does. The radiator murmurs behind Walter's back, the fluorescents hum above.

— Let's go around the circle one by one and share what we're feeling right now, Pam prods, her hands clutching the Kleenex box. — Who's first?

The dusty heat circles Walter, his armpits moistening under his sweater, Pam's words baking together into one long, overcooked sentence. He knows the one debriefing woman is named Margaret or Margarita or Marga, he knows her from a teachers' convention when she gave a panel on how to discipline without appearing to discipline. He nicknamed her Margarine because he couldn't keep all the Margs straight, and this one seemed like she was carved from a block of Becel, especially when she talked about the 'limpwristed' approach to discipline. Whatever *that* means. The beefy one in the grey pants is named Kyle, and then the blonde, bigjawed one Jed. Margarine, Kyle and Jed. Here to save them.

— How well did you know Patrick? asks Pam, her mouth stretched at the first sobbing girl to her right, Madison.

—— Who me? Madison hiccups. — I stood behind him once in the lineup for pizza in the cafeteria. He was in my English class and TA.

Madison pounds her head with her fists, the loudest, most flamboyant mourner in the room, her head slaps sideways into her friend's lap, she's clutching her cellphone. The friend strokes Madison's hair and nods.

Pam tut-tuts, rustling in her jean dress and sloppy cardigan, slips from kid to kid with her box of Kleenex, doling out white puffs. As if Kleenex could be enough. As if any of their debriefing circles could ever loop wide enough to fix a school.

One girl went to kindergarten with the deceased boy. They fought over a green crayon.

— My name's Owen, the next boy in the circle announces. — My locker is right next to Patrick's. I know he's in a better place.

Owen abruptly pushes his chair back and fetches himself another handful of potato chips. Howling Madison shoves a cracker into her mouth and gums it.

The scarfing, the quaffing, the gulping and stuffing as this crowd of grievers cram food into their faces.

The girl named Petra is the only one in this round who isn't eating or drinking, isn't crying, says, *Pass*, when it's her turn to speak. Her back straight, body at attention. Walter will follow up with her later. Her dry, flat-mouthed face more troubling than the hysterics in the room. And maybe the girl with the unicorn bag, Faraday, the grey sweeps of skin under her eyes, her relentless clasping and unclasping of her bag.

He checks the students in the room against the class list he's brought with him — Tomáš Ginger missing. He will call Tomáš's house later today.

Faraday knocks her bag against Walter's knee. — I puked my toast and coffee this morning, she says, the whites of her eyes red and itchy-looking.

Her irises a flat, tissue-paper colour. Like cataracts. Not the colour of regular human eyes. What is she, Portuguese? Maybe Brazilian. Italian? Unicorn hair barrettes, unicorn bag, unicorn binder, unicorn voice.

Next to Faraday, Fumiko licks the tears around her own black-lipsticked mouth. Pam dollops another tissue into Fumiko's hand.

— I took the bus with him almost every fuc— almost every single day, sobs Fumiko, her face melting and streaking, her eyes emerging red and naked as a baby rat's. — Patrick sat in the back by himself and I prefer the benches at the front, y'know, because I can see out the windshield and know where I'm going?

Pam, Margarine, Kyle and Jed nodding, nodding. Walter wanting to brush a fleck of orange Cheezie from Fumiko's cheek.

— He sat at the back of the bus with his iPod on, says Fumiko.

— We as a society all just sit in buses looking straight ahead, and my mother says we as individuals are all stars in this big, beautiful constellation? Like, I thought coming to a Catholic school this wouldn't happen. Are Catholics allowed to kill themselves? The same shitty self-murder happened in my last school, that's why my parents made me leave, what's all this crap about he's in a better place? He's not in a better place, he's in the ground!

Faraday hugs Fumiko, their embrace all elbows and hair and the smell of drowning.

— When's the next debriefing circle? sobs Madison, her head still in her friend's lap.

— Whenever you want, says Kyle, his mouth soft, his eyes brown and wide as a puppy's. — We'll be in the Guidance office all week. More debriefing circles this afternoon and tomorrow all day from 7:30 in the a.m. to 4:30 in the p.m. We're here, he points to his own chest, — for you, he points to everyone in the circle.

Pam nodding violently in agreement. Her cheeks are flushed, her eyes damp and wide behind fishbowl glasses, her black bangs sticking to her forehead.

— Yes, we are here for you, proclaims Margarine, stroking her belly, pursing her lips at the floor.

— Let's go around the circle one more time, says Pam, patting her hot cheeks. — And each of us say one good thing we're going to do for ourselves to feel better after we've left this room.

— Well, says Owen, the plate on his lap dribbling potato chip crumbs. He clears his throat, his Adam's apple so pointy it almost breaks the skin as it elevators up then down. — I'm a really good snowboarder. I'm going to get my brother to help me tune my board.

— Very cool, says Jed. He crosses his arms and nods his blonde head abruptly.

Walter steps over his chair and peels a small cardboard plate off the stack on the refreshment table. He heaps the cardboard with bright, synthetic vegetable nuggets, pours himself a cup of green juice, kids' voices chattering about hugging their dogs, playing *Divinity XII*, playing hockey, getting a sister to help them dye their hair after school. He scrapes his chair back into the circle, back down into the tiny seat, which sighs under him, just in time to have missed one good thing he could do to make himself feel better.

Faraday's body exhales a gust of stale sweater smell as she turns to Walter. X-raying him, her eyes moving from the top of his expansive forehead to the tips of his scuffed leather shoes, her unicorn bag and Fumiko's hands clasped in her hands, Walter's hands tangled into a ball of fingers around the plate and cup on his lap.

— Did Patrick ever come talk to you? asks Faraday.

Walter begins gargling through the soup of a half-chewed, genetically modified broccoli floret, the words dropping from his mouth, a crumbling bolus, when Madison pipes, — There's no more napkins left!

Owen the potato chip boy whose locker is next to the dead boy's and who's a really good snowboarder suddenly slides from his chair to the floor, his body splayed and tentacled with too-long arms and legs reaching across the tiles, the cardboard plate spinning to the side. The crisis team flocks to the fainted boy.

Walter gathers his skin from around his feet where it's accordioned in a heap. Kyle, Jed, Margarine, Pam, Pam, Margarine, Jed, Kyle, Pam, Kyle, Jed, Margarine make Walter want to break wind, spit broccoli gob into heat vents, these Margarines, Kyles and Jeds exactly those kinds of perfect, controlled pricks who peaked in high school, the phys-ed types, the muscled types, the let's-ogle-sixteen-year-old-girls-but-pretend-we're-not types, the pretty, nasty girls, the locker room types who probably would have helped write *u r a fag* on a dead boy's locker.

Walter crams more vegetables into his mouth, his mouth so full he couldn't speak if he wanted to. He cringes away from this debriefing circle the way moles cringe from the light, moths flee the dark, maggots veer from live flesh. The crisis team finding Walter's scab and picking it, even though it stings and flames with every poke and pick, tearing it off, then taking a break to stuff in another cookie or potato chip, while the dead boy is still dead, and the alive ones, including Walter, r all fags.

Owen is escorted to the nurse's office, Pam propping him up by the waist and shoulder.

— Come talk to us in the Guidance office, Margarine, Kyle and Jed murmur to the students, their hands open, their wings folded.

Each point in the circle of students drifts in arbitrary directions, into thinning clots. Walter pretending to study his list of classroom names while Kyle, Margarine, Jed and a stray student pick through the remaining chocolate chip cookies, push the raisin and oatmeal ones in heaps to the sides of the plates. Sip green juice from Styrofoam cups. The consistency of the sour-cream dip flecked with dill degenerating from cream to mucus then to a clear jelly where it touches the edges of the bowl.

Walter snared by another circle, layers and layers of concentric circles, till they touch each harsh point on the curve, they pin him to one sad fact. He didn't do his job. He failed that dead boy. A hundred million squeezing circles.

Not a single person in the room was actually the dead boy's *friend*. Especially not Walter who, as his school counsellor, should have been the star at the top of the tree.

Walter sitting alone with his crinkled papers in the empty room, cookie crumbs down his shirt.

Faraday

After the debriefing circle, her head still manky, Faraday hooks her bag around her shoulder, scoots from the room and stows herself under the graffitied stairwell at the north end of the school in a cubbyhole where no one except the janitor ever goes. She settles herself on the shining concrete floor, thinks about maybe placing a flower on Patrick's desk or taping one to his locker, maybe a red rose. But her wallet clinks only the ugly change — pennies, a nickel masquerading sometimes as a quarter. Her new unicorn bag vacuumed out her bank account and she doesn't know how much roses even cost — she pays for flowers only on Mother's Day and her elder brother Jonas brokers the deals. But someone would knock the flower off; Jésus and his posse would torture its petals. Pluck them one by one like the legs off a spider, and neigh at her while doing it. Why does he always do that? His neighs usually sink into the regular white noise of talking, bells buzzing, shoe soles squeaking, but sometimes one pierces her wall and she has to duck before it spatters her. Unicorns *not* a joke. *Not* an affectation. When her blessing of unicorns finally arrives, she and her unicorns will heal them all.

But Jésus has done much worse to other people. He once lit a boy's hair on fire and knocked the cafeteria cash register to the floor, the horrendous crash, then sucking silence in the cafeteria.

To buck herself up, Faraday draws a unicorn on the palm of her hand with her second-best pen. The legs too short. When will the funeral be? She should have asked during the circle. She wonders why the dead boy chose to hang instead of carbon monoxide or pills. She'd probably opt for car exhaust. But she would never kill herself anyway, she notes in her daily journal for her psychologist, Dr. Linus Libby, because then she'd miss out on her plans to become a large-animal veterinarian. Because unicorns are real, there are websites from all over the world, she isn't the only believer, there are sightings and healings at least once a week.

She's only told Linus and Linus's receptionist (that was a mistake): her own unicorn, maybe even unicorns, will sniff her purity in the wafts of sex-obsessed unvirgins doing it in their parents' houses, in their boyfriends' fathers' Suburbans, the school basement, the football field. And the unicorn's alicorn will heal everything it touches. All this bitterness and stupidity like the debriefing circle and those toolshed debriefing counsellors pretending to reach out while they huddle together over their Styrofoam cups in the hallway after the circle, laughing like best friends. Her unicorn will gash a hole into the giant chain-link fence and she and the unicorn will leap away to a finer place. Which finer place she isn't sure. Finer than under this set of stairs, huddling into herself.

She wishes the dead boy had talked to her; she could have told him divine help would gallop down the hall any day now, she has arranged it, a blessing of unicorns is on its way to save them all, maybe during English, maybe a Monday morning, what a glorious day that will be, a Monday whinnying with unicorns. Even though they never talked at all, only when he ordered his large iced cappuccino at the Tim Hortons where she works Saturdays and Friday evenings. — Sometimes I think about killing myself, she could have said, — Everybody does. Like when I got a D in biology and it cremated my average. She could have grabbed his sleeve and said, — Hey! You! Patrick Furey! There's too much caffeine and sugar in those iced cappuccinos! Then she would say, — Do you like Ellen DeGeneres's talk show? My uncle watches it, and the actor who played Sulu on *Star Trek* just married his boyfriend Brad. My uncle told me about how Sulu and Brad wore matching white tuxedo jackets with black trousers and bow ties, the music was a Japanese koto harp and bagpipes, and they made their entrance to 'One' from the Broadway musical *A Chorus Line*. Isn't that romantic?

She and the dead boy would have made a date, gone to the mall, chewed two-for-one burgers with extra pickles in the food court. She runs her fingers up and down the ridges of her second-best pen.

She lifts her new bag to her nose. Inhales.

— Hey.

She clicks her bag closed, the fabric still stiff. Peeks sideways at who's kneeling down beside her.

— Nice bag, says Petra. Eyes moonstone-blue.

Faraday pulls her bag into her belly. Petra crosses her legs, the ends of her hair falling forward, buzzing and scorching as they dip into Faraday's face.

— Nice bag, Petra says again, her hand resting on the bag's flank. — I saw you crying this morning.

Faraday thinks, *Evil.*

Faraday feels naked as a larva, her skin damp and tender.

Petra's hand rests on Faraday's bag, her fingers spread out, obscuring all but the tip of the unicorn's alicorn. Is Petra evil? Petra didn't crumble cookies or cry in the debriefing circle. Faraday once saw Petra play the cello in the school orchestra, and it felt as though she were stroking her bow across Faraday's body, transforming her blood into light that moved through her belly, breasts and head when she heard the music Petra pulled from those strings, Petra's eyes closed, her silvered eyelids smooth, her mouth a red frown. Could someone who conjured such beauty be evil? Could she *not* be? Petra leans in, the irises feathered around her pupils, jagged fault lines, blue mountainous landscape, and grips Faraday's shoulder, each finger articulated against Faraday's bones. Faraday's skin flinches, ripples.

— Why are you crying when you didn't even know him? asks Petra. Faraday yanks back. Her mouth clamps closed to retard her green-juice breath.

— I talked to him, says Petra. — Did you ever talk to him? I doubt it, but look at my dry eyes, dry as the Gobi Desert. You're crying about someone you never even talked to? You wouldn't have been bothered to wipe your shoes on?

This is not a good question. Faraday thinks of a better one.

— I don't know why you're even bothering with me, says

Faraday, her maggot's mouth poking around in the dark. — So you can hound me to death too?

— I could sue you for that, says Petra. She straightens up, her neck slim as a cello's. — Yes, I'm going to sue you.

Petra wipes her hands on Faraday's bag. Her fingers knobbly and pale. The clasp on Faraday's new bag pokes into her belly. Petra's eyes clear goblets.

— See you in court, says Faraday, her hooves sparking as she kicks at the floor and stands.

Here is what Faraday would write for Patrick's obituary if anyone asked her though no one will. Waiting for the bus home, she composes the obituary anyway, muttering as she kicks snow chunks off the sidewalk, sends them skidding into the road, tears slithering over the hills and valleys of her nostrils:

> **Furey, Patrick** — Passed away sud-
> denly on February 17, harassed to
> death by Petra Mai after he tried to
> hook up with her boyfriend. A nice,
> quiet boy, he had clear skin like in the
> commercials and he could have been a
> model or an actor. No one knew much
> about him, but a true gentleman, he
> handed Faraday Michaels her eraser
> that one time. He liked to drink large-
> size iced cappuccinos. He has left a
> hole in the universe, and deserved a
> better time of it at school. A funeral
> will be held somewhere, maybe.
> Students from his school not invited.

Petra

That boy being dead has nothing to do with Petra and her cello fingers even though all the plebs in this school hush into silence, their faces swinging toward her with military exactness, grenade pins for eyes whenever she walks into a classroom, opens a washroom door.

What about the fact that his nickname was Homo and *everyone* called him that? Maybe he was depressive like her great-grandfather who blew out his own brains with a pistol and was therefore *predisposed* to killing himself? What about genetics?

Petra stretches her shirt cuffs over her freezing cold fingers. She didn't *do* anything. I did not physically knot the cord around his neck and kick away the chair, thinks Petra, tugging a music stand out of the pile in the corner of the music room. I didn't. None of us did. The end. Then she remembers she's supposed to be in chemistry right now.

The dead boy didn't come to chemistry or English class for the first time the day before yesterday. Today is the third day of his not coming to school. In the debriefing circle, Petra listened to the details: he killed himself, poor bugger, her grandmother would say. Poor. Bugger. Bugger. Bug. Her. So he killed himself. So sad. Too bad. So now he'll stop molesting her boyfriend. So glad. All she did was say she was going to rip his dick off. All she said was that she was going to kill him. Of course it was a joke. In chemistry, she faces the blackboard, his stool and table ahead and to the right of her. She can smell that stool, she can smell the dusty death germs crusting it — it smells like two boys instead of one, one of the boys dead. Sad. Glad. The other boy, hers, alive and also absent. Wednesday. Glad. Sad. Not texting her, answering her texts and her calls only once.

There is nothing about the dead boy's stool to distinguish it from any other stool except that the boy who normally sits there is dead. The dead boy scribbled on the wooden edge of the table in front of the stool with ballpoint pen (blue) and pencil (mechanical). He tried to sketch anime faces but wasn't very good, the heads turned out bottom heavy; he drew overlapping triangles in blobby pen and coloured in the overlapping parts with pencil.

She tries to copy down the notes and numbers scrawled in chalk across the board, the chemistry teacher's pants hanging flat as a movie projection screen over his non-ass. The scatter of dandruff all over the shoulders of his black shirt — Petra wants to throw up all over him, then *maybe* he'll break down and wash his hair. She flips through her binder to the periodic table: hydrogen, helium, lithium, beryllium, boron. Boron. The bare tree branches curling and uncurling like agitated fists outside the window, and the sky dribbling with clouds. An airplane slides past, furtive. She tries not to breathe the same air as the desk — but it's futile trying to escape the death molecules in the room. Her boyfriend's chair empty. She texts him now. No answer. After chem, her career and life management class. Maybe she will text him during that class — she already has her career and life managed, and all they ever do in career and life management is watch videos about smoking and people's skulls cracked open from drunk driving. Even the teacher knows that class is a joke, and sneaks from the room after the first five minutes of whatever film she's stuck in the DVD player. Last class the teacher announced that on Friday, representatives from the Royal Bank of Canada would be presenting on compound interest. Wahoo!

Carbon, nitrogen, oxygen, fluorine, neon. She is going to get an A in chem and an A+ in career and life management.

That desk belongs to a dead person, she thinks. A. Dead. Person. Even the wood is infected. She wonders what the dead boy smells like now and how decayed he is. How creeped out she would be if she were to see him right now. She could handle it. She and her dog Chopin once discovered a dead coyote pup in the park and she wasn't creeped out by the rot, although Chopin raised her hackles. Are there maggots nesting in Patrick Furey's eye sockets? He died Monday, day before yesterday. Approximately fifty hours ago. In the movies he would be a hill of maggots. Unless he was cremated. Do ashes smell? No one teaches them anything around here. Probably the chem teacher has all the credentials, but if she asks him, he'll just say, — That's a morbid thought, isn't it? and lean forward, his pupils fast-forward flipping through their own dandruffy periodic table.

Ashes probably smell like fire. Like jumping into a burning lake.

She will smell her uncle Leonard's ashes in the urn in the living room when she gets home. She checks her phone. No beautiful little icon of an envelope waiting to be opened. Last Friday was Valentine's Day. Even though she was kind of mad at Ginger because of the dead boy, her Valentine's Day just a little bit tainted because of the dead boy who wasn't dead yet, she and Ginger made love Valentine's Day, then the Saturday after Valentine's Day and almost Sunday, but then his grandfather rattled the back door with his key before they could get their jeans fully off. Petra sat on Ginger's lap while they listened to the cd she made him of her favourite music from the fourteenth century. They propped their biology textbooks open and pretended their little notes to each other were homework. They ate chicken wraps for lunch together on Monday. While Homo was offing himself. She kissed Ginger goodbye Monday after lunch, texted him Monday night, but when she texted him Tuesday about what a cunt her piano lesson was, he didn't answer. Tuesday night he was a frosty drink. So frozen she couldn't even sip.

Sitting so close to where the dead boy sat, she can hear the germs skittering out toward her and all over the other tables and stools, onto people within the stool's cursed circumference. Germs with hands and feet and claws and hooves. That stool should be in quarantine. She can't accidentally bump it with her hip, she can't inadvertently brush it with her clothes or books or bag. She doesn't even want to walk on the floor near it. She wants out. She wants a hot, disinfecting shower. Brush and floss her teeth three times. No one can understand how much this boy criminally fucked up her life. Her boyfriend. He's caught fag germs. She gazes at the pocked wood of the table. Really, it should be incinerated. She will have to warn Ginger away from that area too. While he's inside her is probably the best time. Maybe she can get her mother to call the janitor. She tries to ignore the cold air around it. *He's* the one who interfered with *her* life, *he* made the choice to encroach on her territory — *he* made the choice to kill himself. Now his dead germs dissipate into the air in this classroom, her clothes, her hair, her nostrils.

His contamination smeared all over the stool, all over his locker — so thick it's sticky.

His locker. Petra wonders if her sweater is in his locker.

Her love, her fury, woven into that sweater — she bends her face forward so the contaminated desk, the chem teacher's pants hanging by a smidge to his old-man ass, vanish behind the dense screen of her hair.

She shopped for that sweater for so long her head throbbed like a car accident — mall-head her mother calls it — but Petra knew a brain crash was worth the right knit, the right shade of ice blue, the argyle pattern. She spent almost three hours jerking herself from store to store, looking for the El Dorado of possible four-month anniversary presents for Ginger, and she's seen him wear the sweater only once, on the day of their anniversary, the week before Valentine's Day, right after he unwrapped it while they were in his car, while she sang the song she'd written for him, 'Winter Anniversary: I Love You.'

In the car after school that anniversary day, Ginger pulled on the sweater, then gave her a shaggy white teddy bear holding a red velvet heart with 'I Love You' embroidered on it in pink, a yellow rose wrapped in a cellophane cone from 7-Eleven, and a giant anniversary card also shaped as a teddy bear.

— This rose is yellow, she said. — Why didn't you get a red one?

Ginger tapped his fingers on the steering wheel. Shrugged.

— Yellow means friendship, red means love, she said. — Are we just friends? Is that what we are? I'll go home then.

She smiled in a way she knew showed off her dimples. She could feel the dimples push into her teeth.

— Uh, n-n-no, he stammered. In the shifting, moving angles of streetlight, his face soft like a girl's. He craned toward her, his hands clutching the steering wheel, and she held his face in her hands. Held off kissing him. Made him wait for her lips.

She expected a *bouquet* of flowers, at least ten, and red for the colour of love. They were in love, right? Ginger sighed and said he liked her perfume. Smelled like jujubes.

Back at her house, the bear was squished and flattened between the pillows, underneath their heads, under his hips, between her thighs, on her bed in her room for the first time because her parents were playing bridge at the Penners'.

Just before her parents got home, Petra and Ginger zipped and buttoned their clothes back on, then drove away for a romantic dinner (or as romantic as it could be since he has hardly any money) at Boston Pizza, then they made love again on his bed in the basement, his deaf grandfather upstairs in the kitchen obliviously slapping around an oversized slab of dough with his old swing music blaring. Ginger had ripped the sweater off, tossed it on the floor. She was rubbing her nipples on his, the small of his back curved and smooth in her hands, when they heard Ginger's grandfather stomping down the stairs.

They bounced to opposite sides of the bed, the blanket splashing to the floor. She dove into her dress, slapped her hands to her Medusa hair and dashed for the corner of the room, not sure what she would find there. Ginger snatched a T-shirt from the floor. She leapt for the blue pool of the sweater, but stumbled back when she saw Ginger's grandfather framed already in the doorway with a tray of milk and cinnamon buns in his hands. She curled her toes so he wouldn't notice her bare feet.

— Thought you might be hungry, the grandfather said, shuffling the sweater into a roll with his feet. — Cinnamon buns fresh out of the oven.

He clapped the tray down on the dresser, glasses tinkling, grabbed up a paper towel from a pile on the tray and offered it to Petra.

— So you don't get any crumbs on your nice dress, he said. Ginger laughed, a quick snort, while he scrambled on another shirt over his T-shirt.

The paper towel flopped over in the grandfather's hand. She kept patting her hair, the nest on the back of her head, Ginger's semen running down the inside of her leg.

Grampa stood in the doorway in his saggy brown pants and suspenders. He had maybe three hairs on his entire head. He held out the plate of cinnamon buns.

— Well, thanks, Grampa, said Ginger.

— What's your name again? asked Grampa.

There was a third glass of milk. He cupped the glass in both hands. Took a sip.

— Who? Me? Petra asked. — Petra.

— Nice to meet ya, said Grampa.

— Hello, Mr. Dobrovolný.

She sipped her milk, her hair hot and gnarled around her ears.

— You've met Petra before, said Ginger. — Remember last Monday? Remember the Saturday before?

— Oh, said Grampa, — I thought she was the other one.

— Very funny, said Ginger, his face flowering into a red red rose.

— What? asked Grampa.

— Nothing! shouted Ginger, flexing his biceps, his jaw.

— Yeah, really funny, said Grampa. — I'm a regular jokester.

— Who's the other one? she asked.

— Nobody, said Ginger. — Grampa's drunk.

— A fine sweater, said Grampa, his movements stiff as he stooped to gather up the soft yarn in his hands. He stood, stretched the sweater out in front of him. — Now this is an old style, he said, thumb stroking the argyle pattern. — I was selling the same pattern back when I worked in the men's department at the Hudson's Bay Company. Before I met your grandmother, back when I was hanging out with the boys.

He folded the sweater to his chest, neatly folded the shoulders, the angles crisp, and set it on the dresser. He stroked the sweater as though it were a new mink coat. — Your other friend wore an argyle vest last time he was here. Brown and red. Now you'll match your friend, huh? Like you're both on a team or somethin'.

— Thanks, Grampa! shouted Ginger, the tendons breaking through his neck.

— Good-looking boy, that one, said Grampa.

Petra furiously wheeling the possibilities in her head of who Grampa could be talking about.

Grampa shouted on his way up the basement steps, — I know you're legally an adult, but I'm not very happy with you down there with a girl and your bedroom door closed like that!

They listened to the graduated creaking as Grampa hobbled up the stairs. The sigh of the floor above them when he reached the top.

— I'm just sayin'! Grampa shouted, and then the kitchen door clapped shut.

— Maybe I should go home, said Petra.

— Okay, said Ginger. He ripped off the shirts he had on before, then poked his arms into a long-sleeved, navy blue shirt, and pulled it down over his head. Then a white T-shirt. Then a brown.

— Really? asked Petra. — I was joking.

Ginger crammed a whole cinnamon bun into his mouth, his back to her.

— Put on the sweater I gave you, she said.

He tugged at the neck of the sweater the whole drive to her house, running his finger along the inside stitching. When she gave him a final kiss goodbye in the car, she squeezed his crotch.

Ginger groaned, and she didn't let go of him until she felt like it.

— Happy Anniversary, she said.

The best anniversary they'd ever had.

Then mid-anniversary week, in between periods one and two, her cello in her arms, Tamsin moaning in her ear about how she didn't know where she'd find a dress to wear for grad, Tamsin's boobs looking like ripe little mandarin oranges in anything she wore so what was the problem, a camera flashed right in her face because suddenly the room turned white and she saw spots — but there was no camera, just the sweater — her sweater — the dead boy wearing it, inside out.

— That's not your sweater, you fag piece of shit, she said to the dead boy, she clutched her cello case, was this close to thumping his nose into the back of his head, but that would damage her hands and she couldn't trust Tamsin not to drop her cello if she gave it to her to hold, Tamsin clumsy as a baby goose.

— Whatever you say, Condoleeza, he said. — I'll try to pretend you're not on crack.

— Who? My name's not Condoleeza.

— Condoleeza Rice knew how to play the piano, stuff a broomstick up her ass and bomb a country all at the same time too. *Talented.*

He tossed a bag of Skittles into his locker.

— You stole that sweater, don't pretend you don't know what I'm talking about.

She poked her finger in the air. Spoke slowly, so he would never forget it, and the words spilled from someone else's horrid mouth even though that someone else's mouth belonged to her face, — You go near my boyfriend again and I'll rip your dick off and then I'll kill you. Now give me that sweater.

He had long, thick eyelashes, like an ostrich's. She would have killed for those eyelashes. His eyes were iced-tea clear.

— I know you like girls, Condy, he said.

She spun to Tamsin, Tamsin sputtered.

Did Tamsin blab about their dozy little kiss two years ago? Petra'd been half *asleep*.

He clattered his skateboard out of his locker, slammed the metal door closed and swept on his coat as he sauntered away. The dead boy wearing her boyfriend's sweater, inside out, skateboard under his arm, and she wanted to slam her fists, two axes, into his back, cello be damned.

He told her she liked girls. Announced she was a freak like *him*.

She wanted him decapitated, a cop stumbling then slipping in his broken brains; thrown from the back of a truck into a ditch, his body ripped in two; murdered and squished into a shoebox; ripped open by a stray bullet; mauled and half-eaten by a Rottweiler; paralyzed and dead from a rotten egg.

She was so angry, pus squirted from her eyes. She almost smashed her cello to the shiny tiled floor. She wanted to break glass; she wanted to poison Patrick Furey to death. She pulled a marker out of Tamsin's pencil case and scrawled hatred on the soon-to-be-dead boy's locker. She would *get* him.

She didn't scream or start crying when she saw Ginger the afternoon she saw Patrick in his sweater — while they fucked in his car in a nearby back alley during their spare. She didn't want to scare the bunny from the bean sprouts.

She unstraddled herself from his lap, her spine snubbing the ceiling of the car. Leaned her head back onto the passenger seat window. Stuffed Ginger's jacket behind her head.

— He stole the sweater I gave you, she said. — You can't deny it.

— He didn't steal any sweater. I have the sweater, said Ginger. He poked at the car stereo, the music exploding.

— Where is it then? You haven't worn it since Friday. I cannot tolerate this song.

— I can't wear it every day. You shouldn't have written that on his locker.

— You wear it never day! You only wore it when I asked you to. Wear it now. Who cares.

— We're having sex. We're busy, he said.

He leaned in, missing her mouth and tonguing her cheek.

— Drive to your house and get it.

— Kinda mean, writing that on his locker.

— Why don't you just tell him to go away? If you just *told* him to go away he'd leave us alone. What do you care? Sweater. Let's get it, bunny.

— Us? What does it have to do with you? You have no evidence.

She could feel forest fire blasting out of her ears.

She shifted her head. The ribcage of a lilac bush crowded the window on her side of the car. In less than a month it would be their fifth-month anniversary. If this was how he felt about her gifts, maybe she'd just wrap up an empty box with pages ripped from a gay porn magazine and give *that* to him.

How she loved Ginger's thick hair under her hands when they kissed, his slick skin. His hurried weight when he was inside her. How he ate calzones, the strings of mozzarella cheese reaching from the calzone to his mouth.

She thumped him on the shoulder.

— You don't have a crush on that boy, do you? she teased, looking into those tiny holes in his eyes, the burbling human machine behind them. She made sure her voice was teasing, teasing him. Teasing information out of him.

He blinked.

— Holy fuck. You fucking cocksucker, she said. — Did you kiss him? Did you let him *fuck* you?

— The sweater's at home.

— You're lying to me you're lying to me you're lying to me you're lying to me, her body shaking the car, shaking the lilac bush.

— Don't …

She kneaded a handful of his T-shirt, twisted, the hairs in the cotton flattening and shredding in her fingers, Ginger's skin hot inside the fabric. She cried so hard the words shredded in her throat.

Knit one, purl two. Here bunny bunny. After school, Wednesday after the Monday the boy died, Petra scoots into a seat by the window on the bus to her piano teacher's house. She chatters with Tamsin, Kate and Angela, reties her scarf when they talk about Patrick Furey and the grief circle and her absent boyfriend Ginger. Closes her mouth and looks at the pattern of the mud splatter on the window when Kate says Patrick was a waste of plasma. She dips her head down and down spills her hair all over her face, the reassuring pomegranate shampoo scent. Tamsin and Kate are in the string section of the orchestra, Angela plays French horn, but Petra's going to be a famous classical pianist or cellist, she can't make up her mind — she should have applied in December for an audition to get into Juilliard but she has settled for the University of Calgary here in town for now so she and Ginger can be together. The bus lurches and spins in the snow, the passengers thinning out as it grinds its way down the streets.

She'd written out loud that he was a fag, and all the fussing about the sweater — she didn't do anything wrong, no one can blame her for anything, come here bunny bunny.

But her stomach is punching her because Ginger hasn't texted her in two days. She needs the sweater back. She needs to pry open that locker with her bare hands, no matter how many witnesses mill about the hallways. She will have to get someone to get the sweater out of the locker. What if the sweater isn't in the dead boy's locker? Her fingers itch.

Ginger won't do it, no matter how much she tugs on his fly with her teeth. If he ever wants her to tug on his fly with her teeth again.

She will sneak to Ginger's house after piano. He can drive her home. Ginger belongs to her. The dead boy's germs sizzling and infecting. Ginger is hers.

She wonders what the dead boy's body is doing right at this moment. Is he bloated? Does he smell? Is he blue? Is he rotting underground? Is he burning? She remembers a black-and-white photo she once saw of the face of a hanged World War II Resistance fighter, the woman's skin bloated and chapped-looking. Petra chews the end of a lock of her pomegranate-smelling hair. It tastes like hair.

Faraday

Faraday leans her thumb on the buzzer. Uncle Suzie's voice crackles out an unintelligible gurgle, the loudspeaker ancient.

— Me! she calls.

The door buzzes and clicks itself unlocked. Because Uncle Suzie has always said that Faraday can stop by, no matter when, and talk about anything she wants. — That's what Uncle Suzie is for, Faerie, says Uncle Suzie.

Uncle Suzie good for a laugh even though he has an apartment the colour of bat poo.

Faraday's father says, — Are you sure, little brother, as in, That's the worst idea her father's ever heard, but Uncle Suzie pokes her father in the chest and repeats to Faraday, — *Any*time.

— Don't piss me off even more, Dave, he hisses to Faraday's father. — My gorgeous niece needs someone to talk to about unicorns for christ's sake. Non-believer.

— That's right. Non-believer, says Faraday. — Thanks, Uncle Suze.

Uncle Suzie, stroking Faraday's ponytail and flinging his brother a throwing-star look. His poor, fucked-up little niece and her unicorn fetish. And she's seventeen years old. He blames his brother Dave and Dave's kidney-shaped wife Shirley for screwing her up so royally. — I wonder if she isn't a touch developmentally delayed, Dave once said and Shirley nodded.

— It's called having an *imagination,* said Suzie, nearly thwacking their heads together.

Poor little fava bean. With parents like Dave and Shirley splitting up and getting back together all the time, never making up their minds, Suzie's surprised it's *only* unicorns Faraday believes in.

Faraday pushes open the door into the apartment when the door doesn't open to her knock. She can smell the ghost of cigarette smoke, hear the bursts of hot air from the heating vents, the erratic bumping sounds of Uncle Suzie digging through a closet in the other room. She drops into the swivel chair in the living room, dying sunshine slipping through the blinds and spotlighting the floating dust motes, and spins.

Earlier, Uncle Suzie at the Walmart, fast as Wonder Woman, using all the power he possesses to swipe umptillion pairs of X-tall pantyhose into his Safeway bag. If the clerks don't notice, well then that pantyhose was destined, right? Uncle Suzie in the spare room now, trying to find room in the closet to stash away his loot.

— You hungry, honey? he calls, dabbing sweat off his forehead, crumpling the Safeway bag with his other hand.

They chomp on nachos with melted Cheez Whiz and mild-level salsa, sip Chambord on ice from perfect crystal glasses with gold rims, click on the TV to Ellen DeGeneres, then watch the videotape of Uncle Suzie's show last Saturday night.

— Oh my god, says Uncle Suzie, — I look like I have a fucking Easter basket on my head. What was I thinking? Oh my god. The rest of me, however, is looking gooooood, yessssssssssss, Uncle Suzette looks *good*. How are you doing, Faerie?

— I like the hat, says Faraday. She dips her nacho first into the Cheez Whiz, then into the salsa. Crunches. — That guy in the audience looks just like my principal, Mr. Applegate.

— So hooooow was your daaaay, sings Uncle Suzie. He lifts out a swath of gold lamé, folds of blood-red tulle, snow-white tulle, three spools of hunter-green ribbon and a spool of black lace from his sewing basket. — That's a nice handbag you've got, he says. — From the Cluny Museum tapestries, I see. One day we'll go to France and stand right next to the real thing. You phoned your folks and told them you'd be home late from school, right? I don't want your dad losing his rag on me.

— Today and yesterday have been preternaturally awful, Faraday sighs. Pokes with her tongue at a fragment of chip wedged between her two front teeth.

— Do tell, do tell, says Uncle Suzie. He unfolds the gold lamé on the floor, unfolds a sheet of paper with a dress pattern printed on it and pins the paper down.

Faraday fingers the stray threads along the fabric's edge, disguises the tears spurting out of her face with a burp.

— You can tell me about your today and yesterday, Suzie mumbles, his mouth bristling with pins. He spits the pins into his palm and pokes them back into the pincushion. The snick snick of purple sewing scissors biting through paper, through cloth, Suzie's tongue sticking out the side of his mouth.

— A boy in my English class committed suicide day before yesterday, says Faraday. She dips another nacho in salsa and crams it into her mouth. She can feel the *s* in *suicide* slide greasy around her tongue and down her throat. The spice in the salsa pricking her palate, her cheeks.

— I don't like Mondays either but that's just over the top! says Uncle Suzie. He leans back on his heels. — How do you feel about that?

— He gave me back my eraser, says Faraday, and tears spurt from her face.

Uncle Suzie snicks the scissors closed while Faraday drops from the chair to the floor and crawls to Uncle Suzie on all fours, Suzie's hands darting and grabbing spilled pins from out of Faraday's path.

— He gave you back your eraser? Uncle Suzie octopus-hugs Faraday in his arms, he can hear his own blood cells rushing traffic jam in his ears.

Faraday starts to babble, — David's too busy working on his marriage to Shirley. He's too busy having intercourse with her so she won't leave him and she's too busy fellating him to pay attention to distractions such as me and my emotional well-being.

She puffs out her chest as she says these outrageous, scandalous things about her parents, she can feel the blood race to her face, and she knows if they knew of Uncle Suzie knowing their family secrets her mother would stop talking for months, for *years*, and her father would swoop into another asthma attack. But in the evenings while she tries to unravel her physics homework, puzzle out another ho-hum novel or play or poem for English, she can *hear* them working on their marriage, hear her father's wet whimpers. Her parents make her want to bury herself like a wasp larva into the back of a dying caterpillar. Her parents make her ashamed to be human and needy in that ugly way. Her head was already boiling and now Patrick Furey in her English class has gone and done *this*.

Uncle Suzie's skin puckers, bubbles and nearly bursts. And why isn't he surprised when just at that moment the phone rings shrill, punches into his ear and of course it's his brother screaming that Faraday is missing.

— Heeey, brother. Yes, she's here, says Uncle Suzie, red-faced, snotty, teary niece under one arm, phone hooked into his ear.

Faraday curls up into Uncle Suzie's armpit.

— Don't — shut up — you! — you listen — Dave! says Suzie. — It's called sensitivity —

— No! says Suzie into the phone. — I will *not* tell her that. Look, if you're married to a crazy bitch that's not my — *I* don't think she's a crazy bitch, *you* — Faraday's having a hard — no, hard day at —

Uncle Suzie holds the phone away from his ear and shouts into the mouthpiece, —Why? Because I know how damaged you are, you fucking-asshole-who-must-have-been-adopted-because-there's-no-way-in-hell-*my*-mother-could-have-given-birth-to-a-Reptiloid-like-you!

Faraday pulls herself away from Suzie, and smooths loose hairs away from her face. She slurps up the final drops of her Chambord and melted ice, licks the sweet off her lips, bites a nacho in half, secretly pleased that there's at least one person on the planet who stands up to her parents. She imagines where her bed could be if she moved in, right next to the window in what's now the furniture graveyard slash sewing room. She and Uncle Suzie could put up proper sets of shelves for her unicorn collection. She could catch a ride to school with Suzie in the mornings. She could study for her departmental exams, and then her university veterinary exams at the kitchen table, and they could play video games when she needed a break. She's told Uncle Suzie over and over again that she would be a superb roommate. They could be Will and Grace, Bert and Ernie. Romeo and Mercutio if Romeo had never met Juliet.

Uncle Suzie holds the phone and its flurry of sound away from his face and snorts.

— Been nice talking to you too, Dave, he says in the direction of the phone. — Love you too, brother.

He hangs up. Thinks hard about the pack of cigarettes in the drawer in the kitchen. Faraday would freak out if he lit up a cigarette and he can't handle another relative turning praying mantis on him.

— Where were we, says Uncle Suzie.

— They told us in —, says Faraday.

— Who told you? asks Uncle Suzie, clasping his hands together in his lap.

— The crisis people.

— Oh. Good.

— They told us —

— When?

— Today. They told us he hung himself. Hanged. They said there was no note, but it was clear that it was suicide. They told us it wasn't our fault.

— Why would it be your fault? asks Uncle Suzie.

— I could have been nicer to him.

Uncle Suzie brushes a strand of Faraday's hair out of her face and tries to tuck it behind one of her barrettes. — Did you ever know him? You did the best you could, Uncle Suzie says. — How could you be better than you already are? Listen to me, I don't fraternize with losers or homely people and I'm fraternizing with you, right? You are the earthshine to my moon.

Faraday pulls the neck of her sweater up over her mouth.

— Okay, Earthshine, says Suzie. I think you better get home before your faaaaather has a coronary. Honey, you have to *call* your parents when you come to see me.

Uncle Suzie grabs a handful of toilet paper from the bathroom and holds it out to Faraday. — Here, Faerie, he says.

— Can I live here with you? asks Faraday, knowing of course what the answer will be. — They're making me into a *crazy* person.

Uncle Suzie strokes his bald head once, twice. He remembers what he was like at her age. He remembers drinking so much at his dragmother's birthday party his bones clanked for three days and he had to pick his own vomit out of his own eyebrows. He remembers fucking his head off with one trick all morning, rushing home that afternoon to change into a fresh T-shirt to go fuck his brains out with another guy he met at a party the night before. When he was *sixteen*. His niece is better off googling unicorn sightings and hanging out with drag queen reformed uncles. He would put her into suspended animation until she was thirty-five if she ever came *close* to being sixteen like he was.

— By not letting you live here, he says, — I am in fact treating you more like an adult than if I were to let you stay here, right?

— That makes *zero* sense, says Faraday. She kicks the baseboard.

— Well, Dave and Shirley are bona fide freaks, but they *are* each other's lovers, you know. They're not just your parents. They've been lovers since they were fifteen, says Suzie. — So of course there's going to be some bumpy spots in their marriage. They were, no offence because I know you hate this word, *kids* when they first fell in love.

— *Awwk*, says Faraday. She kicks the sproingy thing behind the door. She pulls the barrette out of her hair, smooths her hair back, then snaps the barrette back into place. She flicks her hair as she turns toward the door. — I still think we would make a good Will and Grace.

— I don't think I have enough hair to be Grace. Bye bye, Earthshine. Hugs to the brothers.

Faraday tugs open the door.

— You gonna be okay? asks Suzie. — You got a bit of Cheez Whiz in your hair, honey. There. No, *there*. Yeah. All gone now. You know suicide's the most selfish act a person can commit. You know that, right? And it's not like you get to attend your own funeral. Better to just have a party while you're alive. You know what? Wait. I'm walking you home, says Suzie. He shoves on his boots, grabs his puffy silver winter coat from the coat closet.

Faraday pulls the door shut behind them. Suzie's bald shaved head gleams in the bright hallway light.

Ginger

Because the tumbling wind ate all the snow so he has no more snow scabs to peel. He plays *Divinity XII* in the dark in his room, trying to improve on Furey's score, Furey always kicking his ass at this game. Tells his grampa it's a Teachers' Convention Day. — No school today.

— Or yesterday? says Grampa.

— Nope, Ginger says.

— Interesting, says Grampa.

Furey's father, his frame shouldering the doorway, his hands grasping the jambs on both sides of the door frame, says, — What in heaven's name would you want with my son's suicide note?

— It is in heaven's name, says Ginger, twisting the end of his scarf.

— I've never seen you before, says the father, his growl rising. — You ghoul. You jackal. Get the fuck off my property. Coming around here.

— I know for sure he had a locket, says Ginger, he stands legs apart, ready to wrestle, ready for the first pounce, the father circling when all Ginger wants is one thing, the note, the locket, the sweater, the body, just give him the body so he can know for sure.

Because the day after their very last cemetery date, that night Ginger was weak and told Furey love is red, Ginger tossed everything Furey had ever given him, erased everything from the computer, his texts from his phone, hurled the video games, the books, the CDs, the love letters into a garbage bin twelve blocks away from his house. The love fragments and detritus quarantined and then ejected from his sector, more anonymous garbage suspended in outer space.

— It was my grandmother's locket.

— Why would my son have your grandmother's locket? Are you saying my son stole from you? The father's words cracking into the air.

— No, it was his locket. But it's still mine. Where is he buried? Ginger's words dissipate in puffs of white.

— In the ground, says Furey's father, shutting the door.

— Can I at least have the Valentine's card? calls Ginger. — I signed it G! It was supposed to be a *joke*!

Ginger runs his key along the side of every car on the way back home, that sweet whistle of metal etching metal, car alarms beeping, burring and chiming a canticle.

Thursday

Maureen

Maureen, Ms Mochinski, Mrs. Mochinski, Mrs. Alexey Mochinski, Mrs. Mockneeski, Mrs. M., Maureen Mochinski (née Rule), Miss Rule, Ms Ruler, Missy Rules and Regulations, Mistress Maureeny, Maur, Maury, Reeny, Reen. Mo. Now that Maureen Mochinski's husband is trading her in for an uglier, older model, Lorraine, her cousin, should she metamorphose back to her maiden name? Then everyone, including her students, will know how her life has crumbled to ruins, that she has an F in marriage. Men stopped whistling or honking at her decades ago. She whistles at them these days. Her wrinkly lips puckered and obscene. She had her last orgasm in the presence of a man nine months ago. If only she'd known. *Rule* such an obvious name for a spinster teacher. Nothing sexy or provocative about *Rule*.

Ms Rule. Ms R. Miss Arf arf.

She fans herself with her paperback copy of *Romeo and Juliet* while she tries to eat her lunch as quickly as possible, the heat rushing up in a lethal explosion; she fans so vigorously the pages flap the air, the quick buzz of a fly's wings. She tears off her blazer, unbuttons the top buttons of her blouse. She fans her face, gapes open the neck of her shirt and aims the wind from the fanning book between her breasts, the smell of Secret Spring Breeze deodorant, wood pulp and book glue wafting in her face. The paperback cover so frayed and fingered it rubs soft like cloth.

The dead boy's desk a hole directly in the middle of her class. His teacher, Mrs. Maureen Birdie Siobhan Rule Mochinski, burning up at her desk. A witch going up in flames, that's what she is.

A student steps into the room and drops her bag on the floor. Mrs. Mochinski's third eye bats open in the back of her head; she hooks one button on her blouse closed, but the flames prevent her buttoning further.

— Yes? she asks wearily. — Oh it's you, she says.

She says *Oh it's you* instead of the student's name because she cannot remember the student's name even though she's in Maureen's class. Maureen's only had this group since mid-January and knows them only if they sit in their proper seats and she can look at the seating plan, and this student played with her cellphone just this morning in Maureen's class, Maureen slamming down her chalk so it shattered.

— Mrs. Mockneeski? asks the student.

— Yes? answers Maureen Birdie Siobhan Rule.

The student has come to ask a favour, and because the student is an A student Maureen leans in and listens in spite of the fact that she's going to supernova any moment and take the building and this kid with her.

The student's lips move, the girls plastering on the lip gloss these days, the sweat dribbling down Miss Rule's neck, between her breasts, bumping over her ribs, down the middle of her back.

— You know what, says Maureen, — let me get back to you on that. I'll have to talk to the principal.

The student fusses a bit, gently butting her toe against the floor, her voice a snivelling note that erodes Maureen's sympathy, Maureen's voice smouldering at the edges, — No, you cannot go through the contents of Patrick Furey's locker, says Maureen. — I will talk to Principal Applegate and make sure every item in his locker is returned to his parents.

The student mopes from the room, dragging her cello case behind her, and then Maureen remembers her name: Jessica! That was it. How could she have forgotten?

Or was it Jennifer? Erin! It was definitely Erin.

Maureen scoops up her purse. She's going to the bathroom, and she's going to fill a sink with cold water and dunk her head in. She doesn't care what she looks like anymore. The classroom door locks behind her.

She's lost her name and doesn't know where to find it.

Faraday

Faraday's mother and father side-by-side at the dinner table. They used to sit across from each other, opposing kings on a chessboard, but this is their new configuration now that they pay a therapist a lot of money to help them prevent a checkmate in their marriage. Mother sawing through a pork chop, Father crumbling his potatoes into a small heap. Jonas gulping his milk and cutting his pork into identical, symmetrical wedges. The air smoky with pork chop grease. The finches hop around on the newspapers and scattered seed lining the bottom of their cage, their wings fluttering against the bars.

Their mother squints at Faraday and her brothers across the table while she chews her charred meat, then she spears another piece and crams it into her still-full mouth. Her plate almost empty. Her hand clapped on the back of her husband's neck. Faraday, George M. and their eldest brother Jonas all avoid looking at where their mother's arm angles at the back of their father's neck, their mother giving him a rough neck massage; they study the cartons of orange juice and milk, the food on their plates.

Their father shreds his pork into a hill opposite the potato heap. Mashes everything into a single heap on his fork and fork-lifts it into his mouth.

Jonas guzzles his milk down to the bottom of his glass. — George M., pass the milk, he says.

George M. picks up Jonas's glass and slops milk into the glass up to the brim. Milk splashes the table as Jonas swipes the glass from George M.'s hand.

— Dung ball, says Jonas.

— Stop playing with your food, murmurs their mother.

— A guy in my English class killed himself on Monday, says Faraday.

Their father flicks up at her from under his bushed eyebrows. He turns his mouth back down to his plate. — So Uncle Suzie told me. You don't plan on doing that, right?

— No, Dad, says Faraday.

— You'll talk about it with Dr. Libby, right? says her father.

— Yes, Dad.

— I saw you touch the rim of my glass! shouts Jonas. — George M., you are such an ass!

— I will have civility at dinner! shouts their father. He slaps the table with his palm. — Bunch of bloody gorillas!

He rubs their mother's shoulder.

Faraday's family gnaws through the rest of their dinner. Faraday props her head in her hand as she chews through her hunk of mummified pork, her fork upright in her other fist propped on the dinner table. This evening relatively calm except for the dead boy in her head, giving her back her eraser over and over again. And her parents rubbing and massaging each other. She wishes her parents' marriage could be normal again. That both her parents would stop with all the public displays of affection, stop having sex everywhere and all the time even though more effort at physical intimacy is what their marriage counsellor counselled. Her mother told her this one morning when Faraday tried to borrow her mother's hairdryer and found her parents twined like earthworms in the bathroom. Her mother running after Faraday in her nightie and bare legs, her red frizzy hair all rucked up the one side of her head.

— You're not wearing any underwear, are you? asked Faraday, pulling and snapping her hair into barrettes and elastics as fast as she could to stop her hair from wiring into electric curls. She needed the hairdryer. She needed her hair straightener. Her parents were in the way of a good hair day. They were guaranteeing her an awful, awful hair day.

— Do you want me to make you some scrambled eggs? said her mother, her voice gummy. — It's what we need to do to save the marriage. This family. I've been with your father since I was fifteen. Relationships sometimes need reinvigoration. I can add some grated cheese if you want.

Too much information: Faraday couldn't care less that her father now regrets his vasectomy, she doesn't want to know that her mother maybe should have slept with that boy Les Dolecki before she got married just to see what sex with another man was like. — Maybe a virgin marrying a virgin wasn't the best idea, said her mother, flopping the scrambled eggs over onto a plate.

Faraday's afraid to come home early from school — the last time she did, her parents' clothes were strewn around the living room, from her parents' bedroom the sounds of moaning and squishing filigreed the silence, the family dog Shinny panting on the couch, her front legs crossed daintily, ears pointed and alert. The finches beeping and hopping frantically in their cage.

As Faraday reaches for a second glob of mashed potatoes, her father says that he's going to arrange for the whole family to go see the marriage counsellor too because the marriage counsellor also has very interesting theories regarding family dynamics. The family will all go together. All at once. All of them sitting in a circle in the same room. No meal as a distraction.

Faraday deposits a forkful of her mashed potatoes between her lips. She squirts the potatoes back and forth between her teeth behind her closed lips. She just wants to be away from this table, sit by herself in her room and cherish then dissect the spiny, perilous fact of Patrick Furey's death. She just wants to talk to her friends on www.unicornswillsaveus.com or write in her journal or flump on her bedroom floor with her blessing of unicorns: her posters, figurines, stickers, temporary tattoos of anatomically correct unicorns. Uncle Suzie understands the importance of unicorns in her blessing being accurate — the small tapestry reproduction of a *Hunt of the Unicorn* panel on the wall above her bed comes from when he had that dopey, pretending-to-be-wealthy boyfriend who lived in New York and Uncle Suzie visited the Cloisters. Artist unknown, the tapestry the first unicorn in her collection. The Kirin beer bottle Uncle Suzie gave her with the kirin galloping across the label. Not like her mother Shirley who gave her a pink and white porcelain figurine of a horse with a horn and a Disney logo on the bottom. Because real unicorns do not wear fake eyelashes or have muscles that allow them to contort their muzzles into a smile. A real unicorn, like one of the ones she knows are coming, could nod its alicorn and heal the nonsense of her parents' marriage, give her brother George M. a decent personality, give her brother Jonas a personality period, give Uncle Suzie a boyfriend who knows how to clean up after himself, perhaps even resurrect Patrick Furey from the dead. The alicorn all-powerful. All-perfect. If only her parents were less uptight about their credit cards, oh her unicorns and her unicorn art collection would fill the whole house and the garage.

She doesn't need a child psychologist — not even a *real* psychologist — to understand the secret to eternal happiness.

Jonas collects self-help books for children of divorced and/or separated parents. He also chews every single mouthful exactly thirty-two times. He swallows the glob of food in his mouth, turns to their father, and says, — Great idea, Dad!

— Nope, says George M.

Faraday tastes the green mush of the pea she pops between her teeth. She knows seeing a psychologist doesn't apply to her. She still goes to Dr. Linus Libby every second week to 'help' her with her uicorn 'fixation.'

Her father explains to the table but points his fork right at George M. when he says that it would be really nice if some people would stop thinking only about themselves and pitch in to the collective effort once in a while.

— So what you're saying is the needs of the many outweigh the needs of the few, says George M., tinging the edge of his glass with his knife.

— That's right, says their father, patting Shinny's head on the table beside him. They can hear the hollow sound of her skull with the pats, like their father is tapping a melon. Shinny rolls her eyes and exhales a sigh into their father's plate.

— Well sometimes, George M. says, — the needs of the one outweigh the needs of the many. I am that one. He tings his glass again. He burps. — Excuse me, he says. Then he starts to laugh. He is the only one laughing, the only one tinging his glass, the air zinging with the tinging.

— You will go to family counselling! says Dave, his voice low, almost as though he's singing. Shinny thumps her tail under the dining room table. The finches rustle and cheep into the silence.

George M. smacks his lips over his mashed potatoes.

— Why the eff not? says Dave. — How will it hurt you?

— Because *you* need the therapy. There's nothing wrong with *me*. Plus you can't afford it, remember? Faraday's already 140 bucks an hour you and Mother have to pay, and now you want to pay again? Some more?

Faraday wonders what Patrick's family argued about at the dinner table when he was alive. Maybe their arguments made him kill himself.

Shirley shovels forkful after forkful of wrinkly peas into her mouth, drinks from her brimming glass of Coke. George M. tings his glass.

— Enough with the tinging, says Dave.

He pats Shinny's head, her chin propped next to his plate.

Ting, sings George M.'s glass. Ting!

Shinny barks.

— Look, son, says their father. — I'm just trying my best here. Because I love you, Georgie.

— Dad, don't, says George M.

— Give me a hug, son. Their father pushes himself back from the table, about to stand up.

— Dad! Dave! Stop! shouts George M. — I'll go to the family counsellor.

— Okay, their father says, returning to sitting. — We don't need to hug. I just love you so much. I love all of you kids and your mother so so much and it would kill me if anything happened to this family.

He wipes his watery eyes. Sighs. Glances at their mother.

Their mother glumly sips from her glass of Coke; her fourth glass, Faraday counts. Her mother's silence in all this reminds her uncomfortably of the same great silence almost a year and a half ago that followed when her mother loudly clicked closed her makeup case and said she was leaving. In response, their father sat in the basement in front of his tiny TV, replaying his NHL *Great Moments* DVD, stroking Shinny's head, big and heavy as a pot roast, in their father's lap. The dog sprawled across the entire chesterfield, their father squinched into the corner.

— Leave me alone, he said when Faraday or her brothers creaked the top stair, the hockey announcer's tinny bellowing, the organ honking, the crowd shrieking. Then after they backed away he slapshot himself up the stairs and asked them why he was alone in the basement all by himself, were his children all bloody robots? He boiled himself a hot water bottle, talking about how adult men have feelings too, men crying shouldn't be frightening, then clumped back down into the basement, the water bottle cradled in his arms, NHL *Great Moments* cranked up. That first time when Dave and Shirley's marriage spiralled the whole family into a galaxy-sized blackhole.

How their father's grief simmered into an inflammation, and the bad blood infected the whole family, all of them not making eye contact, saying *Leave me alone.*

The air in the house was dirty all the time, too many flies buzzing and squirming. One day, Faraday's father threw a plastic bottle of mayonnaise and splattered the kitchen wall. Their mother retaliated while he was at work by throwing his favourite coffee mug against the living room wall. Two days of gelatinous mayonnaise splatter until Jonas scraped it off the wall and the floor tiles with the sharp, plastic edges of his brand-new university student ID card. Carefully picking up the mug pieces and stowing them in an empty milk carton by the garbage can.

How their mother stood by the shoe rack next to the front door to speak to their father, — Dave, I'm taking the kids with me. Faraday, George M. and Jonas all kept watching their own computer and television screens.

Their father shambled downstairs to his tiny television, and then suddenly he was wheezing, his eyes wide when he suddenly snow-angeled to the floor. Their mother stayed overnight with him in the hospital, her very own Gordie Howe hat trick: taking the kids, leaving the kids, remarrying the husband, all in one night.

That day — thirteen months, four days and six hours ago — Faraday's nose started to bleed. She needed to get away, needed to neutralize the toxins, unearth an antidote to her family's venom, so she borrowed a credit card to buy a blessing of live unicorns on the internet. She knew she could end up in the clink as she pulled open the snap of her mother's wallet, chose arbitrarily from the fan of plastic credit cards, but she did it so she wouldn't nosebleed to death, she did it for her father gasping his asthma attack in the hospital, her mother cooing her love for their father but regret for her youth, Jonas brandishing a spatula as he fried up bacon and egg sandwiches in the kitchen, George M. complaining only once when Jonas insisted they all eat at the table together, or together in front of the big TV at least.

— You don't have to eat anything, George M., said Jonas. — Have fun making your very own salad with the liquefying lettuce head in the fridge, gonad.

Yolk drooled down George M.'s chin as they sat in a half-circle in front of the blaring television, a *Sector Six* rerun, the theme song plinking, 'No such thing as heroes, just a bunch of ones and zeroes,' Colonel Shakira in her gold uniform aiming her weapon at a giant Reptiloid in gold shorts. The Reptiloid called her the equivalent of pig turd in its language, the Reptiloid lunged, Colonel Shakira shot her Rosette Nebular, — I am Colonel Shakira! she shouted.

— That would never happen in real life, muttered George M.
— That Reptiloid skin would repel a flimsy laser like that.

Faraday's raging tears were not so much from the hurricane of her parents, but from her mother shaking the credit card printout in her face after the credit card company had called her mother about suspicious activity on that credit card. Her mother trampled her with the news that the website was a hoax, that she hadn't bought a blessing of unicorns, it didn't matter if there was an official receipt, and a shipment of unicorns was not sailing the Atlantic Ocean on its way to her on a ship from the Black Forest in Germany.

Her mother wailed at Faraday's credit card fraud and the money lost, and her father's voice was breathy in the hospital as he tried to lasso enough air for his lungs. The credit card printout her execution summons on the kitchen table, braying, betraying her.

She decided not to tell her parents about how the company that supplies the unicorns, Einhörner GmbH, asked for a pair of her used panties along with her credit card number and home address. The panties so that the unicorns could know her virgin scent of course. She knew the panty part was maybe a little creepy, but she also knew they were a reputable company. All the customer reviews rated them five stars.

— Do you want to tell me what this is all about? wheezed her father.

Faraday's tears dripped dropped splotched splat.

— The shipment was guaranteed or my money back! she said.
— They can't lie about that. *They gave me a receipt.*

— It doesn't make a lot of sense, he said. — Does spending money on an imaginary — ?

— They're in the Bible! she interrupted wildly, — Aristotle wrote about them, Marco Polo, Pliny the Elder, Genghis Khan, they all knew that unicorns exist, they saw them, Faraday tried hard not to shout. — Are you calling Pliny the Elder a liar?

— Does spending money, her father repeated, — on an imaginary animal really make that much sense to you? Plus, where were you going to put them? In the garage? Because there's no way you could keep a bunch of horses in the house. I'm going to have to take away your computer privileges. For a month. His bony knees poked tents up under the sheets on the bed.

— The mother of Confucius! She wouldn't lie! *They're not horses*, she gritted her teeth.

— I don't appreciate that tone, señorita.

— What *tone?*

— Privileges revoked. Computer. For two months.

— Well, my blessing's on its way, Faraday said, whirling a circle of medical tape on her index finger, slipping her bum off the edge of the bed. — They'll be here. The credit card went through. Money's been spent.

— *Where* are these unicorns? It's been a month since you ordered them.

— They'll *be* here. Ordering a shipment of unicorns in the mail isn't like buying a set of washed-up, olden-times hockey DVDs!

— That's it, said her father, swiping his hand through the air, the plastic tube of the IV violently looping, — Your hair straightener privileges are now officially revoked too.

— Please not the hair straightener, she said.

She raged to Uncle Suzie. He fed her nacho chips and Cheez Whiz, the occasional glass of Chambord. — Not too much, he said. — Or it stops being sexy and just becomes sloppy.

He said, — Maybe you should go see a shrink. *I* saw a shrink. Then I *saw* a shrink. A different shrink. You'd think a therapist would be the most well-adjusted person alive. Uncle Suzie shook the bag of chips and peered into it, hunting for crumbs. — Wrong. And neither were any of his shrink buddies. That's right, they hang out in *packs.*

He took a sip of his drink, the ice tinkling.

— You don't believe they exist either? she sobbed, a fresh burst of grief rippling through her.

— Oh, Faerie, he said, taking her hands in his, his hands warm and strong. — That's not it at all. It's just that, you know, things like unicorns, those important things, they're not things you can *buy*. Like love. You can't buy that. When you try, all you get is something ugly and misdirected that's not really yours. Does that make sense? I know it sounds like a Harlequin romance.

Faraday hiccupping, her face wet, she was dying from the grief, the betrayal.

— What's a Harlequin romance? she asked.

— Everything's going to be all right, he said, patting her hand. — Your unicorns, your parents. One day you'll graduate and flip the big fat bird to high school forever.

— They issued a receipt, she said, slapping one hand into the other for emphasis.

— You stole a credit card, he said, slapping one hand into the other for emphasis.

He lent her his hair straightener.

She loves Uncle Suzie, but she knew he was wrong. The unicorns are on their way. In the live cargo area of a ship currently crossing the Atlantic Ocean, courtesy of Einhörner GmbH, a reputed dealer. She isn't stupid. She did her research.

Her father told her to go talk to Father Tim at their church. She tried to look excited when Father Tim exclaimed about her enlightened decision to remain a virgin, and did she know that unicorns were closely associated with the Passion of the Christ?

— Think about it, said Father Tim and his shiny round cheeks and Santa Claus beard. — The maiden is the Virgin Mary, the unicorn Jesus Christ. You have joined a spiritually wealthy, esteemed tradition, Faraday.

Faraday doubtful of Father Tim's enthusiasm as she picked the polish off her fingernails.

It was the first time Faraday ever heard *fucking* and *priests* in the same sentence. From Uncle Suzie's mouth roaring in her father's face. Then Uncle Suzie coaxed her father to watch a live hockey game upstairs instead of that old, canned Wayne Gretzky. Each of them angled into the opposite arms of the couch, Shinny splayed between them.

Father Tim twinkling and nodding hard at her the next time she went with her parents to church. Father Tim on the way out as her therapist but not her priest. Her first appointment with Dr. Linus Libby only three days later.

— Why a unicorn? asked Dr. Linus Libby. — Why not a regular horse? Why not run away in a car or a bus or a train? Why not a magic carpet?

— It just makes sense, Faraday said. — Cars, buses and trains break down. And magic carpets don't exist. Unicorns are genetically programmed to gore and eradicate the impure. They cure us.

After her father came back from the hospital, her mother clicked her makeup case back open. So Dave moved back upstairs, and now he watches hockey games in colour again. Her parents visit a marriage counsellor once a week. Dave sometimes tries to hug Faraday and George M. in public for no reason, and she just wants to die.

She has a spare Friday afternoons after 2:30, so she gets half an hour at home, then half an hour for the drive to the shrink, one hour with the shrink, and the rest of the evening she works at Tim Hortons because she has to pay her parents back, and besides, they're at home having sex.

— You know, said Dr. Linus Libby one Friday afternoon, you know it's natural to have anxieties — worries — about sex and sexuality. Especially around your age.

— I know what *anxiety* means.

— It's just that … it's just that … there is no scientific evidence to support the existence of unicorns.

— Of course, she lies.

— You believed they were real.

— I was just kidding. I'm not stupid.

— I'm not calling you stupid. I have a very strong reaction to the idea that you would think that. You're very smart. In the top percentile for your age group.

— But not for your age group?

— It's just that — perhaps other students are sexually active around you —

— Of course! It's high school!

— And perhaps you're not as interested and that's okay.

— I'm waiting for the right person. I'm not a virgin freak or anything. I know what sex is. I know what fellatio is. I know that sometimes girls at school charge money for it.

— I'm not suggesting you're a freak, Faraday. How do those words *virgin freak* make you feel when you hear yourself say them?

— Nothing.

— Hmm?

— Nothing. Maybe the right person has a horn growing out of their head, she says. — It's not a big deal. That's all. I'm not prepared to settle for a mediocre product.

— Hmm, says Linus the shrink.

He pulls at his blonde thinning hair, scratches at his skin to match. He has the smell of that sweet pink liquid soap in public washroom dispensers.

— I know you've been facing challenges at home. With your parents working on their marriage.

— Yes, Linus, Faraday says. The liquid soap in public washrooms is pearly in the light, and it always leaves behind a messy tendril on the edge of the sink. Maybe she can talk about that with Linus next time instead of about her parents. She is tired of her parents, their neediness and narcissism, their frantic fornicating, always hogging the microphone.

Faraday wonders how much longer before the dysfunctional family venom completely formaldehydes her brain. How much longer she has to wait before her unicorns come to save them, why they couldn't have come earlier and saved Patrick Furey too.

Walter

Walter the guidance counsellor matches the dead boy's combination lock serial number to the number on his clipboard list, and pulls open the metal door with a clang. A battered runner bounces to the floor. He slots it back into the locker's clutter, next to its mate, then he remembers and places the runners, side by side, into the empty binder box by his feet. Next, a wad of gym clothes. An unruly sheaf of papers puffed from water damage. A blunt pencil stub and half a pack of Skittles. A Japanese comic book and a copy of *The Pride and the Joy*. The book's familiar weight and width in Walter's hand, disturbing the soil he'd smoothed over it. He tries to pat the book back into the locker. He could never have discussed this book with *this* student. An inside-out blue sweater dangling from one of the hooks. He fumbles, and the package of Skittles gapes open, rainbow-coloured candies spinning, bouncing, tumbling, scattering staccato clicks on the floor, metal pings against the lockers.

A torn envelope and a blue argyle sweater. A dried glob of gum thumbed to the door. The boy's fingerprints and spit. Walter pulls a greeting card with a picture of a bowl of fruit on the front out of the envelope and opens it. Tears squeeze out of his eyes — he swipes them away. The card he'll burn. The copy of *The Pride and the Joy* he'll burn too. He folds the sweater neatly into the box.

He fits the lid back onto the box. Kicks and drags the Skittles with the side of his foot into a dusty mound he scoops up with his hands and tosses into a garbage can. Dusts his hands off on his pants. His ears buzz.

The card and the book in the bottom drawer of his work desk.

Walter sits in his car in front of Patrick Furey's house. His family won't think Walter's a creep, they probably don't look out the windows anymore. He doesn't want to look out windows anymore either.

He shoves open the car door and steps onto the pebbly road. The sun a sinking, sloppy peach in the sky.

Patrick's father blinks at Walter in the sunset, the air Kool Aid orange with the falling sun, the grass crisped and brown, and grey, dirty snow crusting lawns, edges of sidewalks, gutters globbed with dead grass and twigs, Barbie doll legs, dead birds and gravel. One of those afternoons when he can almost smell spring on the wind, but not quite. The father's eyes sag as though he has been pulled from an oil slick. — Can I help you, he asks but not as a question. And Walter can only open and close his mouth, the cardboard box full of dead boy pushing into his belly.

— I am the head guidance counsellor from Patrick Furey's school, he says. — My name is Walter Boyle. The words a wet mop dragging between them. — Are you his father? asks Walter. — I just wanted to give you my condolences and bring you the contents of his locker.

The purple bags under the father's eyes pulling his face down past his jowls, so Walter holds out the box and the father takes it between his hands, like they are dance partners with the box a shield between them, — Thank you, the father says, his skin waxy and collapsing.

— I am so so sorry for your loss, says Walter.

— Yes, well, says the father. — As my dead son's head guidance counsellor I guess you should be.

The father flickers in the orange, windy air.

Walter's hands hook onto the steering wheel. He peers out the windshield, he can't remember anymore how long he has framed his life like this, spattered windows and closed doors, close air, dead grass. Once upon a time, this was enough for him, this job. His work life with the students and their girl or homework or timetable problems one thing, his real life with Max another thing: a clear outside, a clear inside. The occasional leak of one world into the other, the occasional charge of seeing his boyfriend by chance in the hallway or at a meeting and Walter secretly gloating *He's mine*, the brilliant reunion trysts at home some days when they could shiver in pretend-but-real fear over how they'd pulled it off another day. They'd have their cake and eat it too, Walter licking the cake icing off Max's fingers. And how wonderful that Max made sure their work life and real life could stay separate, so vigilant: two peas in a pod they were as a couple. Max and Walter undercover. Their electrifying, delicious secret. Not hurting anyone inside their closed doors, Walter always thought, their windows with the blinds drawn, safe inside their secret shell.

Spring is overrated, but a winter that never ends, like this one, feels like it's pushing him closer to lunacy. If he could, he would fall to his hands and knees and drag the green from the ground, yank out blooms from frozen tulip bulbs; the time for spring is now. Now.

Petra

In Tamsin's bedroom, musical notes unfurling, uncurling, ungirling. Tamsin has poured Petra a Diet Coke with secret rum in it, the husky sweetness and fizz rolling across Petra's tongue. Tamsin practises her viola, the sweep and scrape of the bow across the strings, and she frowns as she plays the same bar over and over again, a broken horsehair streaming from her bow. Petra sips her drink, poking at an ice cube with her finger. Tamsin's bow sawing across her viola, Petra's heart cracking at the high notes.

— I'm gonna do it, says Petra, plunking her drink down on the table.

Tamsin's playing abruptly stops.

— No, breathes Tamsin. — You wouldn't.

— I would, says Petra. — I will.

— You still haven't heard from Ginger? Are you sure?

— That's why I have to do it, says Petra.

She pulls on her coat, picks up her bag. Shakes her hair down over her face.

The delight on Patrick Furey's father's face, how he intermittently pats Petra on the shoulder, the smile wrinkles around his mouth deepening.

— You were his friend, you say, the father says. — What a nice surprise, how nice, Patrick's friend.

Petra stammers when she asks for the sweater back, a blue one. — With d-d-diamonds on the f-f-front? she says. She sketches the diamonds on her own chest with her index fingers, brushing her nipples. — I gave it to him as an early Valentine's present, a memento of our new love.

The father smiles so wide he seems like he could break into a pale laugh.

Petra hears a door click open, then closed, and a woman, the mother, comes out. Side by side, Patrick Furey's parents look surprisingly normal. Ordinary. Boring even. Like the kind of boring old people her parents would play bridge with. Like regular parents, but she's not sure anymore, it's been a while since she's had to stare at old people. The mother's smile thin and too long across her face, her lips naked.

— You knew him when? asks the mother. — You were exchanging presents for *Valentine's* Day?

— Yes! answers the father for Petra. — A brand-*new* girlfriend. That's why we didn't know about you.

The mother frowns a little, brushes her yellow bangs back with her hand so bits of bang ruffle straight up into the air before settling back down. The house busting and bursting with white and yellow roses and carnations, lilies, feathery flowers Petra doesn't know the name of. She balls the sweater between her hands as though it's a ball of dung she's gathered for her nest — the bright smell of so many petals.

The warmth of the tears surprises her, the sudden flood of mucus at the back of her throat, the tears running from her nose. She cries so hard and for what? The wails erupting from deep within her gut, she rocks and the father pats her on the shoulder and the mother offers her a hank of Kleenex. The sweater seized in her lap as she leans forward, she's sure she can feel the wool ball beating like a heart. Or the blood in her head from the crying — why is she crying, moaning? They coo around her — a cup of tea steams on the glass table by her knees. The mother pries the ball from Petra's hands and shakes out the diamonds, folds them smooth and lays the sweater next to Petra's cup. Petra drinks the hot tea, the bitter, minty edges.

The father asks her, — Do you want your locket back too?

— What locket?

The bulbous, heart-shaped locket beating in the centre of the mother's palm.

Petra says, — That's not mine.

Walter

Max is at home, 6:30 p.m., eating microwaved, canned tomato sauce slopped on spaghetti. Walter's breath puffing in the cold as he tromps through patches of unshovelled sidewalk snow for a proper meal he's too tired to cook. The giant digital clock in front of the Ethiopian restaurant reads 17:83, incorrect as always. Walter orders two platters' worth of food, plus an extra order of injera.

— Actually, no, make that two, he says to the woman at the till, and holds up two fingers in a peace sign. — Awesome, he says, then pulls out his wallet from his coat pocket. He'll bolt down the food then boot it to badminton. He needs the exercise if he wants to reach a thirty-two waist again this lifetime. He would even be happy with a forty.

The waitress types in the numbers in the cash register, and Walter inhales the roasting food and coffee smells, smells of his ancient home maybe, the waitress's silvering hair pulled back from her face and tucked up into a white scarf, large gold hoops swinging from her stretching earlobes. Once he brought Ethiopian takeout for his father, and the old man smacked his lips, saying, — Tastes just like what your grammy used to make. Then his father belched, — Buraaaaaaap!

— Really? We originally came from Ethiopia? You have proof? asked Walter eagerly.

— Wally, said his father, Sal, — it's not as if your great-great-granny 'n -grampy remembered to pack their travel itineraries and passports when they were kidnapped into the slave ships. What kind of question is that, did the slaves in our family come from Ethiopia and can I prove it. Like I have a magic wand in my pocket. Next time *think* before you speak, Wally.

Walter's father laying out domino tiles beside his dinner plate. — Think, Sal said as he clacked down a tile, — before (*clack*) you speak (*clack clack*).

The waitress presents him with the credit card slip. He breathes heavily as he contemplates how much tip he should leave. It occurs to him that she might be a distant cousin — a romantic, mostly implausible notion, but still he can't be cheap with a woman who might be a relative. He calculates 17 percent, then signs with a flourish and a smile. She doesn't smile back which, sadly enough now that he thinks about it, is why he and Max like this restaurant. No one who works here is that friendly, they don't ask questions. This woman will never ask him if he's married then say she has a single daughter or a younger sister he might like to meet and make him lie and ruin the restaurant for him. And if he told the truth, well, forget it, old people the most judgmental of all. He likes this restaurant because he likes the food, maybe his ancestors come from Ethiopia, and the people who work here couldn't care less about Max and Walter huddled at their regular, isolated table, minding their own business, even though they've been regulars here for almost five years, since it first opened.

Walter hurries back to the house, skidding on patches of ice, hopping over icy puddles, the bag of food sliding and jostling in his arms. He sets down the bag, unlocks the door, the sound of the television, one of Max's stupid DVD spaceship shows beeping and laser beaming in the front room.

— You know, says Walter suddenly from the doorway as he knocks snow from his boots, — why is it that on every single one of these shows there isn't ever a female captain of a spaceship who's a black woman? An Ethiopian woman, for example?

Max's mouth sours. — I suppose Colonel Shakira doesn't qualify?

— Oh, her, says Walter. — She's just some kind of bimbo with a giant rack. She doesn't count.

— How convenient, says Max, as he turns his head back to the television, his arms crossed, the chunky silver band of his watch glittering in the light from the television. He's still wearing his work shirt and tie. Dress pants. His profile sharp and hard and outlandishly beautiful as always. His white hair swept forward onto his forehead, as though he were the model for an emperor profiled on an ancient Roman coin. Or a *Masterpiece Theatre* show about a Roman emperor. Max handsome in that classical, Caligula kind of way, in a way Walter can never tire of even when Max is being his most horrible.

Walter stuffs his toque and scarf in the closet, accidentally jostles a leftover Christmas tree ornament still hanging on the Norfolk pine by the door.

— And you know what? Next Christmas I would like it if for once we could decorate the tree with normal glass balls instead of little spaceships. I would also like a real tree, and not a house plant we glam up once a year. Like normal people who live in the world instead of fourteen-year-old boys.

The tiny Romulan Bird of Prey spins, then spirals to a stop on its side, one of the warship's nacelles hooked on a branch.

— Low blood sugar, *Wally?* snarls Max. Lieutenant Fong stands and stretches, her back arching up.

— What are you running away from, Max? What's outer space giving you that you're missing here on Earth?

Max points the remote control at the television set as though he wants to knight it, pauses his television show. Then he points the remote at Walter, takes in Walter from the top of his balding head to his bulging stomach to his damp, stockinged feet, points the remote at the rustling plastic bag of Ethiopian food swinging from Walter's hand.

Walter pads to the kitchen, plops the bag on the counter, runs himself a glass of water from the sink. Lieutenant Fong curls herself around his ankles in a repeated figure eight. Max named the cat. Walter wanted a cat, so Max researched cats, selected the cat, bought the cat, named the cat. Lieutenant Fong. Max and his little television shows sometimes *so* gay.

— You're going to be late for badminton practice with those people, calls Max. — You say you want to get down to a thirty-two but then you stock up on restaurant food and skip exercising. That makes a lot of sense.

— Whaddayoucare? shouts Walter. — You telling me I'm fat?

— No, calls Max. — Just more of you to love, my pet, just more of you to love!

Walter rushes upstairs to the bedroom, snarfing down a handful of injera and goat meat from one hand, hopping on one foot as he pulls on his sweatpants with the other.

— I'll be home in an hour and a half, he says as he galumphs toward the door, racquet in his hand.

He sticks his face in Max's face, directly in the way of the beeping television screen. Max cranes his neck to look around Walter.

— Where's my goodbye kiss? asks Walter.

They peck. Max's microwaved-tomato-sauce breath. Max's frown.

— That's right, says Walter.

The television beeps goodbye.

Gretta

As the dead boy's mother, you wonder how you got here. You wish he would open his eyes, why won't he. You wish you had stuffed every rope and everything shaped like a rope into the fireplace and burned them all yourself. You wish you wish this was just an elaborate game this expired star collapsing on itself. You wish you wish and you cannot believe your wish is being ignored. You would like to write a letter to the prime minister, the UN, God, light a candle, cast a spell, force breath back into that broken neck, watch the chest expand, hear your boy cough awake, watch him stuff fork after fork of macaroni and cheese and wiener slices into his mouth like he used to when he was twelve, all big ears and eyelashes and warm baby skin. You would drain your savings, sell the house and your grandmother's jewellery, your great-grandparents' heirloom china and silver, the hutch for the dining room you *had* to have, the cars, your ludicrously expensive cheap-looking clothes — those goddamn leather pants — the whole house, yourself in an alleyway to some stranger, you'd give your life to a murderer if you knew you could force a way to open your boy's eyes. You wish you wish and the plates, the glasses, the bowls, the bag of macaroni, the brick of cheddar cheese you splatter against walls and floors make no difference at all.

He told you the hutch was made from an endangered species of tree, and you told him to stop with the crap. Was *crap* the last word you said to him? You couldn't wait, you cut him down yourself with a kitchen knife, that knife so dull, his body so dead you wouldn't believe it, your husband pumping his chest then poking buttons on the telephone, you pushing air into his dead lips, when all you wanted was to inhale and inhale him back inside your body, wrap him in your skin, start all over again, from the beginning, and not be stuck here in this perpetual ending.

Where he goes from here. Interred and quiet in that sloping parkland, a solitary biker, two mothers jogging behind high-tech baby carriages with bicycle wheels, they have babies inside them — where is your baby? — the mothers' legs thin and fleeced. A desperate couple of hormone bags fucking high up among the older graves, you wish you wish you could fuck the whole goddamn ugly world.

His strange blue face, so swollen, his body a bizarre chandelier. You asked the medical examiner, the funeral director, what would happen next. You close your eyes tight but you can't get his round blue face, his hardened body, out of your sight. You open your eyes wide and wish his body back into your sight. You wish you wish. The black dog on the other side of the fence hunches into the shape of a shrimp, squeezes out a thin long shit. Pants black-dog breath.

Open your eyes.

The winter mosquitoes won't leave you alone. Suck all your blood in tiny increments.

You live a righteous life. You make art that sells in reputable galleries — your work has been featured more than once in national newspapers. You attend Mass on the important holidays, you give up chocolate for Lent and never cheat. Give to Feed the Hungry at Christmas. You and your husband pay the maximum on the RRSPS every year. You chat with the neighbours — even the strange couple who made a jagged rock garden out of giant pieces of slate on their front lawn — and you vote most of the time. You sweat on the weight machines and treadmill at the gym and make sure your husband and son eat their vegetables and you usually shop organic. You cream your skin at night, get your hair trimmed once every six weeks and dress well in public (high heels and a smart dress) even for grocery shopping, because why look like the slob you're not? You knew he didn't like school, but you thought, Soon he'll graduate. You knew he was smarter than the report cards said, you knew, but why didn't you ask why he was skipping so much school. You forgot to ask why he spent all his time in his room, who was texting him all the time, his phone chiming like raindrops, why one day he was wearing a locket in the shape of a heart and a blue sweater you didn't remember buying that that strange girl came looking for. That girl no girl your son would ever know, you just know this because he told you in no uncertain terms. You remember wishing he was seven again, all skinny arms and legs wrapping themselves around you like a monkey's, bony like a kitten's, back when you could read his actions like they were your own. You remember deciding to ask about that locket, that piece of girl's jewellery around your boy's neck when he'd yelled at you that there would never be a girl, but you knew enough to know you didn't really want to know. You saw the chain wrapped around and around his throat, the heart cold against his skin, cutting off his circulation, you ripped it off, the chain dissolving in your hands. If you'd known, you would have done something because you always assumed he would be a banker, not a faggot.

You think about killing yourself too. How that would end the grief, just go ahead and jump, toes pointed artfully, into that giant lake of fire. Dump rocks in your pockets, your purse, two of those sturdy shopping bags from your favourite clothing store Tristan and Isolde, and jump into a swimming pool. Inhale water like air, cough yourself into a flood. Why couldn't he just have had a problem with a girl? Why couldn't he just bum around Europe and smoke too much pot, experiment a little with cocaine, like his father did?

Because you are evil, you continue to live. Because funny that *evil* is a noun spelled forward and a verb spelled backwards. Because what you did to your son was the word *evil* as a verb, a verb that means to ignore someone to death, that locket winding around your boy's neck, lurid neon signs, a verb that means to stand by, place your hands over your eyes while someone dies in front of you. The verb of not putting out your hand to save. That verb. That human-chandelier verb. That verb-an-unnatural-colour-of-blue verb. That gold, heart-shaped-letter-he-wrote-to-you-and-only-you verb. You evilled. Your chest heaves, scratching in and out your breath.

Furey, Patrick — Patrick Furey, known to his mother as Peanut or Fishy until he told you to fucking stop it, his name is Patrick, stop treating him like a kid, door slam the exclamation mark at the end of both your shouted sentences. Took his life February 17 in the morning while you were pushing a shopping cart through an aisle at Planet Organic Market and trying to decide if you should change canned tuna brands, your son gasping the last of his life while you stood on another floor of the house stacking the cans of tuna in the cupboard, arranging green and Spartan apples you just bought in a bowl in a way that caught the light instead of fucking running up those fucking steps, leaping up those stairs and stopping him, the glossy green skins against the red, bright apples, a snowy day, snowy apples, glistening tuna, gasping. Your Peanut, your Fishy, Mister Fishy a cluster of cells in your womb, bubbling into bright bones hands pushing out of the skin you can still feel his heel, his skull pushing through your skin, your giant belly, your heavy tender breasts, your fishy. You his mother. His empty body.

Friday

Walter and Max

Walter, the dead boy's guidance counsellor, so hungover he can see into the centre of the earth, isn't at work this morning. He phones in sick, his glutinous voice scratches on the phone to Joy.

— Your flu wouldn't be of the twenty-six-ounce variety, would it? she asks. — Ha ha! Just kidding! That's good. You need to relax. Been a tough week.

Walter's not sure if he likes Joy very much. Or maybe now he likes her a lot.

Max, the dead boy's principal, the dead boy's guidance counsellor's secret husband, has not the foggiest clue where the guidance counsellor is. He taps a cigarette out from his new pack and smokes under the porch light at 5:30 a.m. Last night when he finally started getting ready for bed, selecting his 'I Heart Colonel Shakira' T-shirt to sleep in from the dresser drawer, Walter wasn't ensconced in his Buddha-like way in front of the TV, watching the eleven o'clock news, drinking his regular post-badminton Diet Coke with ice. Then the cat yodelled for her midnight snack; Max scrabbled fruitlessly among and through the cupboards hunting for the stash of cat food tins so he dumped out a can of sardines into the cat's food bowl instead. By 1:03 a.m., Walter still hadn't deigned to call and Max fumed as he tossed around in the blankets that there was no need for this kind of rudeness, how difficult was it to take fifteen seconds and dial in a phone call, and suddenly Max was waking up to a shrieking alarm clock in an empty bed. It's morning, Walter's still MIA, Max's mouth and lungs cry out for a second cigarette, and the cat hisses and angrily switches her fluffy white tail every time Max ventures near her, even after he locates her cans of cat food under the sink and cranks one, two, three, open for her that she slurps up and then promptly vomits on the bathroom floor right next to Max's heel while Max is in mid-shave. Max cannot *bear* being interrupted mid-shave. He steps and slides sideways into the pile of vomit anyway. And Walter, that reprobate, still isn't home, he's started tramping around, the principal just knows it, Jesus H. Christ. That reprobate. That tramp. Once a tramp always a tramp, and a long time ago the principal loved how his husband used to be a tramp and a kleptomaniac and a reprobate who stole bedsheets from Superstore along with Eggos and parsley just because he could, a quasi-criminal with shark eyes who reformed out of love for the principal, a tamed lion padding quietly around the house, my goodness how the principal loves that. That reprobate probably in someone else's bed right now. The principal glances at his watch, maybe he can sneak in another smoke. Yanks his tie around his throat. Twists out another morning cigarette from the package. Coughs a foggy puff into the cold morning air. Shameful. All of it shameless.

When he gets in to work, hangs his coat from its hook, Max phones Walter's office and the phone burps the canned voice mail, — I'm away from my desk but will return your call as soon as I am able. If this is an emergency please dial the following number —

Skipping work!

Thursday night, Walter actually wins a badminton game — the birdie dead on the floor on the other side of the net. Not through deliberate strategy, but brilliant, awesome fucking accident, racquet at the level of his knees when he wants it up in the air, Walter heaving for breath, Ethiopian food lurching up from his stomach into his windpipe, his racquet wilting at just the right time in the path of the zinging birdie. He huffs and puffs, his esophagus burning, he's drowning in sweat, goddammit, somewhere along the way he transformed from a muscular stud muffin into fucking Fat Albert, but his heart pounds like a twenty-year-old man's — then he decides to go to the pub afterwards with the badminton guys and the two badminton gals, Brecken and Louise, and he worries that the cat hasn't gotten her midnight snack, but why is it always his responsibility to feed *their* cat, he smiles a little bit when he thinks about how Lieutenant Fong will yodel at Max and he won't know where Walter's stacked the canned cat food. Then he worries for Lieutenant Fong.

He sucks hard at the creamy head on his beer, trying to ignore his leaping irritation at two of the other guys putting their arms around each other and calling each other *babe* and *honey* in this too public place (why would they *do* that, there are ways *around* that), one of them calling everyone *bitch*, including Walter even though Walter's done nothing except drink his beer, — You enjoying that beer, bitch? 'Sabout time you came out for a beer, bitch.

If Max were here he would have signalled to Walter *Time to go home* and ranted the whole way back to the house about these flamers and public displays of affection giving everyone a bad name, and how he and Walter keep it in the house and only in the house which is the only right way to do it and sexier too. Which Walter would normally agree with. Which is why Walter hardly ever drinks beer with the guys and the two badminton gals, Brecken and Louise, because they're always so *loud* even when they aren't talking. This beer undoing all the benefits of the badminton exercise.

When he pulls himself up the steps from the pub, clutching the railing with each step, the cool air nuzzles his face, the beer still foaming in his head, and he watches winter-muddied cars squish by in the dark. He wants to go home, so he hails a cab to the bar called Home, and he orders another beer while he stands in line at the bar with the trannies and the dykes and the bears and the nellies and the circuit boys and the twinks and the leathermen and the drag kings and the drag queens and the drag hags and the fag hags, then he dances by himself in the steamy, dark dance club with a beer in his hand like he's nineteen again, and if one of them's a student or a colleague or a superintendent or a parent or a priest — if they see him, well, he will also see *them*, he isn't the only one — and for the first time in a long time, he's finally Home. He's once again himself with his own people, he can't remember why he doesn't go Home more often, how zingy and awesome he feels drinking this many beers and dancing in the flashing lights with giant, awesome women and their tucked-away dicks like this giant Colonel Shakira here, how maybe keeping it at home and just between the two of them isn't as sexy as it could be anymore.

He is a middle-aged fat man with an unfashionable goatee, but an electric, noisy peacock tail unfurls around him, and he swirls among its feathers. He sweats under the folds of his sweater, his body gleaming.

All these dancers, strangely flavoured, oddly shaped fruit hanging from branches of the family tree. Tucked behind leaves and flowers, behind wedding dresses, plus and equal signs, and vertical lines heading toward children, grandchildren, great-grandchildren. The abrupt end to a branch. An anonymous, invisible life companion fallen to the ground. A whisper, but no ears to hear. No pens to record.

Walter drapes his sweating body with shining peacock feathers, — Awesome! he shouts, curls his bottle of beer in his hand, next to his heart. Another beer and another beer, he never wants to grow up and leave Home.

Look at that! His old boyfriend Normie Kwong roosted at the bar, just like in the old days. He wonders if Normie's still freezing him out, like in the old days.

Walter's hands grip the cool rationality of the toilet bowl, the water fresh and cold next to his nose until his throat forces his mouth open and zings of beer and Ethiopia waterfall out. Normie — who is still freezing him out — and one of the glamazon drag queens drag him into a cab, her name is Suzette, — But, girl, that just doesn't matter right now, we've just got to get you home, your husband'll be worried sick —

— How do you know I have a husband? Walter asks, then vomits in the gutter bubbling with decomposing winter leaves and garbage.

— *I* told her, you moron, says Normie. — You left me for Max, remember?

Walter rouses himself long enough to blurt his address, not that address, but the other address of the condo where he gets his school mail, and has a phone number under his own name, and utilities, and another mortgage, all under his name, because technically it is his home even though he hasn't lived there for years, he only tells people at work he lives there, he only goes there when Max needs to host a school staff or administrator social event at their house, Walter sleeping by himself on the little single bed, a picture of Max on the night table. Maybe he'll give the address of the bar as his home address to the next person who asks. He giggles.

He falls into his other-home toilet just in time to vomit his heart out, then rinses out his mouth — the taste so bitter, oh God he's too fucking old for this — in the sink. He pulls back the sheet and blanket like the flap on the envelope of his tiny bed, the sheets cool and smooth, the way sheets can feel only when they've been waiting for months, for years, for a body to climb inside. He crawls back to the living room, grabs the wastebasket beside the desk, and sets it near the bed. A glass of water. He slurps a glass of water. Flops into the bed. He doesn't know where he's left his badminton racquet. Or what the score is.

Mrs. Mochinski

Because that little fucker Jésus said to her face yesterday afternoon, right out of the blue, — Who the hell would want to be married to you? in that psychic way children sometimes have. Reading a teacher's secrets like on a billboard.

And she very calmly pointed to the door and ordered him to get into the hallway *right now*, wait for her at the *third locker* to the right of the door right there and *nowhere else*. She has had students throw pencils and crumpled paper balls in her face, tell her to fuck off, draw obscene pictures of her on her chalkboard, tell her she's a lesbian, but nothing has prepared her for this.

Jésus sticking his hand up in the middle of a discussion of Paris in *Romeo and Juliet*, and saying to Mrs. Mochinski, — Who the hell would want to be married to you? I feel sorry for your husband.

The smirk on his face, the truth in him.

Maureen, so hungover from last night because she let herself drink as much as she wanted, anything she wanted. She pulled on her sweatpants right after work, her fluffy pink sweater, and she downed two shots of Alexey's $100 bottle of scotch and then poured the rest down the sink, a very sweet *glug glug*. She drank six glasses of Chianti, the brand that Tony Soprano drinks. She sipped homemade crabapple liqueur her neighbour gave her five years ago, a shot of tequila, she even tried some of the cooking sherry because she always wanted to but just never had. Then she lay down on her stomach on the floor, raised her ass to the sky in downward dog, and did a little drunken yoga because yoga is good for anger management, upward then downward dog, a little pigeon pose to open her hips, the pose that always makes her cry because she carries her tension in her hips, that shows her the centre of the universe, and then she collapsed into corpse pose by nine p.m. Really she needs to go to a yoga class. Trying to do it by herself always leads to drunkenness.

She is not proud of herself this Friday morning. In fact, maybe she is still a little bit drunk as she tells the students they're going to watch a movie today, and she listens to them cheer, Jésus at the back of the class cheering the loudest, of course — Listen, class, I'm just going to level with you, she says. — I'm hungover, my head is splitting, I don't have a lesson. I do have a DVD we could pop in, and if you have homework you're stressed about in another class you can work on that, but it can't be mayhem in here, things are not going well for me, you can put on your iPods if you want or text your friends, my head's splitting, okay? All right? How about *Sector Six: The Movie?* Happy Friday!

Sector Six: The Movie's a good one, that's the emergency one she confiscated from a student once that she keeps in the bottom drawer of her desk. What difference does it make. In her drunkenness she found several truths. The truth that she is no longer Mrs. Mochinski, but just plain old Miss Maureen, even Jésus can tell. The truth that she didn't help Patrick Furey one bit, not one. The truth that one of her ass cheeks is a little flatter, a whole centimetre saggier than the other cheek, and that she is still stuck in high school, she hasn't written that novel she has promised herself she was going to write every summer for the past twenty years that would set her free from high school. Write a book. Make a million bucks. Live on a houseboat with her husband. Cross-stitch pictures of Boston terriers like her neighbour does and lie back enjoying the sunsets. She hasn't even started the book, she has no idea what it should be about because she has done nothing but punch a clock and/or play devoted wife her entire adult life. Even though she had so much potential to be a writer, all her teachers said so back when she was in high school. Had the potential to be whatever she wanted to be.

Walter

Walter surfaces from his hangover. He noses through the earth in his headache pain, he opens his mouth wide, wraps his mouth around the clay and earth and swallows, moves the grit and sand and rocks and roots peristalsic through his vitals and intestines, shits out earth in dark clusters, pushes his way up and breaks the topsoil crust. Walter shaking dirt out of his hair and pulling himself up out of his hole with his arms and his kicking legs. Walter surfaces. His clothes filthy, grit and roots between his teeth. Pulls himself out of bed and showers in time to catch the noon bus so he can make it to work by one.

After rummaging around in closets and drawers in the condo for a set of clothes, Walter steps into the crisp noon light. The wind this week drifted all the snow up onto the lawns — the sidewalks arctic clear. He rocks from heel to toe and back again as he waits for the bus, clouds of breath gusting from his mouth. He climbs up the grimy steps of the big red and white bus that will take him to the school. He clings to the grey rubber strap. The other bus riders hang from their straps, hang on the metal bus poles, and sit bunched in the blue plastic seats like cuts of meat arranged in a butcher's freezer.

In his office, in the midst of smells of photocopier toner and paper, the noise of lockers slamming, students laughing, he unwraps the framed photograph from his condo of Max in his Tilley hat. From that day two springs ago when they crawled up Tunnel Mountain, and Max seized in a laughing fit he couldn't stop. Walter can't remember what Max was laughing at, but it was one of the few times Max didn't frown or have a cigarette hanging out of his mouth or try to turn away when Walter took a picture of him. The sun shining silver through the pine trees.

Walter shoves aside papers, pencil jars, staplers, empty and half-empty boxes of paperclips, then props the picture on the corner of his desk. The inside life now outside.

It's only half an hour before Joy flutters into his office.

— So you made it to work! she says. — I thought I saw you skulking around, Boyle. That's an interesting picture you have on your desk. Her cucumber perfume fills Walter's office. The scent reminds him of car freshener. She's flipped open a small photo album with a transparent plastic cover on the desk so Walter can dote over the pictures she has of Begonia, her new baby niece.

— Yes, says Walter. He pokes an imaginary speck of dust away from the picture frame with his index finger. He flips through the pages, oohing and ahhhing at the pictures of a baby indistinguishable from a newborn kangaroo.

— Did Max give you that picture?

— I took it two springs ago.

— Nice, says Joy.

Then she blathers about how warm it was this morning, how she thought she saw a bud on her honeysuckle bush, while Walter pretends to look at the pictures, wonders what she really thinks of the photo on his desk, his shocking act. Breathless as he waits for the roof to collapse, the guillotine blade to fall. But she hasn't even glanced at it since her first look, instead she talks about how she was tempted to wear her spring trench coat this morning, but now of course the sky looks like snow, and didn't that wind at lunchtime just slice out your bones? The wind ran through her coat like a bunch of needles, right to her skin. And she decided on her tired winter coat, what would've happened if she'd gone with her trench coat! She'd be a Popsicle dropped in a snowbank.

Her hips push against Walter's desk, her arms crossed, her nails short but evenly filed straight across. Suddenly she leans down, runs her finger around the frame on the photo of Max. Taps Max right on the mouth.

— Do you have any pictures of your family? she asks.

— Just this one, says Walter, pointing a pencil at the picture of Max, his heart about to pop from his chest and run away. Max is my *family*, he thinks. He flips more plastic pages in the baby Begonia album.

— It's good to enjoy the company of people you work with, she says. — I can give you a picture of me to put on your desk too. We should do a group photo with all the staff! She throws her head back and laughs boisterously, her chest bouncing up and down.

Walter closes the photo album of Begonia the blob. Snowflakes have begun to drop outside the window.

— It's been a helluva week, huh? Joy says, turning to the window, the white winter sky bleaching out her dress like she's an overexposed photograph. — Poor Patrick. Poor thing.

— He's in a better place, blurts Walter so quickly, so automatically, he flinches. — No, he recants. From now on he's going to tell the truth when he's asked, no matter how bumpy, no matter how job-threatening. — What I meant to say is, yes, a horrendous tragedy.

— We should really do something. A minute of silence or something. The school.

— Can't, says Walter. — Copycat syndrome.

— It's not fair.

Walter rotates the pencil slowly in his fingers. — No, he says.

— Well, the staff should be allowed to do something. I've sent the family flowers and a card on behalf of the school. Maybe all the staff and the teachers, we could have our own private wake. Go to a pub the old Irish Catholic way.

— You — you knew him that well? asks Walter.

— Talked to him once or twice when he had to sign the book for being late. It doesn't matter. He's one of the tribe, right? she says, her voice beginning to shake, her eyes puddling. — The St. Aloysius Senior High School tribe. I'm going to send out a note to the staff. Have our own wake. Toast his life. Will you come?

— Y-yes, maybe, says Walter, his voice wilting. He hands her a tissue from the box on his desk.

— It's all too bad! she says, dabbing the inside corners of her eyes with the tissue, blowing her nose. — Well, she says, straightening and pulling down the bottom of her blouse, her breasts a high and mighty shelf. — You have a good weekend then. Any plans?

Joy has a shred of tissue stuck to one of her nostrils. Walter hesitates. For once he can tell someone at work about what he's really going to do on the weekend with his boyfriend Max. Then he remembers he's left his boyfriend Max and plans on taking full custody of their cat. He fumbles around in his head for the reason why he has Max's picture on his desk if they've broken up. What is he doing? What has he done? What will he do without Max to protect him and remind him? What will he do when he goes back to the inside and there's nothing there?

— Maybe get the cat's nails clipped, he says, flimsily. He clasps his fingers over his protruding belly. One microscopic, out-of-the-closet step at a time. He would like to go to the wake. If Joy knew the truth, she would uninvite him.

— I didn't know you had a cat, says Joy. — What kind?

— A white Persian.

— Max has a white cat too! That's funny.

— Yes it is!

Joy claps her hands together. — I'm halfway through that book you were talking about, she says. — Got it from the library.

— Which one's that now?

— The one with my name in the title of course!

Walter's skin prickles.

— *The Pride and the Joy.* Boy, that's a page-turner. I'm going to give it to my twin brother to read when I'm done. He's the gay one in our family. The baby of the family because he's ten minutes younger than me. He hates it that I'm his older sister and I remind him every time I see him that he should respect his elders. He hates that! she laughs.

Suddenly Walter cannot move a muscle. Not a twitch, not a shiver.

Joy claps her hand to her face, touches, brushes the shred of tissue. — Have I had this on my nose the whole time? She looks at the piece in her hand, —And you didn't tell me? Shame on you, Walter! She laughs again, sticks it back on her nose. — There, she says.

— You have a good weekend now, says Joy, packing up her album. — Tell me if you find any other books like that. It's *really* good.

Joy's heels clicking out the door.

Joy

My picture on his desk? asks Max.
— What about it?
— Nothing, says Joy. — Didn't know you hiked together.
— Just the once.
— Ah.
— That it?
— No. Jésus García Hernández's mother returned your call when you were meeting in the Area Office today. I told her you'd call her back in the morning.
— Okay.
— You okay?
— *You* okay?

Joy will buy Max a box of Belgian chocolates tonight on the way home, he's so obviously flustered by the suggestion of human contact; she feels sorry for him and his robotic, humanoid goofiness. She wants to hug him. Maybe suggest to Isaac they have him over for dinner — they haven't shared a single meal even once in the nine months she and Max have worked together. Not even drunk a cup of coffee together. Max pretending he's king of the school when really he's just the lonely runt of the litter, the last unsold kitten pacing figure eights in its cage.

Joy is also surprised at how pretty Walter looked when he smiled. She's never noticed the gap between his two front teeth before. Although he seems to be bloating up more and more each time she sees him. She doesn't want to be around, she decides, when he finally pops.

Faraday

Finally at the end of this horrible week, in the little pool of time she has before she has to leave the house to go see Dr. Linus Libby, Faraday pulls on her unicorn toque and clips the leash onto Shinny's collar for a dog poo in the park.

It's never occurred to Faraday until right this instant, her breath freezing into white clouds, Shinny's broad shiny back swaying mid-step, that she and her family regularly walk their dog in a park by a *cemetery*. Their house only blocks away from a vast field of dead people. During the first and last driving lesson she had with her mother, she accidentally drove them into a funeral cortège and what bothered her most at the time was not the corpse in the long, white car in front of them, but the fact that she had just driven straight through a stop sign. Her mother wouldn't stop yelling in her asphalty voice and was a *douche*. Funeral cortèges are not a big deal in their neighbourhood.

Shinny sits on her black haunches outside the cemetery fence, panting out dog breath. Ears perked, she noses the air. She leaps and burrows her nose under the snow, her tail whipping back and forth. She pulls out a frozen hamburger bun and starts to chomp. Faraday could pry it from her mouth, but the process is so slimy, and her hands aren't strong.

Faraday remembers once when she was little digging in the backyard for treasure with George M. and Jonas. Their father said, — You can dig for treasure in the corner by the wheelbarrow, but not by the fire pit. Dig down and find the very bottom of that rhubarb plant's root.

Their yard frilly with rhubarb leaves. She remembers how the soil absorbed her and her brothers, the prairie layer of topsoil then clay then rocks and roots all the way down. They wiped clay clumps off a twisted silver spoon. An old beer bottle. Some long, rusty nails. A buried car muffler. Bone fragments. Maybe a pet cat's.

She had sobbed quietly under a tent of rhubarb leaves about the cat, poor Bernard. George M. had decided that the cat's name when it was alive was probably Bernard.

Shinny gulps chunks of bun. Faraday plants her feet in the snow by the fence, the long rows of headstones rolling down the frozen white slopes in front of her. The air cold on her lips and the tip of her nose, and around her mouth the rough wool scarf dampens from her breath. Each headstone stands guard over a dead body. Of course. Maybe Patrick with his perfect skin lies under one of these tombstones. Maybe several Patricks lie under several of these stones, the grief of an entire school enfolding each of them. She grasps the chain-link with both mittened hands. Her boot soles this close to standing on top of the bloody, bony, hairy, dirty cemetery pile. Right this instant, she can't stand her feet on the ground, her feet stepping on Patrick. She snatches up the end of Shinny's leash and runs, flees, all the way home, the dog galloping beside her.

Max

A dead child. His lover the tramp. Friday evening on his way home from the school, the window squeaked down a stitch to fan out the cigarette smoke, Max marvels in amazement at how well he's handled the crisis in spite of Walter fumbling his job:

- He contacted the crisis team immediately.
- Talked to the father and collected the facts.
- Sent a letter to all the other principals in the city.
- Aside from the one girl accosting him in the hallway (her father assures the principal she's seeing a child psychologist), the fallout among the students has been minimal.
- Three parents calling, each thanking him for protecting their child from this nasty incident. Excellent.
- Hysteria at a minimum in general. (Except for Joy's bright red face. At least she doesn't *say* anything. He should get her a secretary appreciation card. He should get her transferred. He's not sure someone so sensitive should work directly under him.)
- Arranged to get the graffiti in the north stairwell painted over within the next two weeks.

So maybe his cigarette budget has doubled with him needing to drive away from the school during the lunch break more often than usual to smoke in his car in a distant neighbourhood where no students, no one, can see him.

Walter hid out at the condo last night — Max's figured this out like the way he's figured out this year's maintenance budget. Why Walter would sleep in that greasy hovel when they have a house in a thriving, orderly neighbourhood with neighbours they never see makes about as much sense as Walter always wasting his money on hardcover novels when he could easily just wait for the paperback reissues or borrow from the library. Probably Walter dug up some old boyfriend at badminton practice because he's always playing badminton with those people, Brecken and her girlfriend, plus those guys who coo 'babe' to each other all the time even though someone might see Walter and jump to conclusions. One night and almost an entire morning come and gone, which would mean at least six men. That's the way Walter used to operate, one guy in, one guy out, two guys in, one guy out, one guy in, one guy in, one guy in. The dead boy's principal thought for sure Walter had reformed, but a worm can't live above ground too long.

Max zips down the window, takes a last pull from his cigarette and tosses it out into the street. He starts the car. Steps on the accelerator. Zips the window back up while he turns the corner on to the main drag. The traffic report tumbling from the radio, Max lulled by the reporter's voice and its deep, rough song as he reports a two-car pile-up on Deerfoot, traffic backed up on Crowchild Trail, one lane blocked for road repairs heading west on McKnight Boulevard. The ruggedness of his voice, the beautiful punctuality and simplicity of his traffic reports. Max idly scans the licence plate on the moving van in front of him, ncc-1701, and wonders why it looks so familiar to him, the van edges forward, he edges forward in his white Toyota, the van inches, he inches, and when the van accelerates forward Max jams his foot down on the accelerator and almost manages to swing the Toyota completely around the corner before he sees he is screeching against a red light and when the other car slams him on the side, right near the gas tank, he thinks *Jesus goddamn Christ the fucking insurance.*

His metal side screams, a punch in his door, the gouged paint, his tire gashed and melting. His car skids and squeals and he wonders how he is going to argue his way out of this one, he has a report to write for the director, he has budgets to balance, he can't fritter away even fifteen minutes worrying about nonsense like this, how many witnesses, he can taste blood, this is no easy speeding ticket he can play stupid with. Maybe he will die, and he guesses dying will solve his problems, but he doesn't want to die, he doesn't want to be in pain, he wishes he could have said goodbye to Walter, Oh Walter, I love you, I'm so so sorry, who cares about a table. Why did he care so much about a stupid table? Someone who cares that much about a table deserves a one-way ticket to Ponoka.

His blood falls from his head to his foot crammed against the brake, hands sticking to the wheel in this strange cold, this electric world, he will die, the world will incinerate, he'll die. The inside of his beating head, ba-dum, ba-dum, the sound of his blood pressure ticking off the scale.

His car facing the concrete wall of the underpass, his body frozen inside a metal and concrete glacier. The window beside his head knocking. How could knocking be coming from the window? Engines knock, not windows. He just paid $1,300 in car repairs. He pours his face against the window.

The most beautiful woman in the world, Colonel Shakira from his favourite TV show *Sector Six*, knocking on his window and shouting at him through the glass. He steams up the glass staring so hard at her beautiful, rich skin on this cold, grey day.

The door exploding outward.

Colonel Shakira gripping him by the elbow, the shoulder, her arm lifting him by the waist, his head on her shoulder, he's always known how tall, how strong she must be, a veritable giantess lifting him up and setting him down like a carton of cigarettes, and he is tick-tock answering questions from a paramedic and a police officer scribbling on a pad, cool rubber gloves patting his head, pulling up his eyelids, pulling down the bags under his eyes.

Colonel Shakira a drag queen ruining her heels and her hair in the snow.

Are you hurting? she shouts at him, her breath mint and cigarettes.

— Is there anyone you want to call? asks a paramedic.

— No, says Max, straightening his shoulders, he is a single, professional man in his late forties and so he doesn't need any help. No one.

— I guess we'd better trade insurance information, says Shakira. — Too bad. I'm going to be so late for my show. Oh well. Drag Queen Time, n'est-ce pas? she says, and blinks, her eyelashes dotted with snow.

— Of course, says the principal.

— Are you sure your fella won't be worried? asks Colonel Shakira.

— My what?

— Honey, listen. I'm doing a show tonight at Galaxy Lounge. Why don't you come? I'll get you in free, you'll have a great time. Bring your guy, make a night of it. We can talk afterwards. Let's not do the insurance shit, okay? I'll dock my starship at my mechanic's, figure out the damage, you just pay me cash, all right?

— Of course, Colonel.

— You know it, darling. What's your name?

— Principal, Colonel ma'am.

— All right, Principal, you're on the guest list. You and your guy, okay?

— Yes, Colonel.

— You're sweet, she says.

Max sinks down on a snowbank, stars in the shapes of snowflakes flutter around him.

Max wipes his face with his gloved hands. He pulls off his gloves, and wipes off grit and melting snow with his bare hands, the soggy inside of his elbow, road grit, salt, and pebbly snow trickling into his collar, grating between his teeth. He announces to the police officers' backs, the tow-truck driver hooking up the Toyota, that of course he would never attend a show like that, for goodness' sake. He hopes the police officers didn't notice he called her Colonel, he was in shock, everyone should know he was in shock. Why doesn't Walter just splash up and take him home?

He sags on the bench in the front hallway of their little house, the little bench that the few guests entering or leaving the house are supposed to sit on when they take off or put on their shoes, but they never do, they're always hopping around on one foot trying to unlace their shoes, leaning against the wall and knocking askew the framed print of a Canadian Rocky mountainscape as they pull up each boot, hook a sandal strap over a heel. The house dark, and the air that settles on his upper lip is cold because the furnace hasn't clicked in to its normal temperature yet. His stockinged feet soaking up snow runoff from his boots. He would like Walter to take him in his arms; he would like to rest his head on Walter's shoulder or against his chest, smell the faint odour of sweat in Walter's shirt, curl against the warmth of Walter's round belly under the wool of his sweater. It has been a hard day in the hardest week, and Walter isn't here drinking Diet Coke in front of the news. The weekends are theirs, when they live their real lives together, ripping up the carpet in the basement, cleaning house, making love. Max really just wants to put on his old sweatpants, pour a beer and watch an episode of *Sector Six*, Walter sitting there next to him, stroking his feet. The Grizom episode, those fuzzy little hamster aliens the Grizoms, the clarinet-dominant soundtrack noodling in the background and the sheepish looks on the actors' faces always make him laugh, but after today's Colonel Shakira hallucination, he is afraid of feeling foolish, even if it's just him and a beer and a cigarette. Maybe he can watch the wasp-woman episode of *The Outer Limits* because that always cheers him up.

Walter will be phoning anytime now, anytime. He would like to be dancing with Walter right now, the way they sometimes groove around the kitchen in each other's arms when they've just polished off a tasty meal and the radio's playing a silly song like 'The Monster Mash.' The way they used to before boys started dying.

He flips through the Tupperware containers and lumpy plastic bags in the fridge. A small circle of steak. He sniffs the steak. Up close, the meat is definitely turning green. He slides it back into the fridge, toward the back of the shelf. Brings into the light a container of Ethiopian beef and another container of cooked spaghetti. He heaps them both on a plate, shuts them in the microwave. Slips the *Sector Six* episode 'Giddy With Grizoms' into the machine, and eats his recycled supper on the couch. The house fills with light and music, Colonel Shakira looking bewildered at all the tiny, furry Grizoms cascading around her in her tight gold uniform. Colonel Shakira brushing off the Grizoms and aiming her Rosette Nebular at a Reptiloid. The Reptiloid roars, the Reptiloid lunges, the Colonel shoots. — I am Colonel Shakira! shouts Colonel Shakira, and Max wants to cheer out loud but restrains himself.

Ginger and Furey

The first time they really met, in October, Ginger and Furey were silent in the weight room, a pond of clicking and clanking steel, the twenty-months pregnant guidance counsellor and his bouncing moobs substituting as their phys-ed teacher shouting out, his clapping and shouting frenzied, — All right, people! Go, people! You got it, people! No pain no gain, people!

Ginger's chest and shoulders popping as he bench-pressed, Furey poised just above him, in the centre of his eyebrows a perfect frown line, Furey's eyes on Ginger's, Ginger could have sworn he'd just been kissed.

Ginger popped up, wiping his forehead with the belly of his T-shirt, and Furey pressed himself into Ginger's outline on the bench, his body cradled in Ginger's damp warmth on the plastic, their bodies humid twins.

They grunted to each other about weights, hey, the guidance counsellor who looked like a whale, yeah, video games — You like playing *World of Warcraft* too? I like *Divinity XII*. You some kind of *Divinity XII* fanboy? Ha ha, yeah, wrestling, music. — You downloaded that song too? Shuddup! They talked about *Sector Six*, — No such thing as heroes, just a bunch of ones and zeroes, Patrick chimed the song. World Wrestling Entertainment, wrestling, wrestling.

That sweating teacher with his whale stomach and Easter ham legs, clapping his hands, — That's it, people! and Ginger blooming on the inside: someone to watch *Sector Six* with, play *Divinity XII* with, a WWE night next Wednesday, his inner nerd bounding free from quarantine.

His grampa's palm clamped to Ginger's forehead that night in October. Ginger zipped open his backpack. Biology test next week. His index finger on the diagram of a bisected human heart. His cellphone purred. Another text from Furey. He clicked the text open. Never knew how easy, how normal, this could be.

Gretta

Your cunt falls out and all you have now is a battered locket. You think it might be eighteen-carat gold.

Vase after vase of flowers — some cadmium yellow, some ultramarine rose, some so zinc white they poke their thorns inside you, all the colours pure — on a table in this room.

You lie on your stomach on the couch, hearing the smell of the mars venetian red wood table polish, a low shriek of nails raking your eyeballs. The locket a large seed in your hand. So clear and cool, so lacking in doubt or blur.

You remember holding your son's hand one afternoon, you can't remember when anymore, and even though you rarely pray you tried to pray to make him different. Why God, because who is this God who transforms your son into a homosexual and then takes him away, what kind of sadistic asshole can this God be, what have you done to deserve these punishments, why does He torture you and laugh at you this way. You would like to forget about this God entirely, you would like to splash layer after layer of Drano on Him and dissolve Him down the drain, but your mind creeps toward Him every time, like ivy, like mould, like a cockroach who's eaten her way under a baseboard through the wall. Your jaws are tired from the chomping, your mouth dry from licking and chewing plaster. You want to taste the promised fruit. You want to push the fruit back into your womb.

And your son let you hold his hand. While you made him promise that he wasn't.

The blues, his colour in death, in the couch fabric flash bright and clawing.

You lurched around the blue grass carpet at the internment. Your hands fanning underwater, mottled coral, that obscene hole in the ground. Your fingernails cerulean blue.

Saturday

Max

The time on the giant digital clock in front of the restaurant reads 70:12 p.m. Max pulls back his sleeve so he can see the fluorescent hands glowing on his watch: 12:45 p.m. The dead boy's principal and his head guidance counsellor scoop up lentils and beef with torn bits of injera between their fingers. Max's beer carbonates in front of him. He can feel his temper carbonating too, Walter refusing to come to the house, demanding they meet over lunch here in public. He drinks from his glass of water; the ice cubes bump against his lips. He would like to gnash an ice cube, but that would electrocute his teeth. He wipes his fingers on his napkin, glances at the door in the dim restaurant every time it swings open.

The restaurant is a fifteen-minute walk away from their house, in the direction opposite their school. Their house a forty-five minute drive from the school on a good day. Still a risk because teachers, staff and parents from St. Aloysius shop and eat all over the city. When he goes out with Walter he is always naked, they are always in someone's crosshairs no matter what, even though Walter usually knows how to be discreet, and once upon a time even seemed to enjoy it, their couplehood a naughty, arousing secret. But nowadays, Walter screws up his mouth like an old grandma when Max says they'll do takeout. Or delivery. — Or invite your badminton friends over for drinks, Max will say. — We don't need to go to a party with those people.

— But it's a Tuesday/Monday/Thursday night, Max, Walter pouts. — We haven't gone anywhere for two months/two and a half months/four months. Feels like nine years.

— So what, Max answers. — You're exaggerating. Walter like a sixteen-year-old girl flouncing into a temper because she's not allowed to go to a bush party or a rave. Once every three months or so, Max capitulates, but they have to sit at the back of the restaurant, right next to the bathrooms and the repeatedly flushing toilets, so Walter can disappear if necessary.

Once Max collided into a superintendent in the aisle of an airplane returning from St. John's, Newfoundland. Once Max waited to buy a loaf of bread in the same grocery store line-up as an English teacher from his school when he and Walter were vacationing in *Florida*. But this restaurant doesn't even have a sign, just a menu taped in the window. It could be a hardware store. Five years they've been eating here, incognito in Ethiopia.

Walter refused to meet him at their house.

Walter hammers food into his mouth, specks catching in the bristles of his goatee. Max nipping at bits, his pinches of food neat. The platter between them a hodge-podge of raw beef, cooked cabbage, lentils in sauce, beets all higgledy piggledy. Max wipes his mouth. Walter scooping handfuls of food into his mouth with his thick brown fingers, the bristly black hairs tufting the backs of his hands, Walter not even done chewing before he scoops in the next handful, Walter's belly *huge*, oh, Max can hardly bear how much more there is of Walter, how much more of Walter there isn't at home with Max in their proper home.

— Joy tells me you have my picture on your desk, says Max, trying to sound casual, dabbing his napkin at an imaginary drop of sauce on the front of his golf shirt.

— One I took two years ago when we went hiking, says Walter, chewing. He gives a small burp.

— I don't think a photograph is at all necessary, Max stammers.

— It's how couples act.

— But the couple you're referring to doesn't act like that. And now you prop my face on your work desk without even asking me. Without telling me. You used to be so discreet. You *loved* to be discreet.

Max remembers the horror, the titillation, of being in the same room as Walter at the school back when he and Walter first started dating. Max the new principal chairing a meeting and trying not to look at Walter, trying not to *not* look at Walter. The edge, the charge, the thrilling, sizzling reunion between Mr.

Applegate and Mr. Boyle at the end of the workday back at Max's house.

Walter chews on a piece of curried goat meat.

— You loved to be discreet, repeats Max.

— I'm tired of it now, says Walter. — I've been getting tired of it for a while but I just didn't know it.

— You could have at least warned me.

— It's not illegal, says Walter, he takes another bite, licks his fingers one at a time, *pop pop pop*, his fingers gleaming with oil and spit.

Max draws back from the table, his body tight. — Not illegal, but grounds for termination in a Catholic school.

— So terminate me. That'll be an awesome show.

— This is unprecedented. This harassment is unwarranted.

— Who's harassing?

Half-chewed food tucked inside Walter's cheeks, slimy across his tongue. Max jolts in his seat.

— You owe me an explanation, says Max. — For God's sake, I've been worried sick about you. Don't make me worry like that. How do I know you're not back at the parks again?

A toilet flushes, water rushing, sucking.

— It's too risky, Max says. Do you know what kind of pressure I'm under at the school? Max leans forward, Walter continuing to chew and scoop, pack his face with food, Max can feel fury and blood flooding his face. — *Joy* is asking me about our hiking trip. *Joy!*

— So Joy said, says Walter. He tears off a piece of injera and scoops up a fingerful of raw beef. A small curl of meat plops into the lentils.

The old lady from the till pushes and waddles through the bright green, yellow and red cloth in the hallway leading to the bathrooms, wiping her shiny wet hands on her skirt.

Walter wipes his lips with a paper napkin and clears his throat. Quaffs from his orange juice. He scrapes the crumb of raw meat out of the lentil sauce toward himself. He wipes the pool of lentil with a piece of injera.

— Why won't you say anything? Just eating and eating and eating.

— Okay, says Walter, suddenly stopping his food train. — This food is awesome.

— Ugh, exhales Max. He fists his napkin into a ball. — The car accident's going to cost over $4,000, the other person's vehicle and my vehicle all together.

— Bad luck, says Walter. He coughs. Hacks. He sips from his glass of water.

— I would really appreciate it if you removed my photo from your desk. It's an unnecessary risk, it's a foolish thing to do. And unwarranted.

— Were you drinking when you were driving? Walter asks. He scrapes up the last of the lentils with a spoon and slides the spoon into his mouth. — I guess you were sober, says Walter. — Well, I'm just about done, he says, discreetly burping into his hand. — I'll ask for the bill.

— I haven't finished eating yet. You've barely touched the beets even though you ordered them. What a waste of money. I want to order more injera. Remove my picture from your desk. Please. I am asking you. It's a picture of me. It's me there on your desk. Where I work. My picture, my job. Please.

Walter plants his credit card on the corner of the table. — We'll split the bill. I'll figure out my share, he says.

— Are you going to call me? asks Max, his voice low.

— What for? Walter asks too loudly.

— Are you going to remove it and stop this attack campaign? I'm not finding this enjoyable, as I think I've indicated to you already.

The waiter refills his water glass, takes away Walter's credit card.

— Don't use your principal voice on *me*, says Walter.

— Why have you suddenly turned? When did I become the evil person?

— *We* have become the evil people, Max.

Max's eyes sting. Walter pushes back his chair, twines his blue-and-white striped scarf around his neck. The snow's melted, but February is back with its ice winds and mood flurries.

— I'm really gratified that you decided to come out today, whispers Max.

Max hops his chair to the right, in Walter's direction, turning his back to the door of the restaurant, the other diners in their jubilant and romantic twos and threes, the music tooting through the speakers.

— I'm glad you agreed to meet me for lunch, whispers Max, a little louder. A little.

Walter buttons his coat. Stands waiting for his card.

— Ah. Look, says Max. — I should have controlled my temper. The house is a much better place with you in it. That hovel of a condo? That's not the right place for you. You need our home.

Walter pulls on his toque, tugs it over his shiny, wide forehead.

— Look. Why don't we go back to the house and talk? I don't think this kind of public place is conducive to proper conversation. Walter, whispers Max furiously, — *I love you!*

— Mm hmm.

Walter stands, dressed and ready to leave. Hands at his sides.

Max draws back, fingers the edge of the tablecloth. — That response is unkind and unfriendly.

— Well, if you want me to say something specific, you should ask the right question.

— Do you feel the same about me?

— I'm tired of our little Tupperware container life, Max.

Max's hands start to shake. — Isn't there something I can do? Some action I can take?

A long time, thirty-six full seconds according to Max's watch, of Walter standing in his toque not answering. — Okay, says Walter. — Come to the bar with me.

— All right. As long as it isn't on a school night, all right, says Max. — We don't live a Tupperware life, Walter. I take offence to your version of our life, he has to add.

Walter rolls his eyes. — Dance with me at the bar. Can you do that?

Of course Max can. How hard can it be? He has two feet. He wants to make a joke about dancing and bars and the reason Mennonites don't dance is because dancing can lead to sex, or no, the reason Mennonites don't have sex standing up is because it might lead to dancing, but by the time he's figured out the wording, Walter has already got his credit card back. His signature a series of stabs into the paper.

— Well then, says Walter. — See you at work, Mr. Applegate.

He leans forward, his face too close to Max's for this public space. — Where's my goodbye kiss? he asks.

Max grabs a slice of dripping beet with his fingers and stuffs it, whole, into his mouth.

— I thought so, says Walter.

— You're needed at home, Max's mouth blurts through the beet, but Walter's already sauntering out the door, scarf pulled up over his nose. Max swallows. His mouth sprouting beet.

Faraday

Faraday would like just one Saturday night that isn't purgatory. She writes about her hypothetical crush in her unicorn journal, about how the crush sends flowers to her (not lilies, she can't stand lilies, not in any colour), how the crush picks her up from school and drops her off at home, texts her poems and love letters. Her crush makes her music CDs because the crush knows all about good music, but she doesn't have to be embarrassed about how she sings along to Miley Cyrus on the radio when she and the crush are driving to make out somewhere — Faraday in her black lace, boy-cut underwear. The crush and Faraday have sex — that's right, Faraday, have *sex* that isn't imaginary or pathetically solo — like normal, well-adjusted human beings, at appropriate times and away from other people's ears and eyes, and the kissing is skilled and dry, without too much tongue (she hates mushy tongue). Faraday's also excellent and athletic in bed, a natural of course; she knows she's a good kisser, the one person she's kissed in her life told her she was a fantastic kisser, but then moved to another province. She's terrified that if she finally has sex she'll suck at it, and she doesn't understand how she's supposed to learn without first poking around the anatomy to figure out the coordinates. She knows how to make herself orgasm, but she's just one person and she's had a lot of practice in spite of her resisting the need as hard as she can. Her teachers teach them about how kidneys and eyeballs function, how Zoroastrians leave their dead to be eaten by vultures, but nothing she can use. Not how to give a good blowjob or get multiple orgasms. What semen or girl-cum truly tastes like. She can't buy the speeches about abstinence and chastity with her parents fornicating their heads off all over the house, and her own mother told her she had already slept with Dave before she married him. Shirley and Dave had their first serious experience with each other when they were both seventeen.

— But don't use me or your father as an example, adds Shirley hurriedly. — If I could, I'd go back and wait until I married your father. Shirley's hair flat on one side, Dave pretending he isn't hiding under the covers in their bed. Waiting to do his wife again. No matter how much it damages the children. Her father who tells her that the secret to Sid the Kid Crosby's attractiveness to young women like her is not that he is a stellar hockey player, but that he has the eyes of a woman. This is her father's advice for how to find true love.

Friday and Saturday nights are when Faraday's body yawns wide open for a unicorn to lay its healing alicorn on the world. As Friday and Saturday nights draw closer, the way they do in their unrelenting cycle every week, the nights for falling in love, Faraday senses her hypothetical crush craving its sugar and caffeine, circling the city closer and closer; the circling agitates her, like period cramps, only a delicious, unquenchable pain. Then she unpacks another box of paper cups, stacks cartons of milk and cream in the Tim Hortons fridge.

But in the lore, a unicorn will only accept a virgin as its companion, and if this crush ever returns her love, she will surely lose her unicorn chance. Brecken, her psychologist Linus Libby's receptionist, told her unicorns are patriarchal crap about the sexual fetishizing of teenage girls, and that single horn is just one great big penis stand-in. — Isn't it obvious? Sorry to break the news to you, Faraday. Then Brecken pressed a button on her phone to alert Linus Libby that Faraday, the wacked-out unicorn girl, was there to see him.

— It's not a horn, said Faraday. — It's called an alicorn!

But solving Brecken's ignorance is no consolation. And as Faraday buttons up her brown uniform, draws on the hairnet and visor, the crush's circle tightens so close it almost strangles her, this is how much she wants the crush. To notice her. This is how much the dilemma of losing her unicorn potential crushes her. If only a unicorn would gallop up right now, hooves spidering windshields and denting hoods as it gallops and leaps from car to car lined up in the parking lot and the drive-thru, its alicorn tossing coffee cups out of people's hands, mending hearts and crumbling doughnuts.

When she reaches out the drive-thru window to take the money this time, it isn't her crush, it's the dead boy.

— Of course it's you, says Faraday. — I've memorized your routine. And she counts out three pennies, then hands over the large iced cappuccino and a paper-wrapped straw. — Want a Timbit with that?

She wishes.

When she reaches out the drive-thru window to take the money this time, it's Jésus in an old white truck saying, — What the ... ? and for once forgetting to neigh. — You work here? asks Jésus.

— No, says Faraday. — I just like to stand in the window, she says and counts out Jésus's change, then hands over the large iced cappuccino and a paper-wrapped straw. The first time she's ever seen Jésus not surrounded by his blood clot of friends, and when Jésus smiles and says, — Thank you, Unicorn Girl, his smile is not so bad at all even though he's truly an asshole.

She thinks about what her crush might look like. Long eyelashes of course — if the crush's face were vaguely animal, she would have no problem with this. Horsey. An excellent, smooth body with nice, toothpaste-smelling breath.

She calls into the mic, — Welcome to Tim Hortons. How can I help you?

— A chocolate Timbit, sputters the speaker.

She waits. Idiot.

— Will that be all? she asks.

— Yeah.

— Fifteen cents at the window, she says. Tool, she thinks.

Jésus pulls up in his white truck.

She slides open the window. — Fifteen cents, she says.

He hands her a nickel and a dime. She hands him his Timbit in a paper bag. Plus three napkins.

— Thank you, says Jésus.

He revs the truck's engine. She slams the window shut to keep from sucking in the exhaust.

— Hey! he mouths. Jogs his upper torso out of the truck and taps on the glass.

— What?

— Aren't you supposed to say 'Please come again'?

— That's McDonald's.

— Well say it anyway.

— Um, no.

The truck thrums away from the window.

Her stomach flutters. Once.

— Can I help you, she says into the mic.

— I'd like an old-fashioned sugar Timbit.

— Is that your boyfriend? asks her supervisor Morris. — Because this better not keep up all night.

Morris barks at Jésus through the window, and Faraday cannot help smiling, reaching into her collar to straighten her bra strap.

— A cruller Timbit please, croaks out the voice.

— Fifteen cents, ma'am, Faraday says. — Please pull up to the window to pay for your purchase.

She laughs into her hand. It smells of pennies and coffee grounds.

Jésus hands her ten pennies, so she has to say, — You're missing a nickel, ma'am.

— Oh did I, Jésus squeaks, and adds a little neigh. — Here you go, he says, — One nickel. Don't spend it here.

He holds out the nickel, and as she reaches out to take it, he slides his middle finger along the inside of her palm.

Her clitoris coughs.

— When're you done here? asks Jésus.

— Sorry?

— When're you done here so we can go grab a coffee from somewhere good?

— Okay?

— So when're you done?

— No. I can't do that.

— Why not?

— I just can't.

— Your loss, Faraday, he says, and his truck jangles away.

The nickel warm and throbbing in her hand.

Miss Maureen

Five and a half months ago, Maureen and her slutty ex-husband, Alexey, forked over a hundred and twenty dollars — sixty dollars each — for Crêpe Suzette's female-impersonator show. Her car lurched and screeched through a September afternoon rush hour; she swore the air foul and jabbed with her middle finger at perfectly law-abiding people through the windshield of a car that revved like it had a space missile for an engine, a car that belonged in a vehicle emergency ward. She broke her rule and drove *into* instead of around downtown, through the jungle of cranes, booby traps of fenced construction sites, and one-day-only, one-way streets, so typical of this stupid city Calgary. She cut out of the school early illegally, whipped on her coat and purse like Zorro's cape and sword, strolled then trotted then galloped out the school's back door. She leapt into her terminally ill car and pressed the accelerator past the floor because this female-impersonator show at the Galaxy Lounge was the one thing that actually counted as a romantic *date* for her floundering marriage and was the one thing they couldn't, didn't fight about. She threw her money at the guy behind the ticket counter and she stuffed those tickets into her purse, risking her job, her car, her life, because she loved Alexey, because he was her husband at the time, and because tickets sold out months ahead and could only be purchased in person during business hours.

But now that Alexey trumpets out his farts and snores in some other woman's bed, clutters up some other woman's house with his baseball cap collection, neither Maureen nor Alexey is willing to give up a ticket to this show. She would rather chew on the Pope's gummy cock; Alexey would rather slice off his balls in a salami slicer. They will each have their ticket, they will each eat their pasta — he will order veal ravioli, she will order linguini in marinara sauce — they will drink their wine and beer and watch the show like they are a married couple, a married couple where the husband left the wife five months before.

Alexey tells her he wants to take his new girlfriend, her cousin Lorraine the macrobiotic-diet eater who's also his new life coach, to the show, and Maureen says, — You have two choices: you give me the tickets and I go with a guy I dredge up on a singles' website or you suck it up and go with *me*.

They sit across from each other on the high stools. She concentrates on the fake palm tree in the corner that looks exactly like the ones at the zoo, remarkable. Alexey is touching his finger to each tine on his fork over and over again, and reading through the menu. When the aproned waitress presents herself at their table, all drippy ponytail and long earrings, he asks her, — Which of these pasta sauces is macrobiotic?

He chooses plain spaghetti.

No, he cannot help himself to some of her calamari. Now that he's dumped her, he can order his own.

She wears her red lace bra and matching thong. He won't get to see either, but she knows what he's missing. Now the bra is cutting into her ribs. Now the bra is wasted and she'll have to wash it clean by hand. Like the past twenty-five years of her life. Pure poo. She doesn't mind her buttocks so unhampered and free, though. Not one bit.

She listens to him slurp and chew. She sips her wine in the clatter of the restaurant, her ex-husband chewing like an old giraffe, all grey lips and eyelashes.

After the waitress and her ponytail clear away the plates, Maureen picks at the wax leaking from the candle. Alexey excuses himself and disappears into the bathroom. The discoball in the middle of the stage begins to twirl, a cancan line of drag queens glides out, her ex-husband knocks over a chair on his scramble back to the table, his fly still open, and Maureen pretends she is here alone, he is some stranger who happens to be sitting at her table, and she is painting the town bright brassiere red.

— Here's a nice couple, says Crêpe Suzette, tracing her palm in a circle on Alexey's bald pate. — How long have you two been together?

Alexey, purple as a grape, mumbles, — Twenty-five years!

— Twenty-five years! croons Suzette. — Why I was just a twinkle in my mother's eye.

The other impersonators, Vaseline Dion and Miss Demeanour, laugh raucously.

— Vaseline, barks Suzette, — does your cane come with batteries?

Sweat drizzles down Suzette's temples, around the artificially bright blue eyes, the makeup caked on her cheeks. His cheeks. Maureen wonders if Crêpe Suzette's mother knows what he does for a living. What she tells the neighbours when they ask. How much he gets paid. If he likes his job. If when he was a boy he ever contemplated suicide.

— Your fly's undone just for meeeee? asks Suzette. — Oh honey, there're some things I don't want this big an audience for. Well, maybe just one or two of you. You over there, yes you, how's about a sandwich later on, just you and me and Mr. Flying Low here.

Suzette gives a giant, blue-eyed wink; Alexey fumbles at his crotch.

— And you, says Crêpe Suzette, giving a graceful hop-kick in her high heels on her way to Maureen on the other side of the table.

— What's your name, honey?

— Maureen, she squeaks.

— Maureen, you've been together twenty-five years with this delicious gentleman. Can you tell us all what the secret is to a lasting relationship?

— We're divorced, squawks Maureen.

— Divorced? Well you better tell *him*, Maureen, because *he* still thinks you're married! You hound dog! says Crêpe Suzette, turning to Alexey, — You, Mr. Flying Low, I guess you ain't nothing but a hound dog, ain't that right, Vaseline?

— We only divorced this week, mumbles Alexey.

The sound of piano notes unfurling and Crêpe Suzette, Vaseline Dion and Miss Demeanour lipsync 'I Will Survive' right to Maureen, and she finally uncurls her fists and claps her hands, loudly, rudely in Alexey's direction.

— I think you can make more fucking noise than that! shouts Suzette, and Maureen whoops, her smile broad and mean, and she twirls around to look at everyone else applauding the timely end of her marriage, all the other women who've been treated like shit by their husbands and who will survive just like her, no matter how much she wishes her husband would just come home.

Gretta

You are the dead boy's mother, one eye green, one eye blue. You switch on the bedside lamp and finger your dead son's locket. The curves, the gold, its antique, brazen feminine heart.

Because you don't believe in God or hell anymore, but you keep a rosary for decoration, for irony, for kitsch, the rosary apparently winding itself around your fingers. You swallow the grief away, the mould creeping into this closed space.

You try to pray, your voice catching in the rawness of your throat: — Holy Mary Mother of God ...

— Our Lord ...

— Dear God ...

— Blessed Virgin ...

Your prayers, suspended below Heaven, above ground.

The phone perches between your head and your shoulder and no one else is on the line but you talk and talk anyway. The way you used to keep talking to your son even after he'd left the room. The way you grasped his hand, tight, tight, that day and willed him to be normal. The day he told you he was gay. — Just be normal, you said. — Sell insurance if you want. Bum around Europe, then come home, go to university, save up for a car. You'll find a girlfriend. You'll be different then. You'll grow into who you'll be.

Your husband in denial. Your husband insisting *it's just a phase*. Your teeth chatter.

Your skin is hard as a beetle's carapace, and when you manage to walk, your beetle armour clicks in the joints. At night in bed you lie on your back, too tired even to breathe, too tired to stop breathing.

The inside of you a tongueless yawn, a pile of contaminated dirt. A handful of hair torn out by the roots and lying in the crab grass and weeds by the side of the highway.

His note to you an antique locket cast in the shape of a teenage heart.

Your husband asks you what the big deal is about a stupid piece of jewellery, and when you try to caw out its meaning, he tells you, — You're imagining things. That's not the way it was at all.

The day after the terrible thing, your husband pounded out an obituary on the computer, praising your son's passion for wrestling, especially WWE on television. Refining, editing, composing your son's death, composing your son. Then your husband retreated to his room.

That flesh and metal heart. Thundering hooves on the roof, on the other side of every door you close.

Furey, Patrick — Patrick Furey, known to his family as Patrick or Paddy, sadly passed away suddenly on February 17. This vibrant young man, who loved his family, who loved to watch wrestling (particularly World Wrestling Entertainment on television) and who had many friends and acquaintances both male and female, will be greatly missed by his parents Gabe and Gretta Furey, and both the Furey and Conroy clans. A memorial Mass followed by a reception will be held on February 19 at St. Joseph's Catholic Church, Calgary, AB, at 1:00 p.m.

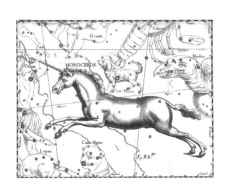

Sunday

Max

Breaking up is not a possibility, so of course Max just flicks the ash off the tip of his cigarette when Walter says he is moving out. — I'm moving on, Walter says, and in response Max snarls a laugh through the doorway and says, — The coffee's not *that* bad.

Sunday morning, six days and three hours after the boy hanged himself and everything started going terribly wrong, Walter stops by the house, — Your own house, Max says to him, just before Max would normally leave for Mass. He flicks through the pages of the scripture reading he's supposed to give today. He didn't know he was supposed to meet Walter at the bar *last* night. At the time, he understood meeting Walter at the bar as just a hypothetical possibility. In the future. And how stupid to break up because Max didn't go to the bar. How can Walter move out? For what? They are middle-aged, who else would want either of them? Where does Walter think he is going to go? To live in that tiny closet of a condo? They have been together for seventeen years and now he tells Max — while scooping handfuls of breakfast cereal straight from the box into his mouth, Max handing Walter a bowl and the milk carton — that he still loves him, but that he is tired, as if seventeen years can roll away from them like an escaped roll of toilet paper wasting itself on a gritty bathroom stall floor. As if love and exhaustion are mutually exclusive.

— You're a very angry person, Walter says, packing all his shaving paraphernalia, his hard-water-crusted shampoo and conditioner bottles into a shoebox. A flake of cereal dots his goatee. Max flings around pots and pans, slams closed the dishwasher. — It's hard to love someone who is so filled with rage, says Walter.

— Your degree is in education! Max screams, his voice escaping him, control of his vocal cords evading him. — Not psychology! *Not real psychology!* You can't even do your job!

— Exactly, says Walter. — You finally got it.

The ripe-vegetable young men they once were. Now freeze-dried.

Max brushes his teeth so hard his brush turns pink. He accidentally stabs his lower gum so his whole jaw throbs, blood splotching in the sink. He turns on the water hard, flushing the sink in toothpaste froth and diluted blood, so that Walter can't hear him sobbing, suspect the salt Max is tasting.

A long time ago Max thought he could do without a man entirely, love the sinner hate the sin, but then he needed this man, his body, his smell. But he needed his job too. Needed the money and the benefits and the pension, Bald-Headed Baby Jesus his pension, he can never give up his pension, does Walter expect Max to quit his job for Walter and give up his pension? And now here is the man he needs, wrapping dishes and packing up books, his two-day-stubbled, goateed man pantomiming leaving, standing next to the china cabinet full of glass and ceramic while he bends and straightens, bends and straightens, breathing hard, sweat stains expanding in the armpits of his T-shirt, pulling out his antique compass collection and packing the compasses with too much newspaper into a box that used to hold bottles of Gato Blanco wine, the white, illustrated cat coiled on the side of the box. Max wants to put his face against its fur, feel its purr buzz his face, the quick pump of its heart, the gurgles and bubbles and pops of Walter's stomach. The short, curly hair on Walter's head, the kneecap smell of his growing bald spot.

— I'm going to take some mulligatawny out of the freezer for lunch, said Max, his hands not shaking. — Do you want some?

Max will call up Bozenna and tell her he can't make it to church today, would she take over his scripture reading? He won't go to Mass today, that should show Walter he's serious, that Tupperware isn't all Max cares about. Quite a few teachers attend his church, so he'll sniffle like he's sick around the office on Monday, but right now he'll play hooky from his outside life, heat up lunch for his man, his oh-so-needed man.

Walter has brought Lieutenant Fong over to the house this morning, allegedly to say goodbye. Lieutenant Fong snakes around the boxes, around Max's legs. Butts open the flap of an empty box at his feet, jumps in. Max wants to jump in after her, bury his face in her fur. How wonderful, how generous of Walter to bring the cat along for this visit, dangle the cat in Max's face. Max's mouth opening and shutting and no sound coming out. As if Walter would ever leave him.

The crackle of newspaper, the clink of plates and mugs. The cat biting a ball of newspaper, grabbing it to her chest, then gutting it with her hind feet.

Today is Sunday, and tomorrow when he is a principal at St. Aloysius Senior High School, a principal who works 7 a.m. to 8 p.m. every single day, he will go to the office as usual, pretending he had a cold on the weekend, which is why he wasn't at Mass, make phone calls and emails, nod understandingly to parents, hunt down delinquent teachers. Pretend that his husband has not abducted the cat and the Cuisinart. Pretend he is gay in the old-fashioned sense because without Walter, well, that is the only gay he'll get to be.

Max piles his arms with boxes from the basement and stacks their insides with the blue-and-white dishes from the second set in the cabinet. He wraps the dishes, the ones stamped with blue peacocks, in newspaper. Wrapped properly, not all willy-nilly like Walter's doing it. Collects a set of matching but unflamboyant cutlery, and the juice glasses with the orange squiggles, the plain burgundy coffee mugs, and he wonders, Why on this particular Sunday? Just after they'd ripped up most of the carpet downstairs? They ripped up the goddamn carpet because they had *plans!* He has to go to Mass. He says, — I have to go to Mass. Unless, he says, wrapping another sheet of newspaper around a mug, — you'll stay for lunch. I'm supposed to do the reading this morning, but I could get Bozenna to do it and skip this one. For you. Stay for lunch.

Walter squats next to a box, shows off a swath of brown, hairy plumber's butt. What's going to happen to all the renovations they were going to do? wonders Max. The carpet in the basement, for example. Max marches back down to the cellar. He digs through boxes. Mouse droppings, larvae husks. He bangs the boxes, punches, stacks them, so that Walter can't hear the tears splurting down Max's face, no matter how hard Max tries not to let them. These are Walter's boxes, Max never would have piled boxes willy-nilly like this. When did the cellar turn into such a landfill? He sets the boxes next to the Gato Blanco ones Walter brought back from the liquor store. Of course Walter isn't leaving him. How could he. One bar. One missed date. Big deal.

Dust under Max's fingernails from helping his lover pack. Dust and dirt drying out his fingers as he scrambles and digs through the boxes in the basement, exhumes the sturdier ones. Ones strong enough for Walter's book collection, his favourite lamp with the polished granite bottom. Who is Walter, wanting to move out like he's a teenager? And Max his mother. Max helping Walter leave him.

— I'm heating up some mulligatawny for lunch, Max yells up the stairs.

He wipes his hands on the dusty thighs of his pants, suddenly aware he's standing with his legs spread, his 'I Heart Colonel Shakira' T-shirt splotched with dust bunnies. Streaks from a rusty bicycle chain on his church pants. He can smell his oily hair and he has to keep smoothing it back out of his eyes. Walter dumping his bag-of-garbage news before Max even has a chance to shower. Maybe if he had a better haircut, quit smoking. One minute later he fishes in his back pocket for his lighter. He kicks aside empty boxes, stacks of newspaper, and puffs on a cigar and walks through the house, trailing the thick smoke in the house he's never been allowed to smoke in. — Freedom, he says. He glances at himself in the mirror at the top of the basement stairs, a cigar the size of a baby's arm doinked in the corner of his mouth, his skin grey and barely clinging to his bones. His hair a tangle of white. Maybe if he'd dyed it Walter wouldn't be leaving him.

— I'll take out the mulligatawny from the freezer for lunch later, Walter calls from the dining room. — Plus, I think you should call Bozenna to fill in for you this morning. You're not going to make it in time to Mass, Max.

Max yanks the cigar from his mouth. — Mulligatawny *I* cooked! he shouts, and kicks another box with a meowing cat stamped on the side. Inhaling cigar smoke. He stomps up the stairs to finish getting ready for church.

Sunday afternoon. Is Walter leaving because he's met someone else? Sunday night creeps in and Walter's sock drawer still contains three pairs of socks, plus one unmatched sock and Walter is still puttering with his growing stack of bogus boxes. Next week the crisis team will be gone from the school and that boy, that boy Furey. Well. Max has to laugh at all the boxes pyramided in the middle of the kitchen floor, Walter's drafting table from when he was actually a teacher folded and on its side, propped against the stove. Like he thinks he's actually *moving*.

— Is there someone else, Max says. — Is this some kind of mid-life affair?

Max opens the cutlery drawer, lifts out the tray and turns it upside down all over the floor, the brisk cascade of stainless steel, spoons bouncing and the can opener gouging, chopsticks splattering.

Walter kicks cutlery aside as he reaches up into a cupboard for a measuring cup.

Pizza arrives. Max runs to answer the doorbell, his slippers bumping, kicking forks and knives across the linoleum floor, zinging the baseboards. One pepperoni, bacon and mushroom and one veg, the pizza man says. The greasy kind with the dips; as if pizza weren't fatty and greasy enough, pizza dip is Walter's thing. Max thinks about eating something healthy — he opens the fridge door and scans the shelves. Grimaces at the sight of the old hunk of steak at the back of the fridge, glowing even more green, the circular piece now shrinking. Max wonders how Walter will remember to pay his utility and phone bills, will he remember to take his migraine pills or at least drink an espresso when he feels a migraine coming? Will he take the treadmill? Max bought it. Over his bloated, stinking body will Walter get the treadmill.

He clenches his fist, his jaws, every muscle in his body when he stands in the doorway to the kitchen empty of boxes and drafting table, cutlery still washed up against the walls. Max left to go buy cigarettes, and when he comes home the house is completely dark and he has to flick on the lights as he moves from room to room, lighting his own way instead of homing in on Walter's light as he normally would. He dumps his boots by the door, walks straight into the bedroom and changes into his pyjamas, then marches to the spare room to see if Walter took the treadmill.

The treadmill handles glint in the same way and the machine stands in the same spot it has always stood since he brought it home. He can't believe Walter's left him burdened with the clunky thing.

Maybe Max is dead now and this house echoing like an abandoned warehouse is what hell looks like. He's stuck in a horror-story television show.

If only.

Maybe now Walter will remove Max's photo from his desk.

Maureen

At the Sunday afternoon yoga class, lying flat on her face, her body hot and sore. She starts to snivel; really, has she no control over her emotions anymore? What is happening to her, for Christ's sake? She smears away a glob of tears with the back of her hand, tears blotting her yoga mat.

So young. He was just a little thing, his voice barely cracked probably, and she thinks about visiting that cemetery in Europe that one time with Alexey and seeing the names of the boys on the tombstones who died in World War I, the same age as the boys she teaches, but those other boys had guns in their hands and they were told to save the world. And all she's been able to think about this week is her stupid divorce from that stupid man.

She wonders how she would feel if Jésus died. Is she evil because sometimes in the past she has wanted him dead? She doesn't want him dead (she breathes in), she just wants him to go away on a long vacation (she breathes out). She loves Jésus, she loves them all, those kids, like baby animals with mouths like truckers and hormones playing pinball. Not their fault. Not his fault. That she is crying is a good sign because it means the anger management is happening.

— Are you all right? asks the flat-stomached little instructor, Deirdre. — Do you want help with your pose?

— No, no, sniffs Maureen. — I'm fine. She cranks her neck and shoulders up into an upward dog, her elbows jutting out to the sides like wings, her lower back crackling. She juts her hips into the air into downward dog, not bad, until Deirdre with her flat little abs and muscled little arms grabs Maureen's hips and pulls her buttocks back and up, no this is good this is good it's good to exercise she didn't exercise enough when she was with Alexey, it's good to think about things other than work, the principal, her ex-husband emptying their joint bank account and claiming it was his money after all, her cousin Lorraine breaking the front screen door on the house when she tried to force it closed during that one visit.

Maureen will concentrate on her chakras, her mula bandha. She clenches the band of flesh between her vagina and her anus, she will concentrate only on that band of flesh and how no man has even come close to that band of flesh for almost a year, that band of flesh a lovely trophy in her sexlessness. Arms up, come to standing, her arms were also up when she shouted at Jésus in the hallway, furious at him for pointing out that of course no man would want to be married to her. She raised her arms, wanting to crash down and crush him, just like she is raising her arms now. A *ting* in her rib cage suddenly paralyzes her, she can lower her arms, but she can't bend over, can't sit on the floor, can only shuffle to the door of the yoga studio, gather her purse and coat from the hook, and hobble out the door and down the street.

— Breathe it out! calls Deirdre after her, her mula bandha no doubt clenching perfectly.

Jésus

He whistles because whistling is part of the calm mystique, he wants to look casual, he's the quantum of solace, like if anyone asks he'll just say — Fuck, yeah, this magazine is mine, fucker, who the fuck you think you is, and he's pleading the First Amendment they hassle him anymore. No one's getting a piece of *him*. Carry the magazine in his left hand, walk around then slip the cherry gum into the magazine. He needs some cherry gum because his breath is rank today, like he ate something that died and then took a liquid shit, that rank. Then to the nail polish row, a bottle of blue nail polish for his mom he cups in his palm to hide from the camera, switch the mag with the gum to the hand with the polish. Blue like he imagines a bluebird's feathers might look like. Or a dead bluebottle fly. Pretty. Saunter back to the magazine row, bend down like he's looking at the bottom rack, slip the gum into the cuff of his jeans, the nail polish into his runner, tucked in the arch of his foot. Slip the mag into the back of his pants. He changes his mind: he'll buy the gum. He makes his way to the cashier, gum in his hand.

— Yes I would like a bag for my purchase, he says to the clerk.
— You have a nice day, ma'am.

The electronic doors slide closed behind him. The winter sun outside the drugstore envelopes him in a bright warm hug.

He saunters down the street, just one of many pedestrians out for a Sunday walk on this crisp, shiny day.

He notices her ass first, neat and round in its little black pants. He approves. The hair gathered up into a sloppy, tendrilly bunch at the back of the head, kind of goldy, kind of sexy the way it's falling down. She has a rolled yoga mat flopped carelessly over one shoulder, and she walks along very slowly, stops at the crosswalk light. Her head turns to the side and he sees that she's old. And not only old, but he knows her, it's Mrs. Mochinski, Mrs. Mochinski his nemesis, out in the real world with real people, out of her

Homeroom of Horrors. He halts his step, watches her from behind as she shifts from foot to foot in the cold, her ass cheeks subtly flexing with each step.

In profile, her cheeks shiny and red and *pretty*. And he remembers that she did let him walk across the classroom on the desktops one day without bawling him out. Mrs. Mochinski's secret identity: *a yoga babe*.

He follows her for two blocks, staying half a block behind as she walks, almost hobbles along. Then he aims for her back, lowers his head and starts to run, runs toward that spot on the back of her coat, bull's eye. X marks the spot.

The soles of his runners slap the bare spots on the pavement. At the very last second he angles around and screeches to a halt right beside her at the red light.

— Hello, Mrs. Mochinski! he chirps, and laughs at the naked shock on her face. — You look nice today!

Then before she can start yelling, he jumps into the traffic, dodging cars, an intrepid winter cyclist, and runs out the other side of the street to freedom.

Petra

To show just how much she loves Ginger no matter what trials their relationship suffers, Petra begins writing him another song. She doesn't need a special occasion to give Ginger a gift. Their relationship is not going through any kind of trial; they still love each other. Incredibly. — I'm telling you, Petra tells her mother, — no one has ever felt this way for another human being.

In her playpen, Petra's little sister Odette sticks both her hands in her drooly mouth and slurps.

— I felt the same way with my first boyfriend in junior high, Leslie Dolecki, says her mother, which makes Petra want to punch her mother's big, lumpy, soccer-mom ass. — Now clean up that bat's nest rat's nest room of yours, madam, her mother says, — before I throw all that crap out into the driveway for the neighbours to see. Odette, what a talented girl you are! What a genius yes you're a genius who's a genius!

Odette burbles, pulls both hands out of her mouth with a soggy pop.

Petra and Ginger's love is as massive and rich as Beethoven's *Ode to Joy* — as eternal, unique and holy as Romeo and Juliet's. No. Petra doesn't want any dead boys in her and Ginger's love story. They're basically betrothed, right? Ginger's love for her is awful and awesome, as in inspiring awe, even though he hasn't been at school since Tuesday, and she hasn't been alone with him since last Saturday night, and he has stopped texting her — she hopes to fuck the reason Ginger missed practically a whole week of school isn't what she thinks it might be. That boy dropping out isn't her fault and no one can say it is — dumb, ugly girls with unicorn fetishes certainly can't tell her it's her fault, and she will beat the living shit out of her if she tries, and Ginger can't blame her, he wouldn't dare. But he never will, especially after he hears the new song she is composing. The first three bars play in her head over and over — how it resonates — that oomph of bells and timpani, jingle and boom, the most beautiful music anyone in the world has ever written. Valentine's Day, Ginger told her he loved her he told her he loved her he told her he told her he loved her he loved her. She will believe him. Oh, the French horn.

Odette dangling from her hip, Petra's grandmother says, — There's no point worrying, you can't stop a man from cheating, it's like trying to stop him from sprinkling pee on a toilet seat. Her grandmother's hair so fine and thin the sun reflects off her scalp as she stands beside the piano. You can't stop a man from cheating from cheating from cheating, you can't stop a man from you can't stop a man stop a man stop that man now play.

Petra knows you can't stop a man, but Ginger isn't a cheater even with that sweater fuck-up. She's written other songs for him without giving him the lyrics, like the song about how she wanted to kill Patrick Furey for trying to steal Ginger away from her, 'November Crime.' Ginger got hard to that one. The other one about how magical it was to give each other their virginities, 'Moth to a Flame,' not so well. He suggested they play a video game.

She's going to the University of Calgary for their music program even though she would prefer Juilliard because Ginger can go to university in Calgary, but his grandfather won't let him go to New York. He told her his grandfather said he didn't have that kind of money. She asked Ginger, — Doesn't your grandfather have a pension?

His grandfather doesn't understand moving to a different city to go to university when Ginger can get a perfectly good education and free room and board here in town.

Petra told him he should point out to his grampa that Grampa's not his mother or his father. Ginger reached for the radio and blasted it on.

— You know, says Petra's mother, her sloppy bum waggling around the kitchen as she prepares Odette's banana and sweet potato gloop, — when I was in junior high and my parents made your uncle Leonard and me move to the other side of the city, I really missed Leslie Dolecki because I couldn't see him often. But it turned out all right. If you and Ginger really love each other, you'll be able to manage being apart while you go to school in New York, Petra.

If there was some kind of guarantee she wouldn't get caught and convicted, Petra would have stabbed her mother through the heart with a chopstick.

Petra plays the first three bars of the song for her grandmother. — It doesn't sound good this way, just on a keyboard all by itself and it's not done, she tells her grandmother. — But the rest will come. Ginger will ask me to marry him. I've figured out the parts. It's the most beautiful song in the world. I'm going to ask Mr. Baker to have the orchestra play it for the end-of-year concert.

— Aren't all your songs the most beautiful? her grandmother asks. Odette natters and bangs things in the kitchen. Petra hears Odette smack her lips as she eats her gloop.

Since late Monday night she's been hearing the beginnings of this song, and she works on it between classes and after school, in bed just before she turns off the light to go to sleep, because it stops her, a little bit at least, from worrying too hard about the graffiti on the locker and Ginger pulling away from her. But she cannot pick it out properly on her piano. The ends of the lines all fall flat, too many echoes and repetition when she can't predict them. She's been practising Chopin's *The Revolutionary Etude* (Op. 10, No. 12) for a month and when she tries to play it her grandmother finally says forget it and leaves to go wipe sweet potato out of Odette's hair and drink coffee with her mother in the kitchen. — She's going to turn into you, her grandmother tells Petra's mother. — All that talent, all of it wasted for a man. My only hope left is Odette. Isn't it Odette my sweetie? You're not going to waste your life like these two, are you? she googoos to Odette.

Petra sits at the keyboard, her fingers itchy in the stretch of black and white keys.

She picks out more possible fragments on the piano, scribbles bits on music-staff paper. Piano and cello, vocals of course — she'll need to figure out words but they can come later — but much more huge, more lush than just piano and voice. Just writing a few words can't make someone kill himself — this part of the song, right here, it rings so clearly in her head but clumps out discordant when she plays it with her fingers. Her first true attempt at orchestration: she wants piccolo trumpet, timpani, triangle, glockenspiel, cymbals, cowbells, bells, bass drum, tambourine, vibes, piano, violin, viola, cello, bass, French horn, trumpet, flute, guitar, trombone, a shaker. She knows exactly how triumphant the piece will sound, how gigantic, and how it will wring the tears from the audience's and Ginger's tear ducts, and once she's heard it properly, she'll finally stop humming it, dreaming it, tapping it out with pencils, pens, forks, knives. Maybe the song came into her head the same second Patrick Furey died — no. He offed himself in the morning, that's when he did it.

The song will spread its ointment over her flaming, heartbroken soul. She wishes she could cry but after crying so hard at the dead boy's parents' house, inside her skull feels *scorched*, Ginger cutting her off, she fought for Ginger, she really did — she is always fighting for him — she can't bear him not loving her, and he hasn't been hers, not really *hers*, since last Saturday, since, since. She will ask the school music teacher, Mr. Baker, and he will be so amazed by her initiative and creativity, of course he'll let the school orchestra play it. What a wonderful opportunity to put the school orchestra and the school choir together. It can be a song added to a concert for the parents. Ginger will hear it and come back to her. Perhaps she'll finally record a cd the way her grandmother's always telling her she should.

She'll get Tamsin, Kate, Angela and the other orchestra students to meet with her and rehearse with her, that's all she'll need, to hear it once hear it again hear it three times then four times and she'll be done.

Finally get this song out of her head. Into Ginger's head. Can't stop a man from.

Her hands clumping the keys, hunks of dead meat.

— What kind of song is that? asks her mother from the kitchen. — It makes me want to cut my wrists! Play something cheerful. It's such a beautiful day. I don't know what someone so young could have to be sad about.

— That song's a dirge, says her grandmother.

For once correct, her grandmother. Petra's writing a fucking dirge.

First Monday After Furey

Ginger

For the first time since last Monday, Ginger will go to school. His grandfather makes him put a thermometer in his mouth, the plastic hard and beeping against his teeth.

— You're not sick, his grampa says. — And even though you are of legal age to make your own decisions, I say off you go to make a life for yourself. Stop being a bum.

Ginger lying on his bed, lying on papers and books and gym clothes. *Romeo and Juliet.*

If only.

He should have.

How could he.

How could she.

Ginger stands at the bus stop swaddled in scarves and toque and his grandfather's greasy red coat because he was shivering and the coat is the warmest one in the house, his grandfather impatiently manipulating and dressing him like a mannequin. Ginger in the old man's coat and clumpy Sorel boots. The inside of his head is pudding, and he'd like his grandfather to just tell him what to do every minute of every day for the rest of his life. Ginger's car refusing to start this morning because no one's plugged it in. He throws up diamonds and rainbows.

If only.

He should have.

Ginger watches the crest of the hill half a block away where the bus is supposed to appear because he cannot manage walking the eight blocks to school. Blasts of wind flick and whip at his face, in the crevice between his scarf and the neck of his coat.

He retreats backwards through the snow into the bus shelter, he steps on cigarette butts, old bus transfers, a Tim Hortons coffee cup, frozen mucus horked from a passerby's mouth. The wind rushes past the entrance to the shelter, the snow fans upward and dervishes in tiny tornadoes. His legs and the wind buckle him backward, and he slides onto the bench, then onto the floor. A book kicked under the bench.

The Pride and the Joy.

The air rushes up from the ground to his face, and he spews out a loud sob. He told Furey, how many times, he didn't want to read that damn book even though Furey wanted them to read it together. He pulls himself up, back to sitting, on the bench.

The cover half buried in snow.

— This your book? asks a voice.

— Huh? says Ginger.

— Your book, says the man. He wears a purple toque and matching gloves.

— Here, he says, handing the book to Ginger. He sits down, his puffy silver coat brushing against Ginger.

The man in the purple toque has sparkling cheeks. The man looks back in the direction the bus is supposed to come, the rising sun glinting stars on the man's cheeks, his tiny gold hoop earring.

Max

It's been exactly one week, but for Max it's been years since:

- Patrick Furey took his own life and threw the school into chaos.
- Walter magically emptied, cleaned and replaced Max's ashtray on the windowsill next to the back door leading to the porch.

Joy has already loaded Max's desk with mail when he toes off his boots at the office, and an enraged mother is on the phone complaining that her son only received 37 percent on an essay and she'd researched and worked on that essay *all night*. Joy informs him that on Friday there was a social studies class without a teacher — the substitute never came in, and the class never got taught. Another mother has written him a letter to say that the school doesn't have enough religion in its curriculum and she's considering contacting the bishop. Oh, and the Spanish teacher's just found out she's three months pregnant and wants him to give her stress leave and find someone to fill her place right this instant.

When he flicks on his computer, Grizoms spill from the monitor; when he opens his desk drawers, Grizoms tumble to the floor. They jump up into his nose from his wastebasket, crawl up his pant legs, burst up out of his shirt collar, burrow up his sleeves.

He dials Walter's office phone. A Grizom pops out of the receiver.

— Mr. Boyle, he says into the voice mail. — I need to see you in my office at your earliest convenience to discuss this year's graduation guest speaker. Max's voice a Grizom squeak.

He hangs up. The phone rings immediately, jarring as a slam.

— A Crêpe Suzette for you, says Joy. — That's a cute name, don't you think? Very funny person. Love his sense of humour.

— Who?

— Girlfriend, murmurs the line. — You didn't come to my show at the Galaxy. I've talked to my mechanic, and our car accident frakked my starship but good. You owe me $2,495.62 for the damage.

— Ahem, says Max, — of course. To whom should I make out the cheque?

— Clement Michaels. M-I-C-H-A-E-L-S. C-L-E-M-E-N-T. May the force be with you, honey. Live long and prosper. No such thing as heroes, just a bunch of ones and zeroes. Get us out from under, Wonder Woman. Why don't you come drop your cheque off at my house, Max? Share a bottle of wine? A cup of java?

— I'll send it through the mail, barks Max, and he hangs up quickly, the plastic receiver clattering into its base.

— Some fun! says Joy through the doorway.

Max's briefcase on the floor, his keys hung up, his winter coat sagging from its hanger in the suddenly roomy hallway closet. 8:45 p.m. and the school day is over. The lights still off. Max's real life just begun.

— Walter's moved out, Max whispers into the phone, in the dark, on the floor, his knees up near his chin. The leftover Ethiopian lamb from the fridge twists in his stomach. He hopes he isn't going to throw up. He is curled against the cabinet doors below the kitchen sink, a cabinet doorknob jabbing the back of his head, cutlery he still hasn't picked up poking his buttock. Maybe a spoon.

— How do you feel about that? asks the voice on the other end of the distress line.

— The house is so empty, whispers Max. — Like an abandoned steel mill. And he didn't even ask for a goodbye kiss.

— It sounds like you're feeling lonely.

The fridge bursts into a loud hum, his stomach groans. The streetlights glare through the windows, angle the shadows so that he's in a house he no longer recognizes. He pushes the phone harder against his ear. The voice hasn't hung up. He can hear breathing.

— I don't know what to do, he whispers, his voice choking, the sea rushing upwards into his throat in a freak tide.

— It sounds like you're feeling indecisive. What are you willing to try tonight, to make yourself feel better? asks the voice.

— I like watching *Sector Six*.

— The television show?

— Yes.

— Well, that's a really good start. Can you watch some episodes of *Sector Six*? Do you have a *Sector Six* DVD and a functioning DVD player?

Above the sound of the fridge's airy machinery, he can hear a car roll by in front of the house, the light screech of a loose fan belt dimming as the car drives past and away. The streetlights beaming in their dangerous geometry can't pin him down if he just stays where he is, on the floor, in the dark, tucked into the L of the kitchen cupboards. The fridge's low hum and the yowling in his stomach shattering his ears.

Maybe he should kill himself too. Just because he is principal of a school, a middle-aged man, doesn't mean he's a superhero. Maybe Patrick Furey had a good idea. He can't remember which boy Patrick Furey was. Like walking every day for years past the same row of houses and then one day one of the houses is a hole in the ground and you can't remember what it looked like. He and Walter were rolling along perfectly until Patrick Furey killed himself, detonated and blew up into a supernova, ruining their Tupperware life. This child. There are no children. They never had children. Walter joked about having a baby with Max a few years back. His belly big enough. Borrow a female badminton friend's womb. But Max just wiped clean the television screen, snickering.

— Who is in your support system? asks the voice.

A colleague at work, a French teacher who quit after one year to stay at home and have babies, once announced to everyone in the main office that people who don't have children are people who refuse to grow up. Which means that Max has been a toddler his whole life. But he has to raise and educate children every day and he is glad when he gets to leave the school at the end of the day. Organizing 1,600 parentless children a day enough already.

All those unnaturally red cheeks arranged in front of him. All those oversized feet and hands — like clown feet and hands — and crusty, acned foreheads. The goth ones, their black lips, their skin plastered with white pancake makeup, the ones who look dead.

Folded on the floor, Max notices the Starship Monoceros magnet clinging to the empty plane of the fridge door. The streetlights angling the shadow cast from Colonel Shakira's toy-sized ship, distorting the shadow of the ship, so that it's almost the perfect size for Max to step into and fly away.

He returns the telephone receiver to its cradle. Switches on the television.

Second Monday After Furey

Gretta

Your Pilates instructor asks how you can go on. You go on because you go on. Because your son is dead, but you are alive, and killing yourself is not an option. Your brother, your nephews, nieces, cousins have left to go back to their own children, their jobs, so of course tonight is Halloween because that was his favourite day even though October is eight months away and you flip the kitchen calendar forward to October, the happiest month. Halloween should be a statutory holiday, your son always said. You buy chocolate bars and jelly beans, fill a scrubbed clean bucket with water and bobbing apples. You put on a black witch cape and coned witch hat you uncover in the basement. Your husband retreats to his library, switches on the cbc radio. You smell pot. Coward.

Why would your boy kill himself with only four months left to go until graduation? Just four months and his problems at school would all have been over. Who was that monster who gave him the gold locket? You want to kill that sicko. And the guidance counsellor squirming like a grub with the box of your son's things in his hands, you want to step on him, and the principal who didn't do his job, and all the parents who still have children, those abominations wheeling strollers in the mall, and giving birth to brand-new boys, imitation teenagers, and your baby snatched away by the neck.

You slam the front door open and stand on the threshold, opening your arms to the street. No goblins. His favourite costume was Little Bo Peep, he went in Bo Peep's dress three years in a row until you decided what had been cute was getting old. You told him he was getting too old to dress as a girl and now he's dead too young. Your biceps straining under the weight of bags and bags of chocolate bars.

Third Monday After Furey

Faraday

Faraday crunches on an apple in the cafeteria at lunchtime, her back to the door, which is the same as sitting with her back to a supernova because she won't know until it's too late if evil has exploded in to engulf her. But she feels more naked and withery facing the door to the cafeteria, the courtyard at her back. She doesn't want to see the evil come in, she only wants to know when she has to, at the very very last minute. At least if she faces the courtyard and anchors her attention to the bare, single tree stretching and spreading its branches, the patch of brown grass bordered by brick and concrete, she can imagine that maybe one day she could be eating her apple or her tuna sandwich, or eating a bag of sour cream and onion chips, and her unicorn would leap from the school roof to the foot of the tree, nickering and pawing the concrete, the patchy grass, as if waiting for her to claim it, the alicorn finally in her hands. Because the Saturday Jésus asked her out on a date, she said no, and that fact has to puke on her sometime soon. She sits at the end, the very edge of a long table of kids who don't mind. As long as she doesn't try to talk to any of them. On the other side of the cafeteria, Fumiko sometimes smiles and waves and once asked her by the chocolate bar rack if she'd picked out a dress yet for graduation. How Faraday wishes she had the strength and the fortitude to stand up from this table and walk without slipping in spilled french fry gravy to Fumiko's table. Sit down with Fumiko at her table. She clenches her fist, bites into her sandwich. She doesn't have the strength. Sitting here, even if it's at the end of the table, is better than gorbing it alone.

Saturday night near the end of her shift, Jésus came back to the Tim Hortons, gunned into the drive-thru, ordered a sour-cream-glazed Timbit, and shoved a picture of a narwhal at her. — Thank you very much, she said. — It's a picture of a narwhal, she said, stupidly.

She peered at the fine print at the bottom of the page. — And you ripped this out of an *Encyclopedia Canadiana.*

— The mighty narwhal, said Jésus, Timbit icing dabbed in one of the corners of his mouth. — That is correct. Otherwise known as the Unicorn of the Sea! They're an endangered species, he said, as though concluding a book report.

She stood in the window of the drive-thru, the paper in her hand. The car behind Jésus's truck honked.

— There are ... , she said, — there ... there are ... reasons why ... I have to stay a virgin, she said.

— Unless you plan on being a nun, that's seriously fucked, he said.

— I know, she sighed. — D'you want a doughnut? she asked.

— What kind?

— Um, grape jelly? It's on me.

— Okay, he said.

Her supervisor Morris bustled up behind her in a cloud of sweat and icing-sugar. — What's going on here? He poked his head out the window. — You again?

Jésus screeched away.

Now, in the cafeteria, if she sees him, she'll have to think hard about what corners of this room she can scuttle into, then wait for the next Ice Age when she can surface again. She blabbed to him that she was a virgin!

Dr. Linus Libby once asked her in his pink soapy way if it bothered her that she had no best friend. She answered of course not.

— Why are you crying? he asked.

— I'm remembering how our rabbit got eaten by a coyote. She dabbed at her eyes with her sleeve.

At the cafeteria table, she splits open the top of her milk carton, drinks from the spout and tries not to splatter milk on the table or her chin. She dabs at her mouth with a paper napkin. She drinks her milk and eats her cheddar cheese and mayonnaise sandwich; she's already pulled out the slimy shreds of lettuce her mother sneaks in.

She floats, a silent, sparkling island at the edge of the long laminated table babble about boys, football, boys, hate her, girls, hate him, graduation, hate her. But it's all right as long as she hangs on to her tree. The dead boy used to sit eating his cheese and lettuce sandwich alone too, in the corner next to the main door, but she remembers it wasn't because he was a loser so much as that he was going to be a rock star or walk on Mars one day. She yanks at the sandwich with her teeth. A slice of cheese, slippery with mayonnaise, slides out and slaps her chin. Or maybe he never ate here — how would she know, she never cared, never paid attention to anything he did until it was too late — and was one of those people who walk around with pizza wedges the size of half a pizza, half-in, half-out of their mouths, from across the road. Maybe he ate brie garnished with pear slices at home, the way that one ex-boyfriend of Uncle Suzie's used to. He would never have condescended to eat in the clatter and pettiness of the cafeteria with Faraday and the rest of them. She would have eaten cheese sandwiches or pizza or brie with him if he'd asked her to. She would have picked the lettuce out of her sandwich and listened to him talk about how sad he was, and she would have said that one magical sentence that would have changed his mind and saved his life. She would have said: *It's worth it.* Or: *It gets better. Time heals all wounds. Let's call the cops right now and get Petra arrested. Abracadabra.*

Faraday scratches her nose and hopes no one's taking notes on how she flipped that piece of cheese onto her chin. She imagines the dead boy sitting cross-legged at the base of the tree.

She is a cardboard cutout of herself. She is a magical, special being with huge beauty and power, this body her sad earthly vessel. The tower she has built around herself growing upward, thickening.

Her back to the door, she hears before she sees Jésus and his entourage clatter into the cafeteria. Her chest seizes, she's succumbing to hypoxia. He's probably fresh from robbing a grave or burning down a casino. She knows people who travel in clots.

George M. hangs out with some kind of goth slash emo crowd; he says he eschews categorization as a rule because it limits his life choices. Really, all George M.'s friends just wear the colour black because they can't colour coordinate. She wants to cry because she doesn't know how to prevent the inevitable Jésus punchline.

But Jésus and his cousins slide around her, as though she were a palm tree in a hurricane, as though Saturday night were a pathetic, *almost*-erotic dream involving too many doughnuts and a boy who basically told her he would have given her a torrential orgasm if she weren't such a nun.

— Neigh, Jésus cups into her ear as he passes, and the boys nearest Jésus snort.

She has no doubt in her mind at all the unicorns will come, but even though she can hardly admit this to herself, she hopes they are worth it.

Max

In the house at night, he can hear the plant roots stretching in their pots as he skims through the hallways, up and down the stairs, spreading dust from the decrepit carpet in the basement to the upstairs kitchen and living room floors. Timetabling spread out on sheets in front of him on his desk — better to work than lie alone in bed.

Today at work, his gleaming computer monitor, his gleaming phone that keeps ringing and ringing, he can hear the breathing of a boy who killed himself. And a man in his late forties, so late that it might as well be early fifties, whose secret husband has left him. He trudges back to his office from the washroom, and in his office sits Jésus, what a surprise.

Max sighs as he scrolls through names and phone numbers for Jésus's home number. Jésus García Hernández, followed by the phone listing. God, how he hates talking to Jésus's mother. Why does it suddenly feel like every day is Monday?

When he retires he and Walter are going to drive without a map and stay in cheap but clean motels all over Alberta and BC even though Walter prefers plane travel. This is Max's plan. They will do a tour of every big statue or icon in Alberta: the biggest kielbasa, the biggest perogy, the biggest Ukrainian easter egg, the biggest crow, the biggest truck. Then they will go on a men's cruise and down sambuca shots, two old trolls in love in their Bermuda shorts. They can eat in a restaurant close to wherever they call home, maybe go to a Christmas Mass at the same church at the same time and sit beside each other in the same pew. When they retire.

Now, he will go and try to win Walter back by going to the old bar and asking Walter for a dance. On the website he sees that certain nights are twenty-five-cent wing nights so for sure Walter will be there. One song. What can be worse than that?

Petra

Petra shops for a graduation dress. She would rather be shopping with Tamsin or even Angela or Kate, but her mother's said that if it's going to be that kind of money, she wants to be there too, Miss Too-Good-For-Outlet-Malls.

Petra pushes Odette in her stroller while their mother fingers through the rainbowed racks of insanely ugly dresses.

— So is Tomáš renting a tux? asks her mother. — Or just a regular suit? Does he already have a suit? We could match his tie and cummerbund to your dress.

— He's renting a tux, lies Petra, watching Odette reach up with her hands for a trailing sash.

— Well, says her mother, — we'll tell him what colour after we get your dress tonight. — Oh Odette, honey, no!

Odette gumming the sash.

— Petra, don't let her do that. Her mother tugs a pink, blobby affair off the rack, fans it open across herself. — How about this one? She holds it up against Petra, the froth around the neck sticking to Petra's lip gloss.

— Looks like an abortion, says Petra.

— Petra! says her mother, turning back to the row of dresses. — I have had it up to here with you. Up to here.

— I'm gonna go get a juice or something.

— You do that, says her mother. — And while you're at it, get a glass of attitude overhaul.

Petra slinks past the brightly lit stores, mannequins gesturing at nothing, she cannot hear the music in the speaker, all she hears is her death song. She peers at Laura Secord chocolate bars pyramided under glass, walls of runners and skis and snowboards in a sports gear shop. She is almost at the Juice Bar when she stifles a scream because she sees him, she's sure it's him. The dead boy pushing a giant philodendron in a grocery cart.

But of course it's not. It's not.

But behind him is Ginger's grampa sitting at a food-court table with a cardboard cup of coffee. And it is Ginger sitting across from him — Petra's heart ticks too quickly, attached to a bomb — also with a cardboard cup, twisting the cup in his hand, unrolling the edges as his grandfather animatedly tells him something. The old man with grey hairs bristling out his ears and nose, Ginger sitting frozen like a mannequin, except for the twisting cup in his fingers. The physical pain she feels seeing him, how she can't catch her breath, how she has to turn right back around without her juice and walk, just walk, back to her mother.

— Mom? she asks.

— I think Odette's just swallowed a button, says her mother.

— Mommy? asks Petra, the thudding hum in her ears.

— Not now, Petra, she says, Odette squirming in her arms between them.

Fourth Monday After Furey

Maureen and Max

Mrs. Meeny Miney Mo Maureen Mochinski and that little shithead Jésus García Hernández sit side by side in the principal's office, pinned into a corner by a tiny round table, the principal clippy in his desk across from them. It was never her plan to take Jésus to administration; normally she's good at isolating the bomb, containing the explosion. Then the little jeezler reports *her* to the principal. She's never ever sent anyone to the principal or the veeps. Not since she was a new teacher with clean, moist hands and her freshly ironed blouse, still believing that education was about teaching, not mob management.

Fluorescent lights buzzing above. Her back kinked into one of those goddamn plastic school chairs. She might as well dig her own shallow grave and slink in right now. Squeeze her eyes tight and jam her fingers into her nostrils as they shovel in chunks of dirt. She has had an okay life, a short life, a life spent sharing a bed with a liar and a cheater, a life spent chasing after mouthy sociopaths the world calls teenagers. A life spent away from her own soul.

— Mrs. Mochinski says you deliberately provoked her by trying to give her an apple, Jésus, says the principal.

— She kicked me in the ass, Jésus says.

Jésus's legs spread wide in front of him. Maureen wonders what it is about males and their having to air their balls whenever they sit down. Principal Applegate's face whizzes across the desk nose-to-nose with Jésus.

— Excuse me, Mr. García Hernández? he says, his nose crinkling.

— She kicked me in the *posterior*, says Jésus.

— Mrs. Mochinski? the principal says.

— I have presented my case, Principal Applegate, says Maureen. — It was not the fact of the apple. It was the way in which it was presented to me. Shoved in my face.

She's angled into the corner, the table edge aimed at her ribcage, and he's making her sit and defend herself against this punky, pukey punk. Jésus did try to give her an apple, a monstrous display of sarcasm and disrespect, and she did kick him in the ass. But no one except Jésus knows she kicked him square in the butt. Luckily with the side of her shoe and not the pointy heel or toe.

— Did you or did you not try to give Mrs. Mochinski an apple, Jésus?

— I did. I thought that's what you're supposed to do with a teacher.

— That's enough elaboration, says Max. — Mrs. Mochinski?

She wants to clock Max good. *He* should try living with someone who doesn't love him. He should try pretending the show must go on when the lead actor in his play has forgotten all his lines, the stage set's on fire, the audience is slithering out the back door.

Max can already hear Jésus's mother squawking on the phone.

— You have a choice, he says. — Your first choice is to apologize to Mrs. Mochinski. Your second choice is to apologize to Mrs. Mochinski.

— I gave her an apple, and instead of saying thank you, she kicked me! says Jésus. — It's assault and battery!

— Mrs. Mochinski? says the dead boy's principal.

— I did not kick Mr. García Hernández, says Mrs. Mo Mo Mocknee-ass. — I am shocked that I would be accused of such an act. We can't deny that Jésus has a fanciful imagination, Principal Applegate. If he'd apply that imagination to his Shakespeare studies, rather than toward clumsy mind games with his teachers —

— Phlpt! splutters Jésus.

— Jésus, apologize, says the principal.

— For what?

— Did you or did you not provoke Mrs. Mochinski?

— You are two very screwed-up individuals, splutters Jésus, twisting his baseball cap right way around, kicking his oversized

197

feet into the table leg. — You both need to see a shrink. I tried to be nice, and she kicked me in the ass. She's lying!

Jésus and Mrs. Mochinski infernal twins. Max scrubs his hands through his thick mass of perfectly white hair. White and thick as a horse's mane. He breathes a long sigh and drops his chin to his chest.

Maureen sits taut, willing the menopausal flames to leap up and immolate them all. Jésus lifts his cap, smooths back his hair, replaces the cap.

Principal Applegate finally leans forward over the table toward them and tents his fingers in front of his nose. He leans his nostrils on his thumbs, pulls at his nostrils until his nose stretches into a pig's snout.

— I'm really extremely very tired, he says.

Maureen rubs her hands together nervously. Max appears to be melting, his body sagging and dripping. Jésus spreads his legs even wider, if such a thing were possible.

Principal Applegate closes his eyes.

He snores.

Maureen

She's so busy trying to staple and Scotch-tape together the pieces of her own construction-paper heart, that the dead boy's teacher, otherwise known as Miss Rule, Ms Mo, Miz M., sometimes forgets about Patrick, his empty desk and chair less and less distressing as time passes. How sad that the hole in the middle of the classroom is thickening into normal. The same kid, Patrick, who moth-fluttered around her at the Pita Pit asking her for advice about his skateboard, her light cold and futile.

She's trying to wipe chalk off her hands with the chalky rag in her desk — why she still insists on wearing black clothes to this job after all these years, her hands cadaver dry from all the chalk dust, she'll never know — when she's sure she hears his skateboard wheels rumbling over the hallway linoleum outside her room. The thought of his skateboard, alone in the hallways, crumples her into a heap.

When she sees the chubby head guidance counsellor in his leprechaun beard galumphing in the direction of the main office, sashaying to the office with a purple binder gripped in his hands, she can't help calling to him, — Hey there! Hey! and she remembers that the rest of the teachers were clicking and chewing in the teachers' lounge about how he's propped a framed picture of Max on his office desk.

— Can I talk to you? she asks.

— Anytime.

Up close, the top of her head only reaches his chin, so maybe he isn't a leprechaun. More of a pookah. Wide as a pookah. Short grey whiskers bristle among the black around his mouth. Men with beards remind her of billy goats. And a billy goat once bit her hard on the finger at a petting zoo.

When she mentions Patrick Furey, his mouth turns down the way her ex-husband's mouth did whenever she told him something important, a fish's flat lips.

— He came to see me once, he says. He slides his hand along the edge of the binder, his body edging back in the direction of the main office, but his feet remaining in place, toes toward her. Polite body language. Barely.

— Well, what did he say? she asks. She slaps her hands against her hips and leaves behind faint white chalk finger and palm prints.

— The conversation he and I had is confidential, he says. — So I can't really go into detail about what we talked about. There's nothing we can do about it now, he says, frowning more. — Just make sure it doesn't happen again. Suicide contagion, he whispers, his billy goat lips bristling in her ear.

Like she can't tell when a bearded pipsqueak like him is trying to evade her. The boy is dead — what does confidentiality matter now? After working for nearly twenty years with teenagers and their *I didn't do it*s and assorted bullshit, she can tell when a stinkbomb's been lobbed her way. She can smell the soap and shampoo, the chemical cleaners, and the lying spray underneath it all.

— You'll have to go through the regular channels to find out how his parents are doing, he says, scratching his stubbly double chin. — The father's really angry, I think.

She wonders how he could ever counsel anyone about anything at all.

Then he leans in again, startling her. — I hate my job now, he says. She can see separate silver hairs glittering in his beard he is so close. — I should take up basket-weaving. I've heard it's hard work, but I can't be any worse at it than I have been at this job.

Maureen wonders if she is dreaming, still asleep in her lonely divorcée bed.

— I'm going to go talk to Max, she says, clapping her hands together. A small cloud of dust spurts up between them. — Patrick was a victim of bullying. He told me so, he came to me and there's no issue of confidentiality and this should be public.

Walter's face breaks open into a summery smile, a charming gap between his two front teeth. — That's an awesome idea, Maureen, he says. — Make Max explain why he didn't help Patrick get his skateboard back. You make this all public.

He disappears through the door leading to the north staircase at the far end of the hall. She swears she hears him whistling.

She will find Max and tell him exactly how pooey it was, the way he handled Patrick and the skateboard situation. She will force him to stay awake while she talks to him, tells the parents, tells the cops, tells the media that the boy was a victim of bullying because he was gay. Or else what? She isn't sure. What if someone asks her why *she* didn't do anything when the boy was still alive? Why didn't she do more? What was she thinking when he came up to her at the Pita Pit? Maybe she won't threaten Max at all, just give him a rubber rain hat and a big stick for when the frogs begin falling out of the sky and four horsemen come a-knocking on the school doors. That boy fell from the sky, and even though it was Max's job, her job, the pookah's job, to hold out the net, no one caught him because no one wanted to get shit on their clothes. She's a gerbil in a wheel, running and running, spinning, thinking she's running a marathon, running to paradise, when really she's headed nowhere at all.

Ginger

He lies on his back among the headstones, among the dark pines. The tree branches shushing in the breeze, the occasional whir and bump of a car driving by on the other side of the chain-link fence. He lies with his hands at his sides, he holds his breath. Pretending to be dead. Imagining being dead. Even in the dark, the black branches of the trees stretching above him, the occasional pinprick of star, the sky washed with streetlight. He's still too much alive. He will never have a chance of seeing Patrick ever again unless he's dead. Ginger closes his eyes.

Because everything's a garble. Every day a Monday, that horrible loop back to the day that Ginger thought was like every day but wasn't. The sun blew up and the world incinerated. He wishes that every night could be like that last night they met here, right on this spot. He wishes he could be dead too. The sound of car wheels, and car engines, the occasional far-off siren. The tree branches rustling, the smell of snow, of fermenting pine needles, the sound of winter chill, of gophers hibernating under the ground. Right here in this spot.

He would like to go lie down on Furey's grave. If he could find it. If he could ask.

Ginger remembers licking Furey's stomach at night, in the cemetery, the safe and luscious dark. The scent of pine trees.

He opens his eyes. Rubs his hand on the cold smooth granite of the tombstone next to him. It's just rock. Everything, in the end, just rock. He wishes a blizzard would swirl in, bury him.

Fifth Monday After Furey

Max

Max is lusting for a cigarette when he bumps into Walter in the graffitied stairwell, and his heart shrinks into the first dimension. *Walter, please,* he wants to say, but he cannot say it and before he can think the words he might say, Walter grabs him in his arms and kisses him passionately on the mouth. The head of Guidance giving a passionate kiss to the principal in the school's north stairwell, the kiss lasting seventeen seconds, their lips and tongues wild and drunk, Walter's mouth tasting of sesame seeds and root beer, how desperate Walter must be, how unhappy, to break their rules and finally give in. Max's mouth finally full of a drug much more satisfying than nicotine.

But the way it really happens is this:

Max, starving for a cigarette, bumps into Walter on the stairwell. His body craters. *Walter, please,* he wants to say, but he cannot say it, and before he can think the words he might say, Walter briefly meets his eyes as he brushes by Max down the next flight of stairs and Max hears the door below click shut. How desperate Walter must be, how unhappy, to break their rules and be in such close proximity to Max. Walter looked into Max's eyes. They almost touched. If they were still together, that would surely mean sex tonight. Walter's blazer flicking Max's hip. Max's teeth gripping the inside of his face.

Petra

Petra and Ginger grind past each other in the hallways stuffed with students. Ginger pushing straight ahead, a car angled too close to a concrete pillar. Scraping. Petra alone and head forward. Pretend.

He studies in the library at a table by himself, standing up and shifting his bag and papers to a new table when she tries to sit next to him. He has mutated into an identically charged particle. During her morning spare, she buys a bouquet of red roses, twelve exactly, wrapped in green tissue paper, tied with slippery blue ribbon, and props the roses on the windshield of his car.

The drooping roses are carefully perched on the concrete parking divider at the end of the day. Wizened roses, tissue paper, shiny blue ribbon and parking lot concrete. She picks up the bouquet, the green paper crackling in her hand. Sniffs the flowers.

Meet me or IL tel the hol skool, she texts him, her hands shaking and cold as she clicks in the words on her phone.

The beautiful chime of a message in her inbox, she tears it open, her lover is finally talking to her!

Then youll B a murderer 2 x, says the message from Ginger.

She repulses him.

She scratches *u r a petra* with her pen into the wood of her desk at home.

The graffiti in the north stairwell painted over with grey, its scribbled cacophony erased. One of the school janitors scrubs off the graffiti scribbled across the dead boy's locker. Scratches a fine, spiralling pattern into the paint. The words still there as ghosts.

Maureen

Mrs. Maureen Birdie Siobhan Rule Mochinski hurries after Max, who seems to be walking, but moves so fast he must be running. She clicks after him, how things have changed, usually it's the other way around: — Maureen, he might tell her in that preachy principal voice of his, — a parent's complained the speaker you brought into your class was inappropriate. — Maureen, he might bark like a sergeant and she a lowly cadet, — you're not fulfilling your extra-curricular obligations so I'm assigning you to cafeteria supervision every other day for the rest of the year.

She walks so fast her hair blows around her face. He pulls open the door to the north staircase, she pulls open the door to the north staircase. She sees the principal pass the pookah head guidance counsellor — they don't know she's there above them in the stairwell too. The door below snicks closed behind Walter and she knows from how they don't look at each other, the arctic cold in how they do not acknowledge each other, that they are in the middle of the kind of shattering war that only very intimate couples can have, what she should have known all along and what the gossip flung around the teachers' lounge has been saying for so long. The principal and head of Guidance are secret lovers. Bastards.

Sixth Monday After Furey

Faraday

Faraday dumps her bag on the stairs and knocks on George M.'s bedroom door. George M.'s smell steaming around her. She drops a box of Timbits on his desk.

— I can't get Patrick out of my head, she says, leaping onto his bed, then rolling herself in the top blanket until there is not a single air pocket touching her, wrapped tight as a burrito, wrapped tight as a mummy. The less room she has to breathe, the smaller the chance of her finding the air to cry hysterically and pathetically about a dead boy she barely talked to, unicorns that are taking forever to come and a boy named Jésus who is suddenly too good-looking for words.

— I can't help wondering if he's cold where he is, she says. — If he's lonely. I know it's illogical. I can't help it.

George M. sighs. He opens the box of Timbits and tosses a plain old-fashioned into his mouth. He makes Faraday watch a video of a decaying piglet on the computer screen over his shoulder. Her lips parted, she breathes through her mouth.

He stretches his neck sideways until it cracks. Stretches it in the opposite direction until it cracks again. — Done yet? he asks.

— Noooo, her voice nasal.

— This too much for you? he asks. He sniffs. Cracks his knuckles. Crams another Timbit in his mouth.

— Naaah, she exhales.

He crinkles his nose as he chews, scrolls down another page of *Decomposition: What happens to the body after death?*

She watches the piglet on its side bloat and then blacken.

— Why are you showing me this?

— Death is a fact of life, toilet brush, says George M. — Just because you don't want it to happen doesn't mean it's not happening. It's going to happen to you, it's going to happen to me. It's natural.

— No it's not. Not like that.

— Oh it's not? Because you're immortal? Are you made of some kind of synthetic material? Ho ho, I don't think so. As much as you want to believe in life after death, it just isn't the case. Certainly not with the body. I wish sometimes I was made of synthetic material, but wishing is ultimately irrational.

— I want to be cremated. I don't want worms eating me.

George M. turns back to the computer screen, and scrolls back to the beginning of the video of the decaying pig. He presses Play.

— Oh, burned instead, he says. — Yeah, that's a big comfort. Especially if you've been misdiagnosed and they put you in the coffin before you're completely dead and you wake up with flames shooting up around you. You'll be dead. You won't have any idea what's happening. You'll be sizzling like bacon when you're shopping for unicorn posters in hell. Ha ha!

The dead piglet on the screen inflates into black bloat.

— Oh *God!* Faraday says. She swallows to keep the tears down, the vomit in, she has no more saliva. Patrick was a perfect gentleman; he gave her her eraser back. He ordered an iced cappuccino from her and said thank you. He had clear, perfect skin on his cheeks, shiny, black hair. He was not a piglet.

— It's a possibility, says George M. — People have been cremated alive before.

Faraday jams the heels of her hands into her eyes. Pulls her hands away again.

Her stomach spasms as she watches the blackened pig burst, then dissolve under an unfurling blanket of maggots. Being buried alive is her second greatest fear. Being burned alive her worst fear of all.

George M. clicks the website closed. Clicks around until he finds a short video about an ant whose body has been invaded by a parasitic fungus.

The narrator has a British accent. The ant curls into fetal position. One of its legs twitches.

Max

The rainbowed lights spin and bob around Max. Twenty-five-cent wing night. Go-go dancers gyrate on pedestals, the one directly under the disco ball resembling an accountant from the chin up, all jaw and horn-rimmed spectacles like he's stepped out of 1955. He's naked to the waist, hips grinding, whirling a glowing hula hoop around his middle in time to the music, flat, muscled stomach shiny, he casually wipes his glasses on a cloth from his army pants, perches them back on his nose, his sparkling, rippling biceps, triceps, deltoids, his astonishing muscled arms rising as he lifts them to the rhythm of the music, the hula hoop whizzing, his achingly beautiful Clark Kent face in the half-dark.

Max will walk in, full speed ahead, Warp Factor Ten, locate Walter sitting at the bar with a heaping plate of chicken wings or at a table scarfing a heaping plate of chicken wings, then withdraw, also at Warp Ten, and try not to transform into an anthropomorphic salamander. Max is wearing a suit and tie, he wants to stick out like a badger in a cage of blowflies. He wants to look like someone's vigorously heterosexual father there to retrieve a lost sheep from this den of iniquity.

That drag queen he knows stilettos by, a seven-foot black Wonder Woman, all shellacked hair and thigh-high crimson boots, delicately toned arms, snapping her gum. Max scuttles behind a pillar so she won't see him. He peeps around the pillar. As Max expected, now that Walter has lost his morals and his marbles, he is leaning against the bar — a drink in hand and a plate of chicken wings beside him. Max ploughs forward to retrieve him. But Walter is bent toward the chemistry teacher, their drinks glowing in the black light, Walter no doubt telling the chemistry teacher about Max, spilling, spewing out the story of their seventeen years together, outing Max, sucking Max's life and career into Walter's corrupt vortex.

Max is like a computer program with a virus.

He is an unembalmed corpse eaten by the bacteria in its own stomach, turning inside out.

The principal ducks between two high tables. He trips over a bar stool and slips in spilled martini, falls backward, legs pinwheeling as his feet scamble on the slick floor. The tangle of stools collapsing in on him, the whirling of hula hoops, and those shiny, beautiful, topless accountants who wear them.

Clark Kent calling to him, the horn-rimmed glasses, Clark Kent mouthing then shouting. Max flings his hands up to his ears. His shoulders brushed, dusted off, a firm hand under his elbow, his suit jacket dabbed with a rag, a pretzel stuck to his knee. Through the jungle gym of table legs and upended stools, Walter and the chemistry teacher are still chatting, laughing on the far side of the bar. Did Walter see Max? Walter wouldn't tell the chemistry teacher about Max. He wouldn't.

Clark Kent and Wonder Woman jostle Max into sitting position. The accountant pats Max's hand, the skin on his chest hot and gleaming.

— Mr. Applegate! he exclaims. — Bryce Campbell! I went to St. Aloysius five years ago. Suzette's gone to get you water. Never thought I'd see *you* here.

Of course he's run into an old student, a topless student, one nipple a pink dot, the other sparkling with its very own earring. *He is ogling a student!* Max about to retch.

— Of course I remember you, Bryce, he gags. — Of course. I'm just here looking for my nephew. His mother wants him home. Good to see you. What are you up to these days? I should find my nephew and head straight home. Well, *this* bar is certainly *different*. His mother's waiting up. School day tomorrow. I've never been in a bar like *this* before.

— I'm studying to be a chartered accountant.

— Top grades in math, eh? Max clutches the table above him and leans himself into standing, stomach lurching. He bends over, clutches his knees. He. Cannot. Have. A. Heart. Attack. *Here.*

Hands framed by Wonder Woman's bulletproof bracelets scoop a plastic cup full of water and ice under his nose. He follows the hands, up the arms, and peers into the mouth chewing gum as though it were an Olympic sport, eyes glowing blue in the black light, head crowned with its golden Wonder Woman tiara.

— Here you go, Max who owes me money, says Wonder Woman.

— Thank you. Max takes the water.

Wonder Woman clasps Max's face with both hands, brings her brilliant blue eyes close to his. Purses her generous ruby-red lips.

— You bruised your forehead. Maybe your brain is bleeding, pushing litres of blood into your skull, and you'll be dead in a matter of hours. Should we call an ambulance? You owe me money. I get my money before you die.

— No! No.

— Or, says Wonder Woman, — you get to be my sex slave for forty days and forty nights. Tell me forty stories, one every night.

Max swallows a splinter of ice, coughs water into his hand, spills his cup on his lap.

Suzette's breasts jut out even more as she takes a great breath. She crosses her arms.

— I'm looking for my nephew, says Max. — His mother wants him home. I'm not here for any other reason.

Suzette blows a large, juicy bubblegum bubble, her tongue sticking out at Max through the bubble. She leans into Max's face and pops it.

The wafting smell of artificial grapes.

— So that's your story? smacks Suzette through her gum, through ruby-red, cherry-red, mercury-red lips. — You owe me $2,495.62.

The drag queen's eyes, the long, beaded eyelashes, the silver eyeshadow, the unnerving blue eyes themselves, brimming with lights and drum machines. — Colonel Shakira? says Max.

— I've got your wallet, Colonel Shakira says.

— Please, Max pleads, — I'm not trying to rip you off. Let me get my wallet. He pats his empty jacket pocket. — Please, he says.

— How about this, pretty man, Suzette says as she flips open his wallet. — I take your driver's licence and credit cards as hostage, what's this, I'll take your video card, your, hoo hoo, your *Sector Six fan club membership card?* Hoo hoo! That's mine too! Your AMA card, your health card — no I'll leave that for when you're rushed to the hospital for your bleeding brain — and your business card. I take a business card for myself, I write my name and phone number on the back of another one just for you. Bryce, hand me a pen.

— Now see here ... , says Max, gathering his principal self together. — You just hold on a minute ... I was just looking for my nephew Colin ...

— Oh, honey. Just let your nephew die a *natural* death.

Suzette folds Max's cards and money into the top of her boot, then scrawls on the back of the business card. — You will phone me tomorrow by 11:59 a.m., but not before 10:59 a.m. because I am *not* a morning person, or I will phone you again at your office, she says, — tomorrow, and this time I will not let up. I will let the phone ring and ring until you pick up the phone because I'm head over heels for you, Mr. Maxwell Matthew Donald Applegate, yes I am, you all confused and Alice looking for your way back to Wonderland. I will come to your office and belt out every love song I know, I will stand naked wearing nothing but a sequined G-string and pasties, singing your name, Mr. Maxwell Matthew Donald Applegate, begging you to spank me, spank me because I've been a very naughty girl, oh yes I have, Mr. Donald, until you give me $2,495.62.

She hands the emptied wallet to Max.

— *Mr. Applegate's gay?* shrieks Clark Kent.

Max retrieves the wallet. Tucks his damp shirt back into his pants.

Clark Kent whizzes his hula hoop around his waist, around his chest, around his neck, around his waist. Clark Kent, the man of steel, watching this whizzing away of Max's disguise.

— Thank you, mumbles Max.

— No such thing as heroes, says Suzette. — Just a bunch of ones and zeroes.

Max slip-stumbles to the door, the spinning lights and music drilling, a declawed, defanged old circus bear shambling in his clown suit.

— I know where you work, 'n' I'm gonna get you, baby! shouts Suzette. She twirls a kiss curl next to her ear, stretches a blob of gum from her mouth with her index finger in one long, elastic string.

— Mr. Applegate's gay, babbles Clark Kent, finally whirling his hoop to a stop. He flips it once completely, jumps over it, like skipping over a jump rope. — Who'd a thunk it?

— Oh, Superman with your Superbrain, Suzette says. — He's not gay. His boyfriend is.

Joy

Joy, Maureen and Pam sip their drinks, each woman sequestered to her side of the table, elbows in, coats still on. Maureen the English teacher and Pam the guidance counsellor the only ones who answered Joy's invitation to a wake for Patrick Furey. Everyone else telling her, — You're new here, huh? Or — That's not appropriate. Or, silence that stunned her worse than a face slap. Joy wonders why she hasn't found a single kindred spirit at this school even though it's almost been a year since she started.

Except for Maureen and Pam. They had to do the wake on a school night because Pam teaches dog obedience on the weekends.

— Well! chirps Joy. — Thanks for coming, ladies.

— I'm not a lady, growls Maureen.

— So you like Guinness? asks Joy, nodding at Maureen's drink.

— You said it was an *Irish* wake.

— She didn't say Irish, says Pam. — She just said wake. You can get Guinness in cans now.

— Really? Who knew, says Maureen. — Anyway, she says, lifting her glass, — here's to Patrick Furey, the boy we all failed, goddammit. Her pale, thin lips start to quiver. She drinks from her glass.

— Yeah, breathes Pam, shaking her head.

— No, says Joy. — We're here to celebrate his life. That's the point. I'm going to stop my watch. Like they did in the old days.

— I'm Italian, says Pam. — I don't know what you're talking about.

— My family's Irish, says Maureen, — and I don't know what you're talking about.

— I'm from Guernsey, Saskatchewan, says Joy. — It doesn't matter. I'll start. I remember him as being a sweet kid. A handsome young man. Polite. And he wore an interesting necklace. A heart locket. He seemed sensitive to me. Artistic.

— I know that he always carried around his skateboard when he could get away with it, says Maureen. — He talked to me in the Pita Pit about how some other kids stole his skateboard.

— That's terrible.

— Yeah, well, kids, like adults, can be right shits. Problem is, I hardly remember him at all except for that time at the Pita Pit. Maureen rubs her forehead. — I know he was a good kid, I just know it. But I can't remember a thing about him except that skateboard, except him telling me they stole it when I was at the Pita Pit. Me ordering a roast chicken pita, no onions, even though I really wanted some onions so I could piss off my ex-husband with my onion breath. I cared more about that, I was so selfish. It's always the fuckers are the ones we remember. Jésus García Hernández. I'll never be able to forget *him*. It's not right. He gave me an apple the other day. I don't know what the hell is going on.

Pam's head down, she lifts up her glasses to wipe her eyes, then blows her nose into her Kleenex, limply wiping away the tears and snot. — He was an angel, says Pam.

Pam's upper body sags in her chair. Joy pats her hand.

— Did he have a girlfriend? asks Joy.

— What difference does that make? Pam pours more foam into her glass.

— Well, I just wonder, you know, maybe that had something to do with it?

— Who knows, says Maureen. — Love's overrated anyway. She lifts the beer glass up to her mouth and drains it to the very bottom.

A man on a skateboard rumbles by their table, glides to the bar, then catches up the skateboard, tucking it away behind the counter. He starts polishing glasses.

Music at the other end of the bar starts up, a woman burbling into a microphone.

— Karaoke, groans Maureen.

— Love karaoke! says Joy.

— You would, mutters Pam.

Joy hops up to the microphone declaring, — I'd like to dedicate this song to a beautiful young man who passed away recently, bless his heart. I didn't know you very well, but this one's for you, darlin', up there in Heaven. The screen behind her announces the song, and Joy launches into 'Wind Beneath My Wings,' — Did you ever know that you're my heroooooo . . .

— Oh God, I hate this song, wails Maureen, her spirit finally crashing. She starts bawling, bawls her head off, tugging her shawl up around her face. — Oh, you poor little skateboarding little jeezler, she says, the shawl catching around her chin. — Oh, Alexey.

The bartender who skateboarded in to work scoots out from behind the bar and pats Maureen on the shoulder, plopping another pint of beer in front of her. — On the house, ma'am, he says.

Pam, rocking in her chair, crumples her damp Kleenex in her hand. Hums along to the song.

Seventh Monday After Furey

Max

The woman swings open the door in a whoosh of hairspray, humongous gold breasts and nyloned bare feet.

— Greetings, alien, she says, and Max nearly urinates his pants in the first 0.2 seconds of disbelief because Colonel Shakira has answered the door. Tears prickle behind his eyes. The woman of his dreams in the flesh; he can even *smell* her. Then it is 1.2 seconds and he realizes, no, it's just someone dressed like her. And 2.2 seconds when he understands, no, it's the female impersonator whose car he totalled, and he deflates. Because this is real life.

Five minutes later, Max perches at the edge of the slumping easy chair in Crêpe Suzette's living room. Just a regular cardboard-cutout Calgary apartment. Decorated with cardboard-cutout Ikea bookshelves, Ikea desk unit, a porridge-coloured sofa, a sewing basket spilling gold and pink tulle, silver ribbons. The computer screen naked and irresistible with the Wet & Wild Guys screen saver. He wants to smash the computer with its rotating photos of glistening gym bunnies, he has to pry his eyes away from them, but they flick back to the screen saver with a compulsion beyond his control. The only art in the apartment poster after poster of different galaxies, the Milky Way, the Andromeda Galaxy, the Sombrero Galaxy, the Antenna Galaxies, the Magellanic Dwarf Galaxy. The man clearly obsessed.

A poster of Colonel Shakira.

— What do you take in your coffee? asks Crêpe Suzette, clinking about in the kitchen. Max straightens his tie. The stale cigarette smell in the apartment tickles his nostril hairs. He aligns the skinny tip of his tie directly beneath the fat tip.

— Tell me how much I owe you and I'll write the cheque, he says.

— Cream and sugar it is, says Crêpe Suzette. She sits down in another whoosh of hairspray. Her tight gold uniform outlining her muscled thighs as she pours cream into his coffee, then crosses her legs. Her eyebrows plucked into lean Marlene

Dietrich arches. Her wig Shakira perfect. — You can make out the cheque to Clement Michaels. $2,495.62.

Max sitting so stiffly, he will permit nothing in this apartment to touch him, not one thing.

— Waitasec, says Shakira. — Are you trying to tell me something? Are you bankrupt or something? I knew I should have made you bring cash. Fuck, I knew it. Fuck.

— No, says Max. — No, that's not it.

— Oh.

Max fishes a tissue from his pocket and wipes his nose.

— Well, I don't take Visa. Is it the coffee?

Max pulls his tie loose with his finger. Then tightens the knot. Then straightens the tips. Clears his throat.

— Did someone break your heart, honey? asks Suzette, putting her hand on his knee. — You look like your best friend got sent on a three-decade cycle to the Andromeda Galaxy.

Max unfolds a cheque from his wallet and, smoothing it out on his knee, he writes $2,495.62 over to a Mr. Clement Michaels.

— Excellent, says Suzette. She folds the cheque exactly in two and tucks it into her cleavage. — Just kidding, she says, opening a drawer in the blonde desk and tossing it in. — Now tell me. I can always recognize the fellow wounded.

Max takes a strained sip of coffee.

— Who will I tell? asks Suzette. — Come on. I have credentials. I once dated a shrink. Turns out, they hang out in *packs*.

— Can I smoke in here? asks Max. — Can I have my identification and credit cards back, please?

— Only if you give me a cigarette too, she says.

He flicks the lighter under the end of her cigarette. They both suck.

— Can I have some more sugar please?

She passes him a small white bowl. — Of course you can, Suzette purrs.

— Can I have my identification and credit cards please?

— Of course you can. As soon as you tell me why you're so sad.

A lock of Max's perfectly white hair falls into his eyes as he puffs on his cigarette, shields his eyes with one hand. Clement Michaels's Starship Monoceros perfection makes him want to cry.

Suzette has sworn to herself she will stay away from married men and closet cases. But this one is a chocolate bean with a brandy centre, a bottle of Veuve Clicquot asking to be popped, now that she finally has her money and can appreciate the finer things. She blows her smoke sideways, away from this poor, crumbling, handsome heap of a man.

— A boy in my school ... where I'm a principal ... killed himself. And my roommate has left me because of it. I don't understand the connection, but it's still breaking me in two.

— I remember you, she says.

— Pardon?

She does remember him from one of her shows. He was the one whose foot she held in her hand for longer than usual, so startled was she by his pulse beating like a trapped bird's, fluttering in her fingers. She had never seen a man so terrified, so she had to leave the closet case with the gorgeous white hair alone and go for his giggling bald dad instead. The gay guy gasping and struggling like a man caught in an avalanche, his foot encased in a sexy argyle sock.

His argyle socks. She can still smell his panic coating her hands.

She had not seen someone so terrified in a long time, and while she held his damp argyled foot in her hand she wished she could have taken him in her arms and said *You're home now*, his body relaxing against her. *Come out of that closet, baby, the air's so bright and disco out here.*

Suzette puts a hand on the poor man's knee. — Now why would your boyfriend leave you because of that? she asks. — It wasn't your fault the boy killed himself? I think my niece goes to your school.

— That's impossible, says Max. — I didn't do what I could, frankly. And neither did Walter. And now he's left me.

— So that boy's killing you now too, says Suzette.

— You're only a character from a TV show, Max responds. His head droops.

She wishes she could have bought that poor dead boy, another soldier fallen in battle, a Crab Nebula cocktail. She wishes she wishes she could tell him to look into the music, look into the lights and feel the cosmos right there, right in his hands and shining down on to his baby head. She wishes she could have told him there was a world full of men hiding in waiter yawns and downtown pubs and night-school hallways and grocery-store aisles and next-door apartments. And that he would meet every one of them if he just hung around long enough.

She moves to sit beside Max until their thighs are touching, his mildewy smell right next to her face. She takes his head to her bosom. Props her chin in his hair. His hair thick, oily. Max refusing to exhale.

— I think I know a place where we can go, she whispers.

— Oh, Colonel, he sighs.

Max drives Crêpe Suzette in the mechanic's car to her club — tonight is a special corporate gig — down dry, tight streets that hold their breath, waiting for green leaves, flower buds. She is scooched into the passenger seat in her fur coat, a plastic rain bonnet over her hair to keep her 'do in place, her long hands folded in her lap. She sings softly as he switches lanes, meticulously shoulder-checks to show her what a good driver he is. Suzette sings 'Do You Know the Way to San José?' and 'Hey Big Spender.' She asks for a song request. Max can't think of a single song, his head suddenly Ikea-pine clean of ideas, and all he can hear is the clicking of the turn signal, the air blasting from the heater into their faces. Suzette finally says she'll sing the theme song from *Sector Six*, — No such thing as heroes, she sings. In the signal-clicking, engine-revving silence following the last note, Max nearly slams the car into a sound barrier lining the road.

— You don't like that song? asks Suzette.

— Here we are, he says huskily, pulling the car up in front of the club's awning. She fumbles for the door handle.

— Let me get that, he says, and he hurries out of the car and leaps over a heap of blackened snow, melted into honeycomb. He tugs open her door and offers her his hand.

— My very own chauffeur, she says, as she steps out of the car.

— Well, he says, her hand still in his. The long curls of her fingernails rest against his palm.

— So I'll cash that cheque tomorrow, she says. — If it bounces, I'll bounce you. Maybe I'll bounce you anyway.

Max holds the club door open for Suzette. Inside, it is hot and dry.

— So you'll stay and see the show? she asks. — I can get you a seat where no one can see you.

— Love it! he blurts. When the alarm clock bludgeons him awake tomorrow, he will be performing in his own sorry show, the sleep-deprivation show, the fourteen-cups-of-coffee show, but so what if tonight's a school night? So what?

— Come in, she says. — Get yourself a drink, and we'll get you settled.

His parents will not believe his luck, scoring a free ticket to a Galaxy Lounge show. If he were living a normal life, he would call them up to brag. Walter would laugh if he knew Max was here, on his own, in his parents' favourite place.

— There's a special person in the audience tonight, booms Suzette into the mic.

The blood in Max's head rushes to the floor.

— My mother's here tonight, folks! Give her a hand!

The audience scatter-claps. Max sits back up, claps, then jingles the keys in his pocket.

— It's my drag mother, for fuck's sake, I think you can make more fucking noise than that! she shouts.

The audience's clapping more boisterous, a short *whoooop!* from the back.

Max is a little disappointed when she changes out of her gold Shakira catsuit into a minidress dangling all over with gold coins, but she is still breathtaking and huge, yes, he has to admit she is the biggest, most formidable woman he has ever seen.

Crêpe Suzette, Vaseline Dion and Miss Demeanour in matching gold-coin dresses fouetté around a giant leopard stiletto in the centre of the stage. They fouetté until Suzette positions her buttocks on the stiletto's lip, crosses her legs, and Max has a brief glance under her skirt, but it is so dark she could have the Milky Way tucked under there. Max sips at his club soda; the music and the beauty, he's in a risqué Berlin club in the 1920s. He can understand how a beautiful woman, carrying a white rose dipped in chloroform and ether, could seduce a whole room. He has to piss, but he doesn't want to miss a single song.

— Forgive me, father, for I have sinned, pronounces Suzette, — It has been twenty-five years since my last confession. Father, I — I — I — I have a foot fetish!

A cymbal crashes.

Suzette fingers socked feet, her terrifying sock inspection, so Max runs on his toes to the bathroom. He can hear the audience laughing, the music, and her voice belting out — Straight! Straight! Gay! Straight! and more laughing from the audience. He pisses at a urinal even though he no longer has to go, and washes his hands. He stands just behind the door in the bathroom, the black veneer, the glow from the lights around the mirrors above the sinks. The entire bathroom is black, with chrome and mirror accents. Reminds him of the room that held the coffins when he went with his parents to select his great-aunt's coffin. The poor attempt to disguise the facts with dark wood panelling, soft lighting and flowers. He jingles the keys in his pocket. He pulls off his blazer, and drapes it over his arm. Another musical interlude begins — she sings 'Do You Know the Way to San José?' this time at full volume — and he pushes open the door. He stumbles on the way to his seat, but quickly rights himself.

Crêpe Suzette flashes her pantyhosed bum at the audience and trash-talks the men lined up at the front tables like a row of crows. Their wives laugh, all lipstick, fingernails and tooth veneers, the men laugh and ram their hairy knuckles in the air in triumph when Suzette spontaneously humps one of their thighs, kisses the tops of all their heads. Maybe Max is starting to understand his parents' love for these kinds of shows, how hilarious they thought it was to dress up as the opposite sex for Halloween parties. His father in a blonde ringleted wig that lurched to the side whenever he turned his head too quickly, his mother in a tuxedo with her hair stuffed up into a top hat, her upper lip drawn with a moustache that curled at the ends. They would scream with laughter as his father pulled the dress down over his shoulders and his mother zipped the back; his mother stuffing a pair of balled-up socks down the front of her pants. His father's thin lips stippled crimson, long false eyelashes curling up from under his bristling eyebrows. A heart-shaped mole glued on his jaw. His mother lowering her voice and ordering Max's father to fetch her a beer, woman. Max knows they aren't homosexuals or perverts. Walter calls them the Nutty McNuttersons. Walter.

And now Walter has left Max, as though Walter asked him to dance, then foxtrotted away with someone else.

Max is pretending to his secretary, Joy, to his vice-principals, to the other teachers, that Walter's having Max's photo on his desk is as natural as the *Hang In There* kitten posters that pepper the bulletin boards in the school. He shrugs when they ask him, says he has other more important issues to think about. Like the shrinking budget.

Will Max have to fire Walter?

The evening and a good night's sleep dribbling away in this demented place.

And, come to think of it, as he fingers his lighter, his keys, watches a guy — can't be younger than seventy — slurping a shooter out of Suzette's mouth, maybe he doesn't really understand what this audience is doing, why they are so giddy, so *gay*, why this kind of thing makes his parents laugh themselves apoplectic, his mother once literally rolling on her back on the floor at the sight of his father in her wedding dress. He thought at the time it was the music — the Barbra Streisand and Liza Minnelli impersonations are the closest they will ever get to breathing the same air as Barbra Streisand and Liza Minnelli. These are all middle-aged people and older. What fallen garden is this? Who is he, biting into these fruits? He isn't exactly heterosexual, Max knows that, but he isn't some old queen either. Maybe he is *relieved* that Walter's left. He is spliced and splayed open, his organs naked, here in this raucous dark. He just wants to drive Suzette home as he promised, then drive himself home and bury himself in his own bed, in his own blankets, or switch on the television. *Sector Six.* Colonel Shakira would never let Lieutenant Fong drink a shooter from her mouth, no matter what drug a Reptiloid might have sneaked into their electromagnetic-generated beverage. He paid Suzette — not Suzette, Clement — the money Max owed him her him.

Max buttons on his coat in the steamy darkness. Jingles the keys, the lighter in his pocket. Takes a last pull from his drink.

— You're still here, she says, her forehead and neck shining with sweat. — I thought for sure you'd beamed out of here.

Max wants Suzette to throw him to the floor and leap on him in that horrible, sinful way that would enrage the parents at his school, force his resignation, strip away his pension, his reputation, and make him live the rest of his life on his gravedigger savings, him and his illegal lust. Spend his afterlife in hell.

— I promised I'd drive you home, says Max. He smiles. His breath thick with almost half a pack of cigarettes, cigarette smoke woven into his clothes. He smoked with each of the waiters as they came out for their separate smoke breaks. They talked about traffic tickets.

What his body lusts for more than anything right at this moment, even more than Suzette, than Walter that Judas, that slut, is to lay himself down in cool, freshly dug night soil, and let the earth open its arms and swallow him back down to where he came from.

Eighth Monday After Furey

Gretta

Since your son died, your studio has lain fallow, a button depressed and the entire room a secret behind an empty wall. Your husband retreats to the television, the refrigerator packed with glass, plastic and rubberized containers bloated with food. The multitudinous flower petals curled and brown, the water in the clear vases mucus-thick. The television murmuring and hissing from your husband's den, the aroma of your husband's pot licking the back of your throat.

You open the door to your studio and you smell the sawdust, drying paint. Your old perfume that makes you gasp.

The envelope in your pocket; inside it, locks of your baby's hair clasped in ribbons and string, two scattered baby teeth and that girly locket. The locket not given to you, but it's yours, a metal heart the size of a peach pit the last thing to nestle against his breaths. You bring the locks of hair up to your nose. One from when he was first born, the second from his first birthday, the third from the birthday after that. The last lock of the collection because by three years and one day old, he had already started running away from you.

Begin.

You twist his hair and fine silver wire into flower petals, a tiny molar glued into the centre of the flower. You will make two of these, one for you, one for his father, and then you will have run out of your son.

His father in his cubby, the TV blaring. He folds his legs away to make room for you on the couch, one arm triangled behind his head, his eyes withered slits — your lover a hundred years old. You tuck up the seat of your work overalls and sit. You hand him a hair flower, he hands you his joint; you note the smoke curling upward from his long fingers. You suck in the smoke, the cherry burning only centimetres away from your lips. Your husband sniffs the flower. A spaceship in a galaxy far far away hovers on the TV screen, the stars peppering the background one mighty constellation. You suck in more smoke. The plinks of a TV piano, the low strains of a cello. A flower twisting in your other hand.

Gabe

Because the silence this second Monday night without his boy is the longest sustained cacophony the father has ever heard, he covers his ears when it wails too close, acoustic waves pulverizing his eardrums, stones flung at him, the silence so loud it crushes, buries him. Sometimes in the thudding, the mangling silence, he cannot help wondering if his boy is cold where he is now, what if he's freezing? Does he have his coat? The father has answered the door at every bing-bong of the doorbell, he is never surprised by what he finds when he opens the door, only one thing would surprise him. He has microwaved plates and plates of spooned casserole, brewed litres of coffee and tea for his wife, written eulogies, obituaries, kept the radio on for days, its buzzing and tinkling, chattering, hissing music strangling notes through the tiny holes in the speakers, and finally Monday night the silence wins, he cannot hear anymore, his eardrums played until they've broken, the milky radio voices, the monochrome music, the bing-bong, the microwave beep beep smothered by his boy's absence. The sharpened silence splintering his bones.

Monday nights before the unsayable event, his boy's television show swallowed the house with its racket and braying.

The father switches on the TV, yanks up the volume, the television's electricity jolts him, the stabs of sound assault. He punches the remote control through commercials swirling with sparkling, plasticized hair, snowy teeth so big they could eat a child; reality shows set on beaches, grubby contestants pulling rickshaws, crying and hugging contestants with manly jaws and swelling breasts, reality-show stars punching their fists into the air in triumph; law shows starring rectangular grey suits, pearl earrings, posed behind polished wood desks and glass doors; lab coats, spilling ponytails and glistening lips, haggard handsome men frowning, stethoscopes looped around their necks on hospital dramas.

He pauses the flicking.

A tall, busty, black woman in a pointy-shouldered catsuit aims her space gun at a giant lizard in gold shorts. The lizard roars, the lizard lunges, the woman shoots. — I am Colonel Shakira! she shouts.

He presses the spongy button on the remote and grows the sound up and up and up.

The TV flicking across his face, and his wife rests beside him on the couch, her hand on her knee, her other covering her mouth, the unlined mouth of a much younger woman, a shiny, sweaty, weeping teenage girl, her profile their son's profile, that gleaming ski-jump nose tip their son's. They watch their son's favourite television show, the one they always nagged him to turn down, could you please just turn it down a *couple of notches* because there are other people living in this house too who want to keep their hearing. Why don't you watch it on your laptop in your room? Don't sit so close to the TV. I don't know why. Just don't.

Colonel Shakira on the TV screen toasting a glass of green drink with the gold-eyed lizard to the closing credits. The boy's father on his knees in front of the sofa, trying to trap her voice with his hands before it darts away.

Clem

The next night, Suzette has a shift at her day job at Emperor's Steak House. She needs to pay for all that criminally expensive lipstick somehow. And her name is no longer Suzette, her name is Clem, and that's what the chef calls her when he says, — There's no more sole, Clem, and Clem rubs her hand across her bald head and pretends to shed big, just-about-to-be-clubbed baby-seal tears because sole is the very popular alternative to steak in this restaurant.

— The salmon any good tonight? Clem asks as she pulls on her waiter's jacket, clips on her bowtie.

— Salmon's always good, says Chef.

— But not as good as the sirloin.

— Never as good, says Chef.

Clem serves the customers plates of meat and potatoes in expensive drag. Scampi-in-herbs-and-butter drag, salmon-in-parsley-and-shrimp drag. Grapes stamped on by Spanish, French and Italian men and women, fermented then poured into bottles: grape juice also in drag.

She slides plates in front of businessmen who specialize in not saying thank you when she puts down the basket of bread, refills water glasses, fetches glasses of scotch or cognac that cost more than all her takings in one night at Galaxy Lounge. That's all right — she knows that if she strutted in here one day all done up, wearing the pink cocktail frock she just finished sewing two nights ago, for example, all of them would be punching each other to go home with her hot tight ass. Or laughing and lapping it up at her show as she makes them drink shooters from her mouth, or mimes them sucking her cock (always later on, toward the end, after the fourth round or so of drinks). Once she has enough money in her purse, once she gets too old and fat for Galaxy, she might take up dressmaking full-time.

— I'd like the sole.

— I'm sorry, Clem says. — We've run out of sole, but the salmon is ambrosian.

— You know, says the woman, looking at her companion, — I don't think I'll have anything. I'll just have a glass of water.

The woman covered in fine layer of sawdust. She wears a suit of coarsely woven silk, brown in one light, violet in another, the fabric swishes and whimpers around her as she shifts in her seat.

— That's a beautiful suit, says Clement. — Is that raw silk? It is! Stunning, my dear, she says. — I sew myself. The salmon is really quite delicious.

The woman strokes her sleeves, strokes the silk across her lap. Is this waiter what her son would have become? This fey man with perfectly plucked eyebrows and little gold earrings? No. Maybe he would have. Yes! He would have been the best waiter ever. Her son a phoenix, a unicorn, rare and beautiful. He would have been perfect even if he'd decided to wear a frothy, sherbet-pink ballgown and sing 'Some Day My Prince Will Come.'

— I'll have the salmon, she says.

— Very good, says Clem.

After work Clem and the other waiters crowd a long table at the Ethiopian restaurant, the table scattered with menus and water glasses, the standing waiters clapping the backs of these sitting waiters. She'll just have a couple handfuls of lentils because she's trying to watch her figure, she throws her head back as she tips her lite beer into her mouth. Makeda, the waitress in the white head-scarf, kisses Clem on the very top of her bald head and the whole table laughs.

Maureen

Maureen still wobbly and sticky-mouthed from the wake at the pub, the perplexing waves and waves of tears, a bottomless Martian sea washing from her face, about what, she can't remember, but she thinks it must have been about everything: the dead boy she can't remember and couldn't save; the thought of her husband sloppily sucking her cousin Lorraine's toes the way he used to suck Maureen's; how this unit on *Romeo and Juliet* never seems to end; how she's never gotten around to just sitting down one summer and finally writing that novel she's always wanted to write, basically she's done nothing with her life; the run in the nylons she's never worn before, she just pulled on the first leg and whammed her toe right through, the nylon laddering up from her big toe to her goddamn knee. She and Pam at the karaoke mic caterwauling 'Take This Job and Shove It,' then inhaling a mountainous plate of suicide salt-and-pepper chicken wings and bbq short ribs; Maureen resuming an encore and singing 'Get Over It,' dedicated to all those whiny parents; Maureen creeping her car slowly slowly along all the dark back alleys and small side streets at two in the morning, gravel crunching under her tires, the occasional lurch and thump of a pothole under her car, until she finally pulls up and into the cold automatic light of her garage because she's not *drunk*, she just wants to be *safe*.

But today will be a new day.

— I need to talk to you, she snaps at Max, not in his office trapped behind a desk, but standing up, face to face like *adults*. On the polished tiles of the main floor hallway, five minutes before the bell and chaos.

— Yes, frowns Max, stopping on his way to the main office. His thick white hair falls in his eyes.

— You, she points at him, at the knot in his navy-blue-and-red striped tie, — you told Patrick Furey that because his skateboard was stolen off school property, that you couldn't help him. And now he's dead.

— That is correct, says Max, smoothing his tie down his front. — I told the boy that I couldn't help him with his skateboard, but it's not a logical leap to suggest that because I did not help him with his skateboard, he then passed away.

— Well, sputters Maureen, — that's just preposterous, it's preposterous.

— It's policy, says Max. — Will that be all?

— I've heard that Walter has a picture of you on his desk.

— So I've heard, says Max dryly, glancing down the hallway to the main office, then at the very tip of his pointy tie.

— Well?

— Well what?

Maureen's head thumps with old Guinness, old suicide-flavoured short ribs, old songs about crappy jobs and bad love affairs.

The bell sounds, its low drone an annoying poke.

Max regards her in that supercilious way of his, his face all edges and angles, the straight nose, the broad, angular jaw and chin. The freakish, prematurely white hair.

— I would recommend you go see one of the crisis team counsellors, Mrs. Mochinski. Do you want me to set up a meeting for you?

— No.

— So you'll do it yourself?

— Yes, Mr. Applegate.

— All right then, says Max. — Let me know what the outcome is.

Students asteroid around and between them, jostling and bumping, sweeping Maureen up and away to her room in their wake.

Walter and Max

Walter humming as he chops carrots and celery into neat, low-cal matchsticks on the cutting board, the knife thunking the vegetables, the plastic cutting board.

Max a wooden cutout on the floor in the condo's living room.

— What are you going to do, Max? calls Walter from the tiny kitchen. — Fire me? Ha! Do us *both* a favour.

Walter chewing a juicy chunk of carrot, Walter chopping. He fishes a radish out from a plastic bag. Cuts slits into it, then plops it into a bowl of ice water.

Max hunched. An unsmoked cigarette rolling between his fingers, the neat, smooth roll of paper, the perfume of the tobacco. He's been smoking more than ever since Walter left him. His lungs on fire. His life on fire. That word, *fire*, Max a butterball turkey spinning on a barbecue spit.

— Fire, says Max, sniffing the cigarette as Walter lumbers into the room. — I could. Max cross-legged on the condo floor, littering Walter's turf. — You have only three years until you retire, Walter, says Max, looking up, his whole face, his head, one giant tired bloodshot eyeball. — It's not so long. It doesn't need to be difficult this way.

Walter pushes a plastic container over the carpet toward Max. — Carrot?

Walter bites into a radish. Crunches as though chewing radishes is an Olympic sport. — I never knew how awesome radishes could be, says Walter. — I'm learning how to make radish roses. Found out how on the internet.

— All I'm saying is the photo and my reputation ..., says Max.

— All you're saying is all you're saying.

— There's no need for rudeness. We can get you stress leave.

— I'm leaving the picture on my desk, says Walter, peeling open another container of chopped celery. — And I'll get a T-shirt with our faces on it framed in a pink heart. I will spray-paint your car: *Max Applegate is a Flaming Faggot.* That's what I'll do. Walter pops another radish in his mouth. — Awesome! Radishes have basically zero calories.

— Marry me, Max, says Walter. He grins, a radish-rose smile unfolding petal by petal on his face.

Marriage a fountain of fire, a lake of fire, a towering inferno.

— There's no need to attack me, Walter, says Max. He flips the filter end of the cigarette into his mouth, pushes open the balcony door. Fumbles his lighter out of his pocket. The reassuring smell and hiss of the flame.

He's chosen two colours. Black and red.

The joy that floods him as he shakes the spray paint cans up and down is the kind of joy he feels when he pops open a first can of beer, bites the head off an Easter bunny, the little metal balls inside the paint cans clicking ready, the cans' weight easy in his hands for he has done this many times, he is an *artiste*, and this is what he was meant to do.

The terrific spray and sizzle as the paint follows his hands sweeping fast and smooth over the perfect grey concrete canvas of the north stairwell wall, the smell of success, the smell of completion as he announces his message to the world, for he is a fucking prophet:

THE UNICORNS ARE COMING
THE UNICORNS ARE COMING

Max

I confess to Almighty God, says Max, — and to you, my brothers and sisters, that I have sinned through my own fault, in my thoughts and in my words, in what I have done, and in what I have failed to do.

The inside of the confessional dim and tight, but velvet warm. Unambiguous.

— Father, forgive me for I have sinned, says Max. — It's been a week since my last confession.

— I was jealous of my neighbour, sighs Max. — For one moment I coveted his vehicle because my vehicle was so badly damaged in an accident I worry that it won't operate as well as it used to. I shouldn't be thinking such superficial thoughts.

— I was unnecessarily sharp with my assistant and made her cry. She's still new. I should be more considerate.

— I had unkind thoughts about the mother of one of my students. I know she's just trying to do her best with the lot she's been given.

— Um. I watched far too much television this week. I watched television when I should have been doing work.

Max wipes his eyes.

— I am sorry for these sins and all the sins I can't remember.

Max hears Father Tim rustle on the other side of the screen. Father Tim intones in his jolly baritone about impatience and envy, and some scripture he could recommend to help Max deal with these feelings, and Max thinks about going home to his empty house, grey and dense with the smell of single-man cigarette smoke, the lights out, the spirit gone. Nothing but a wooden structure holding some tired plants, stray cat hairs, one oversized television.

— Your sins are truly forgiven, finishes Father Tim. — Go in Peace.

— Thanks be to God, says Max, and his knees creak, the wooden kneeler creaks as he unwinds himself up to standing.

Walter

Pop, Walter tells his father. — I'm a fairy.
     — No such thing as a black-man fairy, Wally, says his father.
— And I'm moving to Vancouver.
— No such thing as Vancouver, Wally, says his father.

Applegate, Max — Will you sleep with Crêpe Suzette on your date? asked Walter.

He sat on the edge of the bed, Max standing and holding up ties against his shirt, the jacket he wanted to wear. Jeans and polished cowboy boots because he wanted to show he knew how to relax. He whipped a tie around his neck, folding end over end, and pulled it tight. Straightened it while looking in the mirror. Tightened. Tightened.

There's such a thing as a tie being too tight, Walter said.

Max pulled the tie even tighter. I like it straight. Is it straight? he asked.

Let me fix it, said Walter. I just have to get something.

He rummaged in the bedside drawer and turned to Max, slicing the tie off with scissors, with a stainless-steel chew and chop.

That's better, said Walter. He grinned, but he also tasted grit between his teeth, his whole body slumping into glum in this beige bedroom and in the company of this beige man who used to be his.

Max clapped both hands to his throat and turned to the mirror. In his stump of a tie, he looked like he was ten years old again, about to go on his first date with a girl, Madeleine from Sunday school. Holding hands with her on a park bench, their hands chilled and sticky, their mothers making cooing noises that sounded as though they were perched and fluttering in the trees.

I guess it is, said Max. He loosened the knot from around his neck.

Walter was going to retire early.

Walter hugged Max goodbye when he left their house, now Max's house.

In the screaming silence of the condo, he zipped closed his suitcase, a suitcase the size of the house he was leaving behind, wrapped a towel around Lieutenant Fong and plopped her into her carrier. He loaded the bag, Lieutenant Fong and her litterbox into the rental car. He would drive west and keep going until he hit the ocean and the most homosexual neighbourhood in western Canada. Lieutenant Fong would finally know what a hydrangea was, what the sea smelled like. Walter would get a haircut, or maybe get a pedicure, and if anyone called him a sissy, his answer would be Yes.

Mochinski, Maureen (née Rule) —
As Maureen dressed for work that
Monday morning, poking her legs
into a hot pink thong with a red heart
embroidered on the pubic mound,
then her nylons, a grey blouse and
black jacket, she snagged the blouse
on the sharp corner of the bathroom
commode and pricked a tiny hole in
the right front panel. She snaked her
arms into the blouse, buttoned it
closed, tucked it into her black slacks.
Buttoned on her blazer. She did a
half-pirouette in front of the mirror to
make sure the jacket draped evenly in
the back, smoothing and tucking the
blouse, the collar, pulling the jacket
straight. She draped a towel over the
mirror. She inserted her pinky finger
into the tiny hole in the front of her
blouse, thought of the boy, his face,
his skateboard in the river, and she
pulled with her finger, unzipping a
larger tear in the fabric, her pink
camisole shouting through the hole.
She did a big yoga inhale, a big yoga
exhale. She unhooked her purse from
the closet door, her bag spilling with
red-inked essays, and locked the door
to the empty house behind her. The
school website would need to be
updated, the name taped to her
mailbox redone. Today she would tell
Joy in the main office that her last

name was Rule. Only fifteen more years, then she could retire, could finally be free. Ms Rule.

Mai, Petra — Petra swept her hair out of her eye, swept away the sad smell of her pomegranate shampoo and hummed as she marched across the stage, shook hands with Mr. Applegate and collected her diploma. She adjusted the mortarboard on her head and walked down the steps, headed out the auditorium doors into the rest of her life. Her grandmother and parents clapping their hands, their faces smiling wrinkled and gooey, her mother runny-nosed and red-eyed. Petra had brand-new shoes on her feet, the heels clicking hard and firm as she walked to the beat of the song still yammering in her head. She would hear it properly once she started university in September. Her feet hammering, a fleshy metronome.

Tomorrow was Tuesday, and she still had to go to school even though she had graduated. The outside smell of buds on the trees washing out her nose. Going to school was what you did on Mondays, go to school, but she was bursting with being done, soon she would stop being controlled by her parents, her grandmother would stop giving her granny-style underwear decorated with bright green frogs, pigs with eyelashes and corkscrew tails. Ginger in another part of the alphabet, accepting his diploma, his grandfather Mr. Dobrovolný hugging him, clapping him on the back. Ginger strode past Petra. As if she were dead. One day the Mondays would stop, it would be Tuesday, and she could take a breath.

At home Monday night after the grad ceremony, she stuck her hands into the armholes of the blue argyle sweater, pushed her head up through the folds and bunches of wool. She held her breath as she nudged her head through the blue, nudging for the round hole of air. Her hair covering her face, her hands lost in the long sleeves, the boy-cologne, the smell of Ginger belonging to someone else. She fingered her hair out of her face, tucked the strands behind her ears. The sweater hung down past her bum, the sleeves at least a hand's length longer than the tips of her fingers. She saw a streak of silver on the wool hairs of the sweater, then another streak, warm water falling out of the front of her face. She had acted cruelly, selfishly, but she was not a murderer. She was just in love. Petra in love, and Ginger in love with someone else.

As she crossed her arms and pulled the sweater up over her head, stitches in the armpit ripped when one of the sleeves hooked on her blouse button.

She heard each stitch unzip, the seam of the one arm, then a seam on the right side, the argyle diamonds sliding and pulling apart, puddles of ice and glass and navy blue wool hanging on to each other by threads when she finally tugged herself free of the sweater; it fell to pieces around her feet.

Max and Suzette — The digital clock at the T-intersection in front of the Ethiopian Restaurant clicked 26:72 a.m.

He sat at the table the furthest back and waited for Suzette. The red lampshade above and behind his head, a photo of an Ethiopian coffee field on the wall to his right. Ethiopian sun. Ordered a Guinness. They would sit just like a regular couple, and for the first time in his life, he would not glance at the door whenever another customer swung in, he would not flinch away from talking too close. He might even kiss her. Right here at the table. He might even ask her to meet him in another restaurant after this date. A restaurant *downtown*. Just a regular man and his beautiful girl.

Max stepped to the washroom to wash his hands with pearly pink soap. Checked his tieless self in the mirror.

Suzette finished her cigarette before she entered the restaurant, butting it against a brick wall and slipping it into the trashcan beside the restaurant entrance. Last night she did her Dance of the Sixty-Nine Veils, and she wished Max had been there, he would have appreciated her hair, the way she beckoned people in the audience to each tear away a clump of veils until she was naked in her gold Shakira catsuit.

One of the waiters in the Ethiopian restaurant, Solomon, slapped her on the back and shouted hello; his mother Makeda toddled over and smothered her in a hug. Suzette exclaimed over Makeda's new lipstick, Suzette's head smooth, four o'clock shadow bristling awake on her cheeks and chin. She wore a hint of shimmer on her cheekbones. Her wig and the pink sherbet frock she picked out to wear tonight soaking in the sink because Vaseline Dion dropped her waterproof eyeliner brush on them. The straw that broke the drag queen's back. She pulled on a plaid shirt and jeans. Vaseline Dion promising to buy Suzette caffe lattes for the rest of their lives.

Come watch me now, Suzette thought, hunting for Max in the restaurant.

Max straightened his tie and closed the bathroom door behind him. His time had come. He licked his lips. Dry.

Tuesday

Gretta

The doorbell, bing-bong, and you hunch deeper into your chair, the paintbrush between your fingers, the tiny square canvas, the size of a baby's face, clamped in place on the easel in front of you. Your husband's mumbles, the loud tooting of another man's voice, and booted footsteps clobbering across the floors. You wipe off the brush with a rag and dunk it into a jar of grey water.

You can't imagine who this visitor might be, intruding on your fortress. Your husband waving more strangers into your house.

— Who are you? you snarl at a man in overalls and baseball cap in your kitchen, quite rudely, for this is yet another person asking for money in connection to your dead son, of course it wasn't preplanned, who preplans for the burial of a seventeen-year-old kid? The casket, the vault, the embalming, the plot, the grave marker, all that stuff flushed out an entire bank account because who saves up money for the burial of their seventeen-year-old son? Who's picked out a casket for their teenager? Who in this world? Who?

You reach for the wall to prop up your crumbling body when two more men trundle into the kitchen carrying a long, thin, granite headstone between them, you rise and start to scream and thrash, wild with your claws and fangs, at this headstone in your house, more death in your house, who has died? Whose name will be on that headstone? Whose? Your husband grabbing you by the shoulders, shouting and speckling you with his saliva and stabbing you with his jagged, rancid breath, his hands rough and hard as his fingers dig into your upper arms, — Stop Stop.

The men set the first half of the granite countertop on your floor. The headstone a pool in the middle of the room, a cupboard already down to nothing but wood skeleton, whoofs of sawdust, the tang of raw wood. The cupboard just a pocket of space decorated with wooden bones, circled by a pine ribcage.

— Empire Kitchens and Baths, the first man says, the big, stupid galoot.

— Oh no, you say.

— Here to do your kitchen counter and cabinets.

— Maybe you could come another time, you say.

— Stay, says your husband. He has a hammer in his hands, he plans on smashing things.

The freezing starts on the soles of your feet, the frost creeping crystal, grabbing handfuls of you as it travels up your legs, coats your belly, crusts your mouth, you can smell your skin lotion, perfume and sweat, the rosewater and sage shampoo in your hair jump up and out as the skin that covers all of you shrinks and tightens. Your skin clammy as your son's.

His name is Chuck. The other workmen are Callum and Zenon. Zenon looks nineteen. He looks like he might have gone on a date with your son.

Chuck's saw and crowbar claw and rip through the cupboard above the sink, Zenon hammering and prying, exposing. Chuck, Callum and Zenon's grunts, the guitar, drums and the voice of a writhing singer filtering in from your husband's television set. You, in the other room, slumped in front of an empty canvas the width of a baby's face.

Ginger

Ginger doesn't want to understand, but he reads *The Pride and the Joy* to the very end, the paper so thick he can see some tiny specks of the wood pulped into it. He reads it even though it's like trudging through thigh-high mud, even though they rough him up and choke him, those mirror words.

He pulls the sharpest knife out of the drawer, skims the blade under running water against the whetstone. He holds the blade against his skin, the metal warm and spotted with droplets of water, and he slices an F over his heart, not enough to need stitches, but enough so that it will bleed, will scar, so that he will remember, the angle of the knife at first hard to negotiate, he is startled at the sharp, the pain, the flinching response of the meat shell that covers him, he doesn't want to die. He presses a wad of tissue onto the cuts, another wad he claws from the box of Kleenex, his chest pouring, the tissue soaked and dripping, the box empty, one of his T-shirts gathered up and stuffed against his chest, the stains on his fingers, the gobs of tissue so red, the T-shirt horror-movie gory, until the blood stops welling and tearing along the lines of the F, then he flushes the paper down the toilet. Four flushes total. He dabs at the cuts with disinfectant, pats on some gauze from his grampa's first-aid kit, tears off pieces of medical tape with his teeth, the stabbing on the lunar surface of his chest.

He sits down to dinner with his grandfather, sits with the book tucked in the small of his back against the back of the chair, dumplings and goulash tonight, his favourite. His grandfather pouring himself a beer and arguing that there's no such thing as drinking too much beer, how can a person drink too much beer, that's like saying you can drink too much water, there is such a thing as having so much education you can't enjoy life anymore, people telling you what you should or should not do getting in the way of living a happy life, right Tomáš?

— Interesting, Ginger says.

— Proud of you, boy, says his grandfather.

Faraday

We didn't know him well
But we knew him gone.
What was wrong he would not tell,
His face now only dawn.

Patrick, we think about you,
A Great Guy we now all kiss.
Without you, our school's so blue,
Think of us, when Angels you kiss.

Fumiko reaches for her Brown Cow in a crystal glass rimmed with gold, and a swirled chocolate and vanilla cookie. The glow of the computer screen reflecting off her whitened face, her kohled eyes and black lips. Faraday crunches on her own cookie, the flavour not quite vanilla not quite chocolate on her tongue. She scoots her chair closer to Fumiko's so she can get a better view of the screen. She bites again, scattering crumbs on the floor, wondering if anyone would fault them for rhyming *kiss* with *kiss*.

— Uncle Suzie! she calls. — Is it okay to rhyme two identical words?

Uncle Suzie in the other room, the hum of his sewing machine as he polishes off the hem of Faraday's graduation dress.

Furey, Patrick — Under two tonnes of dirt, Patrick's eyelids and lips curling as he dehydrates, his skin suctioning to his bones in air so dry it makes the noses of the people who walk above him — his own little solar system — bleed, their cuticles crack and peel. In a semi-arid city such as Calgary, Alberta, the problem is maggots, but the boy was young, his remains found almost immediately after death, and the decomposition arrested before it could really begin. It was a very thorough embalming. George M. would be impressed.

The boy a supernova in this unicorn constellation.

The Unicorns

Faraday lies in bed in her unicorn flannel pyjamas, contemplating her blessing. The tapestry above her bed, the glinting Kirin bottle on the edge of her little white desk strewn with binders and papers, the poster and paper reproductions of four-hundred-year-old unicorn woodcuts and engravings taped to the ceiling and walls all around her. The figurines on the shelf ricochet the dull lamplight. There's no such thing as being normal, she's figured out. And now, more than ever, no matter what Dr. Linus Libby and Brecken and Jésus and all the rest of them say, unicorns are all she needs. Unicorns stand serene and uncomplicated, even if all she's got is pictures, sculptures, souvenir trinkets.

She abruptly jumps up on her bed to standing, the quilt sliding to the floor. She bounces lightly on the mattress as she unsticks the poster of the Quedlinburg unicorn from beside her bed, her feet landing in a solid thump on the floor then back up on the mattress as she replaces the Quedlinburg for the Jonstonus camphur on the other side of the room. The paint on the walls peeling in patches because of the pieces of tape she's stuck and peeled and restuck.

She clicks off the lamp. Gathers up her fallen quilt and burrows back into her bed. There.

She yanks the quilt edge up under her chin, pulls it in around her hips, then works it in around her shoulders so there's no cold air pockets. She's slung her unicorn bag, the one she bought the day she learned that Patrick died, from her desk chair. The unicorn faces out so even in the dark it's looking at her. She closes her eyes now. Goodnight, Patrick Furey. Her digital clock glows 11:11 p.m. Goodnight.

On the city's outskirts, the trailers' brakes exhale to a stop at a red light, their cargo clopping nervously on the trailer floors at the sudden stop. The light clicks to green, and the trailers inhale back into diesel motion, picking up speed, rolling faster and faster. Three trailers speeding through the periodic cones of light along the highway, the whine and windy blasts of oncoming trucks, the trailers jostle, belch scat stink, cloven hoofs inside the trailers shifting, clopping from side to side. The trucks trundle down the Trans-Canada highway toward Faraday's house.

Under glittering streetlights, the trucks and their trailers bullishly manoeuvre the tight corners of the inner city, bumping up over curbs, bending stop signs, ploughing over pylons. Alicorns clang against the inside trailer walls with the lumbering over potholes and too-long meridians. Abrupt lurches at lights, streets narrowed by rows of parked cars. Hooves occasionally stamp and circle the rubberized floors, nostrils snort in the Stygian dark inside the trailers. The route to Faraday travels past St. Aloysius Senior High School. The traffic light in front of the school unfortunately red.

The convoy pulls to a brief stop at the red light, in the deserted heart of downtown, under the ring of red lights on the alicorn that is the Calgary Tower.

Simmering in the dark, exhaust fumes coiling, the unicorns inhale the smell of the school, their heads swinging as they snort, their tails swishing. The residual smell of Faraday, her locker stuffed with books and papers redolent with her odour, they smell it in the school, they need to turn toward it. They bump their shoulders and hips against the constricted insides of the trailers, against each other, they paw the floor, the wall, thump, bang. They scent her, they belong to her, they want her. But they also smell the school's sweaty, seedy smell of death, sweat squeezed out by fear and judgment. The blessing of unicorns seizes, ears pinned back, teeth bared, they begin to whinny. Eyes roll back, they bite the walls, strike the walls with their front legs, kick high with their hind legs. Pissing and shitting in fury, one shrieks. They all shriek.

Hooves slip. Hooves stamp kick bash burst the rocking trailer doors, welds pop, the doors slap open, hinges screaming. Unicorns gallop, hooves sparking asphalt, leaping the cracked concrete sidewalk, they lunge for the sleeping school and its enraging scent of failure, guilt and grief, unicorns crashing through the door frames, pounding through the doors. They careen on the slippery floors around the hallway corners, gut, gore the walls, stab, shatter fluorescent lights, their lions' tails whipping as they litter the floors with their shit.

They rush into the principal's office, the vice-principals' offices, kick over the desks, gut the filing cabinets, smash the windows.

In office after office, classroom after classroom, papers explode and flutter, books fly and shred. They stamp through the gymnasium, trampling the wood floor, stumbling in the growing, splintering holes.

They slash with their alicorns, stampede; driven mad with vengeance, they batter cabinets, puncture trophies, windows, desks, televisions, computers, pry chalkboards from the walls. Fluorescent lights crumble, walls crash. They tear the lockers from the walls, dented, sharp metal shreds. The roof buckles above the cafeteria, caves in above the chemistry lab, the roof yawns opens and exposes the school's guts to the stars. In the blessing's wake the clawing smell of billy goat, of carnivore, corruption, unicorns glutting, a giant aneurysm, a cardiac arrest speeding down venal corridors.

They crash out the back walls of the school, a blessing, a reckoning, a wall of fury at full gallop, they bunch and lurch into the river, leaping into the brown water, bobbing, sinking, snapping legs, alicorns, necks, unicorns flailing, a breaking blessing. The school gored, broken, and now empty.

Credits

The unicorn images on the section title pages are from the following sources:

P. 9: *De Monocerote.* 1551. *Historiae Animalium; liber primus, qui est de quadrupedibus viviparis* by Conrad Gesner. Turning the Pages Online (National Library of Medicine). Web.

P. 17: Detail from the broadsheet *Come, come all you that are with Rome offended, come now and heare from whence the Pope descended, The lineage of locusts or the Popes pedegre.* 1641. Early English Books Online. Web.

P. 57: *Tab XI: Monoceros seu Unicornu Iubatus / Einhorn mit Mahnen.* 1678. *A Description of the Nature of Four-Footed Beasts: With their Figures Engraven in Brass* by Joannes Jonstonus. Trans. by J. P. University of Wisconsin Digital Collections. Web.

P. 89: *Tab X.* 1678. *A Description of the Nature of Four-Footed Beasts: With their Figures Engraven in Brass* by Joannes Jonstonus. Trans. by J. P. University of Wisconsin Digital Collections. www.fromoldbooks.org. Web.

P. 117: *Tab XI: Onagur Aldro / Wald Esel.* 1678. *A Description of the Nature of Four-Footed Beasts: With their Figures Engraven in Brass* by Joannes Jonstonus. Trans. by J. P. University of Wisconsin Digital Collections. www.fromoldbooks.org. Web.

P. 141: *Unicorn and a Stag [Tertia Figura: In Corpore est Anima & Spiritus.]* 1678. *Musaeum hermeticum reformatum et amplificatum* by Matthaeus Merian. Images from the History of Medicine (IHM). Web.

P. 177: *Fig. Rr.* 1690. *Prodromus Astronomiae* by Johannes Hevelius. National Digital Library Polona.Web.

Pp. 185, 187, 195, 203, 207, 219, 229: Adapted from *Figura sceleti prope Quedlinburgum efossi.* 1749. *Protogaea* by Gottfried Wilhelm Leibniz. Ed. Claudine Cohen and Andre Wakefield. Trans. Claudine Cohen and Andre Wakefield. Chicago: U of Chicago P, 2008. ,cademic Complete. Web.

P. 253: Master E.S. *The Wold Woman and the Unicorn [Queen of the Beasts, from the Small Set of Playing Cards]* / *La jeune licorne.* 1450–1467. *The Illustrated Bartsch. Vol. 8, Early German Artists.* Photograph reproduced with permission of the Warburg Institute, University of London. Artstor Collections. Web.

The author gratefully acknowledges the following for permission to reproduce quoted material:

Lyrics from 'No Such Thing as the Future' by Immaculate Machine. Copyright Mint Records. Used by permission.

Lyrics from 'Wind Beneath My Wings' by Larry Henley and Jeff Silbar. Copyright 1982 Warner House of Music and WB Gold Music Corp. All rights reserved. Used by permission.

Acknowledgements

A big thank you to the many people who helped me write this book: Nicole Markotić, Rosemary Nixon and Nancy Jo Cullen — my divine writer/editor/ass-kicker peeps who read and reread and re-reread and kept me on the path; Alana Wilcox for her amazing editorial eagle eye and brutal (always in a good way) questions, and Evan Munday and all the folks at Coach House Books. For the other important miscellaneous, thank you to Lisa Brawn, Susan Bercha, Ally Flynn, Friedrich Mayr, Allison Lynch-Griffiths, Susan Holbrook, Lori Kennedy, Alice Zorn, Jonathan Ball, Luke Cullen LeBlanc, Melissa Jackson, Belén Martín Lucas, Deb Dudek, Jacqueline Larson, Andrea Kwan, Ulrich Mayr, Rose-Marie Mayr, Wendy Beaver, Julien Mayr, Stéphan De Loof, Alanna Callaghan, Louise Belanger, Birdie and Tequila. Thank you to the people who let me interview them: Steven Peters, Carly York Jones of Carly's Angels, Dev Drysdale, Kathy Cloutier, Gord Baldwin and Keith Johnson.

Texts that were extremely useful: *Prayers for Bobby: A Mother's Coming to Terms with the Suicide of her Gay Son* by Leroy Aarons, *Edmonton River Queen* by Darrin Hagen, *The Mourner's Dance: What We Do When People Die* by Katherine Ashenburg, 'Do I Disappoint You' by Rufus Wainwright, *The God Box* by Alex Sanchez, *Blackbird* by Larry Duplechan, *The Unicorn* by Nancy Hathaway, *Disenfranchised Grief: Recognizing Hidden Sorrow* ed. by Kenneth J. Doka, *That's So Gay!: Homophobia in Canadian Catholic Schools* by Tonya Callaghan, *Lettin' It All Hang Out* by RuPaul, *Don We Now Our Gay Apparel: Gay Men's Dress in the Twentieth Century* by Shaun Cole, *Speak* by Laurie Halse Anderson, 'Blue Sky' by Nicole Markotić.

An extra, *extra* special thank you to Tonya Callaghan for making this text possible and livable, and for continuing to laugh at my jokes.

About the Author

Suzette Mayr is the author of three previous novels: *Venous Hum,* *The Widows* and *Moon Honey*. *The Widows* was shortlisted for the Commonwealth Prize for Best Book in the Canada-Caribbean Region and has been translated into German. *Moon Honey* was shortlisted for the Georges Bugnet Award for Fiction and the Henry Kreisel Award for Best First Book. She lives in Calgary.

Typeset in Bell and Bolero
Printed and bound at the Coach House on bpNichol Lane, 2011

Edited and designed by Alana Wilcox
Author photo by Tonya Callaghan

Coach House Books
80 bpNichol Lane
Toronto ON M5S 3J4

416 979 2217
800 367 6360

mail@chbooks.com
www.chbooks.com